TREASURED HORSES COLLECTION®

DEBORAH FELDER 🐎 JAHNNA N. MALCOLM 🐎 SUSAN SAUNDERS

Riding School Rivals
Pretty Lady of Saratoga
The Stallion of Box Canyon
Kate's Secret Plan

BARNES & NOBLE
NEW YORK

TREASURED HORSES COLLECTION®

Barnes & Noble, Inc.
122 Fifth Avenue
New York, NY 10011

ISBN-13: 978-0-7607-4131-3
ISBN-10: 0-7607-4131-X

Printed and bound in the United States of America

10 9 8 7 6 5 4 3

RIDING SCHOOL RIVALS

The story of a majestic Lipizzan horse
and the girls who fight for the right to ride him

Written by **Susan Saunders**
Illustrated by **Sandy Rabinowitz**
Cover Illustration by **Christa Keiffer**
Developed by Nancy Hall, Inc.

CONTENTS

CHAPTER ONE

The Girls at Birchwood Stable

Cassie Sinclair had taken hundreds of riding lessons over the past four and a half years. But she knew that she could take thousands more and never get tired of them.

Cassie was eleven. She figured she would still be riding when she was forty years old. Or fifty. Or maybe even sixty! And there would always be something new for her to learn.

Every Saturday morning at ten o' clock, Cassie, her best friend Amy Lin, Sara Gerson, and a new girl named Hillary Craig took group lessons from Trisha Prescott at Birchwood Stable.

Riding was Cassie's passion. Besides the group

lesson every Saturday, she had a private lesson in jumping on Sundays. And when she wasn't riding, she was thinking about riding.

Cassie daydreamed about jumping in the Olympics someday. But if she ended up half as good a rider as Trisha Prescott, Cassie would be happy.

Trisha owned Birchwood. She knew more about horses, and riding, than anyone Cassie had ever met. Trisha had been a champion hunter rider and had trained dozens of horses that had become winners. Not only was Trisha a terrific rider and horse trainer, she was a wonderful teacher as well. She didn't put up with any nonsense from students or horses. But Trisha was patient, and she was always fair.

Right now, Trisha was standing at one end of the indoor ring at Birchwood. She was always perfectly turned out, even when she was just hanging around the barn. Today, Trisha was wearing spotless beige jodhpurs, brown paddock boots, a blue-and-white pin-striped shirt, and a dark-brown leather belt with a sterling silver buckle.

Trisha had wavy brownish-blond hair and clear gray eyes that never missed a thing. Right now they were trained on Amy and Freckles as Amy put her horse through his paces. Amy had been taking lessons for two years. It had been hard for her at first, because she was a little afraid of horses. But the horse she rode, Freckles, was one of the smaller horses at Birchwood. He was small and round. That was fine with Amy, who was short and round herself.

Waiting their turn near the gate were Cassie, Sara, and Hillary on their horses. Cassie was watching Amy intently as she trotted around the ring. Even when she wasn't riding, just watching the other girls in her Saturday group and listening to Trisha taught Cassie a lot.

Cassie was blessed with a straight back and long legs that made her look great on a horse. She had skin the color of coffee ice cream and long, black hair that she wore in a thick braid. Gold earrings in the shape of tiny horseshoes gleamed in her ears.

At Birchwood Stable, Cassie had been riding a chestnut mare named Allegra for the past two years. Allegra was a dependable horse, and she tried hard. But now that Cassie was getting more advanced in jumping, she wished that Allegra were younger and livelier.

On one side of Cassie and Allegra, Sara Gerson fiddled with her reins. Sara was ten, and a year behind the other girls in school. She was small, with a pale, heart-shaped face and shoulder-length dark hair. She rode a neat bay horse named Charlie that her parents were thinking about leasing for her.

Sara had been taking lessons from Trisha for three years. She was a much better rider than she gave herself credit for. But she had terrible stage fright. She even got nervous riding in front of her Saturday group.

Hillary Craig was eleven, the same age as Cassie and Amy. But she was a bigger girl, taller and heavier than Cassie, with reddish-brown hair that she pulled back into a ponytail.

Hillary was a good rider. She was quick to announce to the other girls that she had been riding almost since the time she could walk!

Hillary had recently moved to Maryland from California. She had been taking group lessons from Trisha for a couple of months, long enough to annoy practically everyone at the stable with her snooty attitude.

Hillary took private lessons in jumping, too. Her class was right after Cassie's private jumping lesson on Sundays. Usually, Hillary made a point of arriving early to watch Cassie and Allegra work.

At first, Cassie thought that maybe it was Hillary's way of trying to make friends. But when Cassie tried to talk to Hillary, the girl could barely be bothered to answer. So Cassie decided that Hillary came early just to keep an eye on her.

Hillary definitely felt she had an edge over Cassie and Allegra because of Bliss. Bliss was the black gelding Hillary rode at Birchwood. He was young and strong and a good jumper.

"Hillary doesn't want to be friends, Cassie," Amy Lin had said more than once. "I think she's trying to jinx you!"

"Amy, let's see your trot," Trisha was saying now. "Shorten your reins."

Amy tightened her reins a little more. She squeezed her legs once to make Freckles pay attention, then twice more to speed him up.

As soon as Freckles trotted, Amy began to post. She leaned forward slightly and let the horse's movements raise her out of the saddle on the first beat. On the second beat, she lowered herself.

"Easy now," Trisha called out to Amy. "Please don't bounce, or you'll lose your balance. Keep your heels down . . . down. And look straight ahead, Amy, not down at Freckles."

Amy giggled. She had heard all of these

instructions many, many times. As she had said to Cassie, though, "I can't be expected to remember everything, can I?"

Cassie had smiled with her friend.

Now she heard a loud, cranky sigh coming from her right. It was Hillary, letting everyone know that her valuable time was being wasted.

Not satisfied with just sighing, Hillary leaned toward Cassie to mutter, "I can't see why you hang around with that girl. What if her bad riding rubs off on you?"

"Amy is my best friend! And she is trying really hard!" Cassie whispered, her eyes still on Amy and Freckles. Trisha expected everyone in the group to pay strict attention.

But instead of watching Amy, or listening to Trisha, Hillary hummed loudly and stared down at the toe of her boot.

"Let's try a canter now," Trisha said to Amy. "Sit deep and tall."

Amy nudged Freckles again, and he broke into the "one-two-three" beat of the canter. Amy sat back in the saddle and rocked along, enjoying herself.

"You're looking good," Trisha called out. "Okay . . . take hold . . . slow him down . . . now . . . stop."

Amy brought Freckles to a halt.

"Back up," said Trisha.

Amy squeezed on the reins . . . let up . . . squeezed . . . let up. Freckles took a few steps backward.

"Well done," Trisha said to Amy. "Sara, let's have a look at you next."

Another loud sigh escaped from Hillary as Sara rode into the center of the ring.

"What's her problem?" Amy murmured to Cassie, turning Freckles around beside the gate.

"I guess she's bored," Cassie whispered back.

"So why does the great Hillary Craig take group lessons, if we're so boring?" Amy said in a louder voice.

Cassie had wondered about that herself. Why didn't Hillary just take two jumping lessons instead? She certainly didn't seem to be getting anything out of her group riding lessons.

"Quiet, girls, please!" said Trisha, without taking her eyes off Sara.

Sara immediately lost her left stirrup and had to grab the front of her saddle to keep from slipping sideways.

Sara blushed bright red. Cassie could see it even in the low light of the indoor ring.

Hillary snorted and stared at the ceiling.

13

"That's okay, Sara," Trisha said. "Why don't we try posting to the trot without stirrups? It's great for balance."

Sara nodded, pulling her right foot out of the stirrup, too. "Wait. I think everyone should do it," said Trisha. "Cassie, you go first. Then Hillary, next Amy, and Sara at the end."

The four of them crossed their stirrup leathers in front of their saddles to get them out of the way. Then the four girls formed a line, as in follow-the-leader.

"Legs under your body, knees bent, calves against your horse's sides, toes higher than heels," Trisha said. "Eyes straight ahead. And let your horse lift you into the post."

Posting without stirrups wasn't easy. But it was a great exercise for balance, muscle control, and learning to move with the horse, all of which Cassie needed for jumping.

She and Allegra were circling smoothly around the ring when suddenly the mare jumped forward. Cassie lowered her hands to Allegra's neck to steady herself. And she stopped posting.

Allegra bounced forward again. Cassie glanced briefly to one side, and there was Bliss's head, about to bump against Allegra's rump! Was Hillary trying to run over her?

"Hillary, take hold of Bliss!" Trisha called out sharply.

"Sorry. He can't stand not to be first!" Hillary called back.

"And neither can you!" Cassie felt like yelling at Hillary. But she didn't. Trisha liked things at the stable to go smoothly. More than once, Cassie had heard Trisha say, "Don't let personalities get in the way of your riding."

"Well, our hour is up anyway. Slow down . . . and stop," Trisha said to the girls now.

She walked over to open the gate for them to ride out. "Girls, Robert is away for the morning"—Robert Martin was Trisha's stablehand—"and I would really appreciate it if you could help me out by grooming your horses before you go," she added.

"Sure," Cassie and Amy said together.

Cassie's mom would be picking them up that day. But the Sinclairs' house was only a couple of miles from the stable. And Mrs. Sinclair usually waited for Cassie to call her on the phone, because Cassie often liked to spend extra time at Birchwood after her lessons were over.

"I'll help, too," said Sara.

But Hillary said, "Sorry, Trisha, I can't. I've got a dentist appointment." And she nudged Bliss through the gate ahead of the other horses.

Amy rolled her eyes at Cassie, meaning, "Oh, right! The truth is that Hillary is just too good to groom her horse with the rest of us!"

"Please unsaddle Bliss before you go, Hillary," Trisha said. Then she said to Cassie, "I wanted you to hang around for a while, anyway, Cassie. I hope to have a surprise for you later this morning."

"A surprise for me?" said Cassie, puzzled. "What kind of surprise?"

Hillary tugged on Bliss and paused to listen.

Trisha just smiled at Cassie. "I think you'll be pleased," was all she said.

Majesty

The four girls led their horses into the barn, where Hillary exchanged Bliss's bridle for a halter. She hitched the lead rope to a cross tie and then walked away with only a wave to the others.

"And thanks for helping out, Hillary," Amy muttered.

Cassie, Amy, and Sara put halters on their horses, too. Then the girls unsaddled all four horses and led them out of the barn to the grooming tree. The grooming tree was a spreading oak, comfortably shady on even the warmest days.

Trisha carried out brushes and curry combs. "I'll bring a bucket of warm water for their tails," she told the girls as she walked away.

Cassie, Amy, and Sara got started on Allegra, Freckles, and Sara's horse, Charlie, with rubber curry combs and body brushes.

"I can't figure Hillary out," Cassie said as they worked. "She says she's been riding for years, so she must really love it. But if she loves it, why doesn't she seem to care about her horse, or learning anything from Trisha, or . . . "

"I don't think Hillary loves riding. I think she loves winning!" Amy declared, circling Freckles's back with a curry comb.

"Maybe Hillary just hates losing," Sara said suddenly. "My parents met her parents at a party last week."

Sara so rarely spoke that Cassie and Amy both stopped brushing to give her their full attention.

"My mom said that Mrs. Craig talked the whole time about the prizes Hillary won in shows in California," Sara told them. "And how Hillary is just like her dad."

"Her dad rides, too?" Cassie said. Sometimes she wished her dad or mom were more interested in riding.

"Um-hmm. Mrs. Craig is sure that Hillary will make enough points to go to the big horse shows at the end of the summer," Sara went on.

"Cassie's a hundred times better rider than Hillary is!" Amy said huffily.

"I don't know about a hundred times," Cassie said, smiling at her friend. "What else did Hillary's mom say, Sara?"

"That she and Mr. Craig talked to Trisha about finding Hillary a really special horse to jump on," Sara said. "They'll lease it or maybe even buy it for her."

Cassie allowed herself a small sigh.

Riding lessons were expensive enough. Buying a horse was too much for the Sinclairs' budget. And even leasing a horse would be a big expense for Cassie's parents.

In the hunter classes at horse shows, the classes in which many of Trisha's students competed, it was the horse that was judged, not the rider. And if Hillary had a great horse . . . Cassie was afraid that she and Allegra might be left in the dust. And she had to admit she wanted to beat Hillary.

"What about Mr. Craig? Did he have anything to say?" Amy was asking.

Sara shook her head. "No. Just Mrs. Craig, talking about what a great rider he was when he was younger and had the time to train for horse shows."

"And Hillary wants to follow in his footsteps,"

Cassie said. Just then, she heard a horse trailer rattling down the lane leading to the stables. The rattling grew louder and louder.

Allegra, Freckles, Charlie, and Bliss all raised their heads to listen, their ears perked.

"It sounds like Trisha's horse trailer," Sara said.

Sure enough, Robert Martin pulled Trisha's blue trailer into the parking area beside the barn. Trisha hurried outside, spoke to Robert for a second, and peeked inside the trailer. Then she waved to the three girls.

"Come take a look!" Trisha called to them.

They dropped their combs and brushes and rushed over. When they reached the trailer, Robert had opened the door and fixed the ramp.

"Is it a new horse for Birchwood?" Amy asked Trisha.

"A very special horse," Trisha said, adding, "and I think that Cassie will be one of the few students riding him."

"Me?" Cassie practically shrieked.

"You've gone as far as you can with Allegra," said Trisha. "It's time for you to trade up, and this might be the right horse for you."

"Excellent, Cassie!" said Amy.

Now Cassie was so excited she could hardly

breathe! She tried to imagine what the new horse would look like.

There was a clatter of hooves inside the trailer.

"Here he comes," said Trisha.

Robert walked out of the trailer, holding the lead rope. Just behind him was the most beautiful horse Cassie had ever seen. He was beyond anything she could have imagined!

The horse was a gleaming, milky white. His legs were short and strong, his body powerful. He had a heavy, arched neck, a large head, and huge brown eyes that shone with intelligence. The horse stepped proudly out of the trailer as if he were a king and Birchwood was his new kingdom.

"He's gorgeous!" Amy gasped.

Cassie could only nod in agreement. She still hadn't found her tongue.

"Girls, meet Majesty. He's a Lipizzan," Trisha said.

"Wow, a Lipizzan! I thought all the Lipizzans were in Austria, at the Spanish Riding School," said Sara, who had read practically every book ever written about horses.

"There are a few Lipizzans in the United States," said Trisha. "They're wonderful dressage horses, and they're excellent jumpers, too."

"Jumpers?" a voice said from behind them.

It was Hillary, still hanging around. Her curiosity had gotten the best of her.

"Is this my new horse?" she asked Trisha quickly. "The one my parents asked you to find for me to jump on?"

Cassie's heart sank. What if this wonderful horse wasn't going to be hers to ride, after all?

"I thought you had a dentist appointment, Hillary," Trisha said dryly. She added, "No, this isn't your horse. Majesty will be a Birchwood horse. And Cassie will be riding him if they're a good match."

"Oh, we will be." Cassie felt like shouting it. "I just know we will!"

By a "good match," Trisha was talking about personalities, as well as size and strength of horse and rider. A less experienced rider, like Amy, should have a horse that is slow and steady, like Freckles. A nervous rider should have an even-tempered horse, like Sara and Charlie. Trisha was good at matching horses and riders so that it worked out best for both.

But Hillary's face had settled into a scowl. "And what if they're *not* a good match?"

She was working herself up into a real snit.

"It's not fair! I'm a better rider than anyone here!" Hillary said, glaring at Cassie. "I've got more ribbons already than any of these girls will ever have! You're just playing favorites. I deserve the best horse!"

"I'm looking for the right horse for you, Hillary. And in the meantime, you're already riding Bliss," Trisha pointed out. "Bliss is a very good jumper."

"Let Cassie ride Bliss, then, if he's so good!" Hillary yelled.

Trisha frowned. "Hillary, I have heard enough," she said quietly but sternly. "I will not permit a student to tell me how to run Birchwood Stable."

"But . . . ," Hillary began. She was glancing around as if she were looking for someone. "Mom? Mom!"

A car door slammed at the far end of the barn, and a tall blond woman walked quickly toward them.

"Mom, speak to Trisha for me," Hillary ordered, when her mother was within earshot. "I want this horse!"

"He looks nice," Mrs. Craig said, glancing at Majesty. "Of course, your father will also want to see him before we decide."

"Mrs. Craig," Trisha said, "I bought this horse to use here at the stable. I am looking for a jumper for your daughter, and I'm . . ."

"Mom!" Hillary whined. "I want Majesty!"

"Can you believe this?" Amy murmured to Cassie.

And Sara was so embarrassed by all the fuss that she looked ready to sink through the ground.

Now Trisha was really annoyed. "Mrs. Craig, we'll talk about this in my office," she said firmly. Then she turned to Cassie, Amy, and Sara, and added, "Thanks for helping with the grooming, girls. Robert will finish up."

"Nuts!" Amy whispered to Cassie. "I wanted to hear the end of this!"

"So did I," Cassie said. After all, she had the most to lose. Or gain.

But she headed toward the tack room and the pay phone to call her mother.

Cassie wouldn't know until the next day if the Lipizzan was hers to ride. Or if she'd already lost Majesty to Hillary Craig.

CHAPTER
THREE

Trouble with Hillary

Amy had lunch at Cassie's house that day. The two of them told Cassie's mom and dad all about Majesty—and about Hillary.

Mr. Sinclair said, "Hillary may still be adjusting to the move from California. It's a big change to leave your home so far behind and move to a new place where you don't know anyone."

"Well, maybe that's part of it," Cassie said. "But Hillary doesn't seem to want to know anyone. When she first arrived, we were all friendly to her. When the theater had that film festival on horses, I invited her to go with Amy and me, but she said she was busy."

"Maybe she *was* busy," Mrs. Sinclair said.

"And I invited her to my birthday party," Amy said. "She never showed up."

"Finally we got tired of inviting her. It was clear she didn't want to be friends with us," Cassie said.

"And she's horribly jealous of Cassie," Amy said. "Hillary hates it that Cassie is such a good rider."

"Hillary's a good rider, too," said Cassie, trying to be fair.

"But that's not enough for Hillary," Amy said. "She has to be the *only* good rider at Birchwood. Or maybe in the world!"

Sometimes Amy did exaggerate. And Cassie could see from her parents' expressions that they couldn't completely accept what Amy was telling them.

"At any rate, Trisha Prescott has already made her decision about the Lipizzan," Mr. Sinclair said to Cassie. "She told you that you would be riding Majesty. If I know Trisha, she's not going to go back on her word."

Cassie hoped he was right. But she supposed that Mrs. Craig could be very stubborn, if she was anything like Hillary. And Trisha hated conflict at the stable. Would she give in to the Craigs to smooth over an unpleasant situation?

Before Cassie biked to Birchwood for her jumping lesson the next day, her mother said, "Don't give up on

Hillary. Try to be nicer to her, and she might warm up to you."

"Okay, Mom. I'll try," Cassie said.

But she knew in her heart that Hillary Craig was not at all interested in having Amy and her for pals. Hillary seemed to have a one-track mind that didn't allow for friends at Birchwood.

Cassie's Sunday lessons began at two o'clock. She was usually so eager to start that she got to the stable fifteen or twenty minutes early. This Sunday, Cassie biked over a half hour early.

Amy was waiting for her under the grooming tree.

"What are you doing here?" Cassie asked, delighted to see her friend.

"I thought you might need me here for some support," Amy said. "And I'm glad I came. We're not alone."

"Who's here?" Cassie glanced around the paddock, where some of the horses were running and playing in the sunshine. Then she looked at the two outdoor rings. She would be having her jumping lesson in the nearer one. The jumps were already set up. "Check the gazebo," Amy told her.

The gazebo was a round, open, little house with a peaked roof, built on a low platform. It stood between the two riding rings, so that onlookers could watch

the action from there without getting sunburned.

In the gazebo, a girl leaned back in one of the white chairs and stared straight ahead, waiting.

"Hillary," Cassie said.

Had she come to gloat because she'd gotten Majesty to ride, after all? Or was she here waiting for Trisha to make a final decision?

"She was already sitting in the gazebo when I got here," Amy said.

"Have you seen Trisha?" Cassie asked.

"I think she's in the barn," Amy said.

"Let's go talk to her," said Cassie. "I can't wait one second longer. I have to find out about Majesty!"

ꞌ She and Amy hurried into the barn and up the alley between two rows of horse stalls. They passed Freckles—Amy fed him a carrot on her way by—and Charlie, Bliss, and Allegra.

Then Trisha stepped out of a stall at the end of a row, and spotted the two girls.

"Hi there," she called out. "I was just about to saddle up Majesty."

"Does this mean that I'll be riding him?" Cassie practically shrieked.

"I believe it's about time for your lesson, isn't it?" Trisha said, as though there had never been any question about it. "Let's get him saddled."

31

Even in the gloom of the stable, the Lipizzan
seemed to glow. There was something almost magical
about his gleaming white coat and his huge,
intelligent brown eyes. Cassie wouldn't have been
surprised if he had suddenly spoken to her, or maybe
even sprouted wings!

While Cassie was helping tack Majesty up, Trisha
told the girls a little about him.

"Sara is right about Lipizzans. At one time, all the
Lipizzans in the world were at the Spanish Riding
School in Vienna, Austria. They were used for a
complicated kind of dressage," Trisha said. "Then, fifty
years or so ago, during World War II, an American
general brought some of those horses to the United
States. A little later, more of them were imported. But
there still aren't many Lipizzans here, so each one is
quite special."

As Trisha held up the bridle, Majesty lowered his
beautiful head so that she could slip it on.

"It looks as if he's bowing to his subjects," said
Amy, bowing back and giggling.

"Who owned Majesty before you bought him?"
Cassie asked Trisha, buckling the throatlatch on the
bridle.

"A friend of mine did. She used him for jumping.
But she retired from the horse-show circuit and felt

that she just couldn't put in the time with Majesty that he needed. She knew I would give him a good home and plenty to do, so she sold him to me," said Trisha.

She had picked out a saddle pad and placed it gently on Majesty's broad back. Next came the saddle that Cassie used.

Cassie reached carefully under the horse for the girth and buckled it up.

Trisha fastened the breast collar across Majesty's broad chest and stood back.

"We're all set," she said. "I want you to ride Majesty in the indoor ring for fifteen or twenty minutes, Cassie. It will warm him up for jumping and also give you a chance to get used to each other."

Cassie still couldn't quite believe that she would be riding this magical horse. In her excitement, she forgot all about Hillary. She and Amy, and Trisha and Majesty walked down a side alley to the indoor ring. A few moments later, Cassie was in the saddle, looking down at the powerful white shoulders and strong neck of her new horse.

"You'll have to make some adjustments," Trisha told her. "Allegra is a slower horse, less quick to respond to your aids."

Trisha went on, "Majesty is bigger than Allegra, too. He'll feel rather different to you."

Cassie nodded. Even sitting still, she knew she was riding a much larger and stronger animal.

"Let's start out with some circles and figure eights," Trisha said, walking to the sideline. Amy was standing just outside the ring, watching through the fence.

Cassie felt a little nervous and jittery, but at the same time she was almost bursting with eagerness to try Majesty out. She nudged the white horse forward with her legs, first in a medium walk, and then in a trot. She could feel Majesty's powerful legs moving under her in perfect rhythm.

"Good, Cassie. Now the canter," Trisha said.

As Majesty moved into the "one-two-three" beat of the canter, Cassie relaxed in the center of the saddle. She was thrilled with this new horse! Other students would also ride Majesty at Birchwood, but none could love him as much as she already did.

Suddenly, there was a loud bang from somewhere inside the stable. Startled, Majesty shied away from the noise, jumping to one side. It all happened so quickly, and Majesty was so strong, that Cassie's feet were jerked out of the stirrups. She slipped sideways in the saddle. If she hadn't grabbed hold of Majesty's mane, she would have fallen off.

Then Trisha was at their side, her hand on the

headstall of the bridle to steady Majesty. As she spoke soothingly to him, the horse pranced nervously in place for a few seconds. Then he calmed down, although his eyes and ears were still focused on the door that led into the stall area.

Once Cassie had gotten herself settled in the saddle again, Trisha called out, "What *was* that?"

Amy was peering through the door toward the rows of stalls, her back toward the ring. At the sound of Trisha's voice, she turned to answer.

But before she could say anything, Hillary appeared in the doorway. "Sorry," she said. "There was a metal bucket in the alley, and I stumbled over it."

Cassie could see Amy shaking her head. Did she mean that Hillary had kicked the metal bucket on purpose?

"Please be careful. We're having a lesson in here," Trisha said sternly to Hillary. To Cassie, she added, "Ride Majesty around for a few more minutes, and then we'll go outside and try some jumps."

Cassie had learned to jump in stages. She had begun by riding Allegra over a single pole lying on the ground between two uprights, first in a walk and then in a trot. Next, Trisha had added two crossed poles behind the single pole. Cassie learned to jump that at a trot.

She moved on from two small jumps in a row, still made of crossed poles, and still riding Allegra in a trot; to jumping them in a canter; to several different kinds of low fences in a canter. Now she was jumping two-and-a-half-foot fences on Allegra.

For Majesty, Trisha started Cassie out with four two-foot fences in a large oval. As they took off over the first fence, Cassie realized that jumping on Majesty would be a whole new experience.

She remembered to do all of the things that a rider should do, such as leaning her upper body forward as Majesty gathered himself to jump. She looked straight ahead, and her weight stayed in the middle of the saddle. Her legs were steady against the girth. Her back remained flat. And Majesty did the rest.

Cassie had a feeling that the strong white horse could have easily cleared jumps two times higher than this one without straining. He seemed to hang in the air for several seconds before landing smoothly on the far side. Then he went sailing over the second jump. And the third and fourth.

Allegra had been fun to jump on. But jumping on Majesty was the most exciting thing Cassie had ever done in her life.

They moved smoothly around the course a second time.

"Well done, Cassie," Trisha said. "Why don't you walk him for the rest of your hour?"

Cassie was sure that Majesty could have jumped for another hour. The horse wasn't even sweaty.

Amy had been sitting alone in the gazebo, watching Cassie put Majesty through his paces. She met her friend at the gate to the outdoor ring when the lesson was over.

"Hillary kicked that metal bucket on purpose, I'm sure of it," Amy said to Hillary as they walked back to the barn. "She was hoping to cause problems between you and Majesty."

"Well, we'd never be able to prove it. And even if we could, Trisha hates tattling," Cassie said. "Maybe now that Hillary's seen what a great team Majesty and I make, she'll get her mind on something else."

CHAPTER
FOUR

The Missing Hat

Cassie didn't think about Hillary much that week. She thought mostly about Majesty, and how exciting it would be to jump on him at horse shows, and maybe even win.

She also wondered who else would be riding Majesty. All of the horses at Birchwood were shared among the students. It had never bothered Cassie that a younger boy and girl rode Allegra, too. But she had to admit to herself that she wished Majesty were hers alone to ride.

The next Saturday morning, her mom drove her to the barn half an hour early. First Cassie stopped by Majesty's stall. She wanted the horse to learn to recognize her right away, so she'd brought him some fresh carrots and apple slices as a treat.

She laid her riding hat on the shelf outside Majesty's stall door and took the snacks out of a plastic bag. The white horse accepted them gently and politely. He didn't snatch or gobble like Freckles. Majesty plucked each carrot and apple slice neatly from Cassie's hand with his velvety upper lip. Then he bobbed his head up and down as he chewed, and Cassie could tell he was enjoying them.

When she had run out of carrots and apples, she walked outside to watch two of the older riders taking their horses over some high jumps. Every time one of the girls cleared a four-foot fence, Cassie imagined herself on Majesty doing exactly the same thing in the not-so-distant future.

Then Amy's dad dropped Amy off. When she and Cassie walked into the barn together to start tacking up their horses, Hillary was already there, saddling Bliss with Robert.

"Hey, Hillary," Cassie said casually.

Hillary barely nodded before she led Bliss down the alley toward the indoor ring.

"We'd better hurry," Amy said to Cassie as Robert helped them finish saddling Majesty and Freckles. "Sara's saddle is gone. She's already in the ring."

Trisha didn't like them to be late to a lesson. And if a student was too late, Trisha would start the lesson without her.

"I'll catch up with you. I just have to grab my hat," Cassie said.

Cassie led Majesty out of his stall and reached out for her riding hat, but the hat wasn't on the shelf.

Cassie was stunned. She was absolutely certain that she had placed it on the shelf outside Majesty's stall door. But it was nowhere to be seen. And she couldn't ride without her hat. It wouldn't be safe.

"The hat didn't just walk away," she said to herself. "Maybe it fell off the shelf and rolled out of sight."

Cassie led Majesty back into his stall and latched the door. She looked around on the floor of the stall. But the hat wasn't there.

Then she looked up and down the alley. No hat.

Cassie heard Trisha calling her name: "Cassie, we're waiting."

"I'll be right there!" Cassie called back.

She searched feverishly over, under, and behind everything at that end of the stable.

Finally, Cassie uncovered her riding hat in a pile of dirty straw, soon to be carried off to the trash by Robert.

How had it gotten there?!

Cassie barely had a moment to brush some of the straw off and jam the hat down on her head. She raced back to Majesty's stall and led the horse to the indoor ring in a brisk trot.

By this time, Cassie was out of breath and totally frazzled. And for the first few minutes of the group lesson, she didn't look like much of a rider. In fact, she wasn't even sitting in the saddle very well. "Stop slouching. Line up your ear, shoulder, hip, and ankle!" she repeated crossly to herself.

Cassie's mind was still on her hat, buried in the pile of dirty straw. Who had hidden it there?

"As if it could have been anyone other than Hillary," she thought in disgust. Hillary probably hoped to prove to Trisha that Cassie and Majesty weren't a good match. Well, she wasn't going to give Hillary the satisfaction of seeing her plans work. Cassie was *not* going to mess up with Majesty, no matter what Hillary tried.

When Trisha said, "Cassie, show us what you and Majesty can do," Cassie gave orders to herself. "Get your mind on your business! Straight line from elbow to hand to rein to mouth. Feel the horse under you."

Cassie knew that her riding style would change now that she was riding Majesty. For starters, the white horse was used to being ridden on a much shorter rein than Allegra. Cassie was always in close contact with his mouth through her hands on the reins. His body was more tightly gathered together, too. And his movements were shorter and higher, almost like prancing.

For the first time in her life, Cassie felt as though she was riding a real show horse, even though all she was really doing was going through her exercises in the indoor ring. Thoughts of Hillary faded, and she was aware of nothing but the big horse beneath her.

Cassie's face must have shown everyone how pleased she was. As she and Majesty walked to their place near the gate, Hillary rode past them for her turn in the ring. And she gave Cassie such a dirty look that Cassie's heart sank.

Cassie wanted to be able to focus her thoughts on the most important thing while she was at Birchwood—improving her riding. She didn't want to have to waste time worrying about what Hillary might do next.

"I guess I don't have a choice. I have to talk to Trisha about Hillary," Cassie said to herself. "And I might as well get it over with." As soon as class was finished, she asked Trisha if she could speak with her privately.

Amy raised her eyebrows. And Hillary frowned.

"Of course you can," Trisha said. "As soon as you've unsaddled, Cassie, come to my office."

"What's this all about?" Amy whispered to her outside the tack room.

"Tell you later," Cassie whispered back, because she could see that Hillary was listening.

In Trisha's office, Cassie told Trisha what Amy had said about Hillary and the metal bucket. Then she told her about her riding hat disappearing from the shelf.

"Hillary's angry with me about Majesty," Cassie said. "I think maybe she's trying to play tricks so that Majesty and I don't work out."

"Hillary isn't right for Majesty," Trisha said straight off, which cheered Cassie up immediately. "Majesty needs a gentle touch, and Hillary sometimes rides heavily on the reins. And sometimes she leans heavily on people, too," Trisha added. "As to the hat, I agree it does look suspicious, but you have no real proof that it was Hillary, do you?"

Cassie was forced to shake her head. "But it had to have been Hillary. None of my friends would play such a nasty trick on me."

Trisha nodded sympathetically. "I know Hillary can be difficult, Cassie. On the other hand, she isn't having an easy time of it herself."

"You mean, moving here from California?" Cassie said, remembering her talk with her parents.

"Yes, that," said Trisha, "and the fact of having a stepfather whom she still doesn't feel certain about, and . . ."

"Mr. Craig isn't Hillary's dad?" Cassie said, shocked.

She'd thought that Hillary's real reason for riding was to be just like her father.

"No, Hillary's father died when Hillary was quite young. Mrs. Craig remarried a year ago," said Trisha. "I don't approve of gossiping, but I'm telling you this to help you understand some of the reasons that Hillary sometimes acts the way she does."

"Did her real father ride, too?" Cassie asked, recalling Hillary's announcement that she had been riding since she was an infant.

But Trisha was shaking her head. "Hillary started riding three years ago. And she rides remarkably well for just three years." Trisha smiled at Cassie. "Almost as well as you do," she said.

"Do you think Hillary *likes* riding?" Cassie asked. "She sure doesn't seem to like the group."

"Hillary's in the group because her mother wants her to make friends," Trisha explained.

Cassie rolled her eyes. That certainly wasn't working out!

"As far as liking riding—it's a good question," said Trisha. "Hillary's good at it. But I don't know if she likes it, or if she's doing it because she thinks it will please her stepfather, especially if she wins."

"And if Hillary wins at horse shows, she thinks her stepfather will like her more?" Cassie said.

"Probably," said Trisha.

Trisha nodded. "Now you understand what I mean about Hillary's worries," she said. "Not that I'm excusing bad behavior on Hillary's part," Trisha added. "And if you ever feel that she's doing anything to cause you difficulties on purpose, I'd appreciate it if . . ."

Suddenly, the door to Trisha's office burst open. It was Hillary, her face beet red. "I know what Cassie's been saying. And I didn't hide her stupid hat in the straw!" Hillary yelled at Trisha. She was so worked up that she threw her own hat on the floor. "Cassie's just trying to get me into trouble!"

"No one has said anything about straw," Trisha replied calmly.

"No? But . . . ," Hillary fumbled, realizing she'd made a mistake.

How could she have known about the pile of straw, if she hadn't hidden the hat herself?

"Cassie is jealous of me because I ride better than she does!" Hillary said.

Which was so unfair that Cassie couldn't think of an answer.

But she didn't have to, because Trisha said, "Hillary, this has gone far enough. I'm not used to having pointless and unpleasant scenes at Birchwood." Then she added, "And I *won't* have them. Please ask your mother or father to get in touch with me."

When Trisha mentioned her parents, Hillary's face faded from red to white. "But I . . . ," she began rather weakly.

"As soon as possible," Trisha said firmly.

Hillary backed out of the office so quickly that she left her hat behind, on the floor.

Trisha shook her head. "I'm afraid that Hillary isn't going to be much help when it comes to reducing the tension around here," she said. She looked at Cassie for a moment, and went on. "Maybe you could try to get on better terms with her. Would you do that for me?"

"How?" Cassie asked, wishing she never had to deal with Hillary Craig again.

"That's a hard one," Trisha said. Then her gaze fell on Hillary's riding hat, which had rolled under her desk. "Here," she said, handing Cassie the hat. "Maybe you could return this to Hillary on your way home.

Show her you want to be friends. Or, at the very least, not enemies."

Cassie took the riding hat. "I'll try," she said, willing to try it for Trisha.

But Cassie didn't have any great hopes. And she didn't think Trisha did, either.

CHAPTER
FIVE

A Wonderful Surprise

Trisha gave Cassie Hillary's address on Lilac Drive, a street in a brand-new subdivision not far from the stable.

When Cassie's mom drove up to the curb in front of 22 Lilac Drive, both Cassie and Amy gasped. It was a huge, two-story brick house, with big columns across the front, a circular driveway, and a tennis court to one side.

"That's the biggest house I've ever seen," Cassie said.

The Craigs' house was also brand-new, so new that it was hard to believe anyone had moved in yet. The emerald-green lawn was perfect. There were no

bikes, or skates, or toys to be seen.

"It looks like a public library," Amy added, "but without any people."

"Are you sure this is the right address?" Mrs. Sinclair asked Cassie. "It does look empty. Or maybe the Craigs just haven't had time to add any personal touches."

"It's the number Trisha wrote down," Cassie said, rechecking her slip of paper.

"Well, go ahead, honey," her mom said.

"Want to come with me?" Cassie said to Amy.

"Uh-uh. I'll wait in the car with your mom," said Amy.

Cassie walked toward the front door, with Hillary's riding hat under her arm. Her feet moved slower and slower as she got closer. She climbed the steps between the giant columns and rang the front doorbell.

Cassie could hear chimes echoing inside the house, but no one came to the door. She was just about to leave when the door finally swung open.

And there was Hillary, taken completely by surprise to find Cassie standing on her front steps.

"Hi," Cassie said.

"Hi," said Hillary, staring past her at Mrs. Sinclair's car, with Amy peering out the back window.

"I'm on my way home from the stable. Trisha asked me to bring your riding hat," Cassie explained, holding it out to her.

"Thanks," Hillary said, taking the hat without inviting Cassie inside.

Behind Hillary, a large glass-fronted cabinet covered one wall of an entry hall. Inside it, Cassie could see the gleam of gold and silver trophies.

"Wow!" Cassie exclaimed.

The trophies seemed to pull her forward. Without thinking, Cassie stepped around Hillary and into the entry hall to take a closer look.

The cabinet held at least twenty large trophies decorated with horses, plus a handful of smaller ones, and many colored ribbons.

"Did you win these at horse shows?" Cassie asked Hillary, feeling very outclassed.

Hillary answered, "Some of them are mine. But most are my stepfather's."

Now Cassie was close enough to read the dates on the trophies and ribbons. Many were fifteen years old or more.

"I have an important engagement to get ready for," Hillary said in her snobbiest voice. "Thanks for stopping by to bring me my hat."

Cassie shrugged. "Sure."

She couldn't think of anything more to say to Hillary, anyway. She'd done what Trisha had asked her to do, and it hadn't made a bit of difference.

But as Cassie turned to leave, she heard voices at the back of the house. Then, "Hillary?" a man called out.

"In here," Hillary replied.

A small, thin man with curly, dark hair stepped into the entry hall. "Oh, you have a friend with you," he said briskly.

"Dad, I've told you about Cassie," Hillary said.

"I'll bet you have!" Cassie thought to herself.

"Nice to meet you, Cassie," said Mr. Craig, shaking her hand. Then to Hillary he added, "Lunch will be ready in a few minutes."

Hillary nodded. "I'll be right there."

Mr. Craig smiled at Cassie. "Are you keeping Hillary company for lunch?" he asked.

"No, thank you, I can't," Cassie said. "My mom is waiting for me. Goodbye."

She slipped out the front door and hurried down the walk toward the car, still shivering a little from the Craigs' air-conditioning. Cassie found herself actually feeling sorry for Hillary. Hillary had looked pretty lonesome in the huge house.

Cassie and her mom dropped Amy off at her house. Then they joined Mr. Sinclair for a quick lunch of chicken salad sandwiches at their kitchen table.

When lunch was over and they'd put their dishes in the dishwasher, Cassie's dad said, "Your mom and I would like to take you for a short ride in the car."

"But I planned to bike over to Amy's this afternoon," Cassie said. After all, she and Amy hadn't had time to really discuss her visit to Hillary's house.

"This won't take too long," said Mrs. Sinclair. "And I think you'll find it interesting."

"Okay," Cassie said. "Maybe you can drop me off at the Lins' on the way home."

They got into her dad's car and drove here and there for fifteen minutes or so, until Cassie finally said, "Dad, where *are* we going?" Her mom said, "Bill, don't tease her."

Her father grinned, made a couple of right turns, and ended up on Middle Road, the same road that Birchwood Stable was on.

"We're going to drive right past Birchwood," Cassie pointed out.

But they didn't drive past the stable. Her dad turned into the lane and kept going until he reached the barn.

"Why are we here?" Cassie asked, more puzzled than ever.

"We wanted to check out our investment," Mr. Sinclair replied, opening his car door.

"What does he mean?" Cassie asked her mother, as the two of them climbed out of the car.

"He means Majesty," her mother said with a big smile.

"We've leased him for you, Cassie," her father added.

Cassie couldn't take in what they were saying for a moment. "You've leased . . . ," she began, and stopped. "Majesty is all mine to ride?" she shrieked, understanding at last.

"All yours, sweetie," said her dad. "I spoke to Trisha Prescott about it on the phone this morning, and she's preparing a contract for us to sign."

Cassie thought she would burst with happiness. If her parents had leased Majesty, she wouldn't have to share him with anyone else at the stable. Plus, she could ride him every day if she wanted!

But first she had to ask, "Can we afford it?"

"Yes, because I'm working on a big, new project," her mother said. Mrs. Sinclair was a technical writer for a computer company.

"And we'll take a cheaper vacation," said Mr.

Sinclair. "So, let's go see this remarkable animal."

"Oh, yes!" cried Cassie, eagerly.

"Before we do, we have to stop by Ms. Prescott's office to sign that contract," Mrs. Sinclair reminded them.

Hillary in Hot Water

But Trisha's car wasn't parked outside the barn. Robert was leading Freckles and Charlie back to the paddock. After he said hello to Cassie and her parents, he added, "If you're looking for Trisha, she's teaching a class in Milford. She should be here in the next half-hour or so."

Cassie took her parents to the barn instead. "In the meantime, I'll show you Majesty," she told them.

The three of them walked up to the alley toward the Lipizzan's stall.

"Majesty?" Cassie called out, expecting the big white horse to poke his head out over the stall door. But he didn't.

"He's probably taking a catnap," Cassie said.

"Don't you mean a horse nap?" her dad joked.

When they peered over the door, Cassie was surprised to discover that the stall was empty.

"Maybe he's out in the paddock," Cassie told her parents, a little uneasily. Now that Majesty's was hers alone to ride, Cassie wanted to know where he was every second of every day.

"Robert?" Cassie called out.

"I'm in the tack room," Robert called back. He stepped into the alley to talk to Cassie.

"Where's Majesty?" she asked.

"Oh, he's in one of the outdoor rings," Robert said.

"An outdoor ring?" Cassie repeated. "Why?"

Trisha never turned the stable horses loose in an outdoor ring for exercise, because jumps were usually set up there. The horses might get tangled up in the jumps and hurt themselves. Outdoor rings were for riding only. Did that mean someone was riding Majesty?

Robert answered Cassie before she even asked. "That Craig girl is riding him."

"What?" Cassie said. How could that be? Majesty was hers now.

Mr. Sinclair placed his hand on Cassie's shoulder to calm her. "There must be some mistake. We've leased Majesty for Cassie. I spoke to Ms. Prescott about it only a few hours ago. No one else should be riding him."

Robert shrugged and shook his head. "I guess Trisha forgot to mention it to me," he said. "Hillary and her father drove here about forty-five minutes ago. And when I told them that Trisha wasn't around, Mr. Craig insisted that Hillary try out the Lipizzan. He wouldn't take no for an answer."

"I made it clear to Mr. Craig that he would have to square it with Trisha when she got back. He said there wouldn't be a problem, that Hillary had talked to Trisha and had gotten her approval," Robert ended.

Cassie found it hard to concentrate on what Robert was saying. She was too angry to listen to much more than the words pounding in her own head: "Hillary Craig is riding my horse!"

She stormed out of the barn, while her mother called out after her, "Wait, Cassie, I'm sure there's been a misunderstanding."

"There's no misunderstanding," Cassie muttered to herself as she marched toward the outdoor rings. "Hillary knew Trisha would be away all afternoon, giving her the perfect opportunity to ride Majesty. She'll do anything to ride him, including lie!"

Mr. Craig wasn't sitting in the gazebo like a visitor,

watching Hillary ride from a distance. Cassie heard him talking from inside the far ring, giving Hillary advice from close-up.

Cassie saw Hillary's dark-brown riding hat bobbing up and down above the tall fence as she cantered across the outdoor ring. Hillary and Majesty were headed toward the line of jumps.

"Stop!" Cassie shouted.

Hillary didn't seem to hear. She was focused on the jumps in front of her.

"Don't squeeze him with your legs, Hillary," Mr. Craig called out to his stepdaughter. "Look straight in front of you."

Cassie started to run toward the gate of the ring where Hillary was riding.

Mr. Craig was still giving instructions. "Let the reins move with his head. Your legs are behind the stirrups, get them under you."

As angry as Cassie was, she wondered, "How can Hillary possibly manage to follow all of those orders while she's trying to ride a strange horse over a jump?"

Cassie unlatched the gate to the outdoor ring and shoved it open in time to see Hillary and Majesty sail over the last jump.

On the far side of the jump, Hillary pulled Majesty

up hard, pinching his mouth. His ears flattened with annoyance as he felt the pinch.

Cassie shouted at the top of her lungs, "Hillary Craig, get off my horse!"

Mr. Craig was standing near the fence at one side of the ring, still watching Hillary. But when Cassie shouted, he turned quickly around.

"Why, it's Cassie, isn't it? What do you mean, *your* horse?" He sounded truly surprised.

Majesty is my horse now. My parents leased him for me," Cassie said.

Mr. Sinclair hurried through the gate. "That's right. We leased the Lipizzan for Cassie this morning," he said to Mr. Craig. "Hello, I'm Bill Sinclair."

"Andrew Craig." Mr. Craig shook hands with Cassie's dad. "Did you speak to Ms. Prescott about the horse?"

"Absolutely," said Mr. Sinclair. "I made the arrangements by phone. My wife and I are here now to sign the contract."

"I'm sorry," said Mr. Craig. "There must have been some confusion between Ms. Prescott and Hillary."

Instead of riding Majesty back to the group at the gate, Hillary had steered him toward the back fence. She was bent over, pretending to look at her right stirrup.

"Hillary!" Mr. Craig called out.

"Yes?" she called back, as though she had no idea what might be going on, with Cassie and her dad standing right there.

Mr. Craig waved his arm to let Hillary know he wanted her at the gate.

Hillary pulled Majesty to a stop behind Mr. Craig and slid down from the saddle.

"Cassie tells me that this is her horse," Mr. Craig said.

"Since when?" Hillary was dumbstruck.

"Since this morning," Cassie replied, looking Hillary straight in the eye. "That's when my parents leased him for me."

Hillary scowled, and her face turned dark red.

"When did you speak to Ms. Prescott about riding Majesty?" Mr. Craig asked.

"Why, right after our lesson, I think," Hillary mumbled.

"No, you didn't," Cassie said. "I was in Trisha's office right after our lesson, remember?"

"So that's that, Hillary," said Mr. Craig. "We'll just find you another horse. I don't know how you got the idea that this one was available."

Cassie saw Trisha coming toward them. Mrs. Sinclair was right behind her.

"I want to know exactly what is going on here," Trisha said, as she joined them near the gate. "Hillary, you did not have permission to ride Majesty, even if the Sinclairs hadn't leased him. I have been looking for a horse for you. And I will continue to do so, if you can convince me that you're the kind of student that I want to have at Birchwood Stable. You will have to change your attitude, though."

Mr. Craig said, "Ms. Prescott, I'm sure Hillary meant no harm."

Trisha said, "Hillary, hand Cassie the reins, please."

Hillary thrust Majesty's reins in Cassie's direction, her gaze fixed on the ground.

"Let's talk about this in my office," Trisha said to Mr. Craig. "I'll meet you there in a few minutes."

Hillary hurried away, in the direction of the barn.

Mr. Craig turned to Cassie's parents. "I'm sorry about all of this," he told them.

When Mr. Craig had left, Cassie rested her cheek against Majesty's warm neck. She closed her eyes and imagined herself on Majesty, sailing over the jumps at the first horse show.

Trisha smiled warmly at Mr. and Mrs. Sinclair. "So what do you think of Cassie's horse?"

"He's just beautiful!" Mrs. Sinclair exclaimed, standing back a little. She was a bit leery of horses.

"He's one powerful-looking fellow," said Mr. Sinclair. "Cassie, can you really handle this horse?"

"Would you like to show your parents how well the two of you work together?" Trisha said to Cassie.

"I'd love to!" Cassie said.

She was still wearing her riding breeches and boots. And Trisha had brought out a hat to lend her.

While her parents sat in the gazebo and watched, Cassie put Majesty through his paces in one of the outdoor rings. Once he was warmed up, she jumped a few fences for them, too.

Her parents and Trisha clapped as she and Majesty cleared the last fence with a couple of feet to spare.

Cassie pulled in her Lipizzan and thought, "This is turning out to be one of the best days of my life!"

CHAPTER
SEVEN

Hillary's Horse

Cassie planned to ride Majesty at least a couple of hours every day. "I want to be sure that you're getting your money's worth," she said to her parents.

"So you're doing it for us, not for yourself. Is that what you're telling me?" her dad joked.

And her mom said, "Two hours a day in the summertime is one thing, Cassie. But when school starts, you may have to cut back."

"Even more reason for me to get in as much riding as I can now," Cassie said.

There were also some local horse shows coming up. The show at Barker Farm was only three weeks away, and Cassie needed to practice, practice, practice. She hoped she wasn't thinking like Hillary, but she did want her parents to feel that they weren't wasting their money leasing Majesty for her. A trophy or a ribbon would be nice!

Cassie preferred to ride in the morning, before the sun got too hot, and before the riding rings were too crowded. All of the Birchwood horses were fed around seven o'clock every morning. Cassie would get to the stable, ready to saddle up, before nine. Since Trisha didn't schedule any classes before ten, Cassie and Majesty usually had an hour to themselves.

But on Thursday that first week, Cassie rolled up to the barn on her bike to discover quite a crowd already on hand. Besides Trisha's blue truck and trailer in the parking area, there was a green station wagon and a white horse van with "Herricks' Horse Farm" painted on the side. Tied to a hook on the back of the van, a stocky bay horse was switching flies with his tail. He whinnied at Cassie in a friendly way as she walked past.

A couple of men in jeans were sitting on hay bales just inside the barn, talking to Robert Martin. And as Cassie headed down the alley toward Majesty's stall, she heard more voices coming from the indoor ring. She recognized Trisha's voice, and another voice sounded a lot like Hillary.

What would Hillary be doing at the stable so early on a Thursday morning? Curious, Cassie turned around and walked toward the ring to take a look.

The first thing Cassie saw when she stepped through the door was a striking chestnut horse with two white feet and a blaze on its face. Then she checked out the rider: It was Hillary, looking excited, and maybe a bit nervous, too.

Trisha was standing beside the horse. Cassie could hear her talking to Mr. and Mrs. Craig, who were outside the fence.

"I personally think he's a little too much horse for Hillary," Trisha was saying to them. "He's a Thoroughbred, he's high-strung. I think she would do much better leasing the bay. He's steadier, he's used to young riders, he's been to many horse shows and has done well at them."

Mr. Craig shook his head. "I disagree. Hillary's an excellent rider. She needs an excellent horse, and the Thoroughbred's just the ticket. What do you say, Hillary?"

Hillary shrugged. "I don't know. I like him, but I really want a Lipizzan." Her lower lip jutted out as she pouted.

"I couldn't find another Lipizzan on such short

notice," Trisha said. "The bay is a fine horse. I recommend that you lease it for Hillary."

"The bay is a horse for a five-year-old," Mr. Craig scoffed. "Hillary won't win any ribbons on a tame horse like that."

Trisha rubbed her forehead as if she had a headache. "That's not so, Mr. Craig. The bay has brought in his share of ribbons. Why not let Hillary try him out next?"

Hillary took her father's side. "The bay looks as if he should be pulling a farm wagon! And he plods—I won't win anything on him. If I can't have a Lipizzan, I want the Thoroughbred." She appealed to her mother: "Mom!"

"Hillary, you know that I know nothing whatsoever about horses," her mother said.

"Maybe neither horse is quite right for Hillary," Trisha suggested. "Why don't I talk to a few more people, and . . ."

Hillary might have gone along with Trisha's suggestion if she hadn't caught sight of Cassie just then. Seeing Cassie—and perhaps thinking about Majesty—seemed to make her twice as determined to lease the Thoroughbred.

"No!" Hillary said, shaking her head. "I want this horse. The horse shows start soon, and Thor and I are going to make a great team and beat everybody. I'm sure of it!" She stared straight at Cassie as she said it.

Trisha looked at Mr. Craig.

He grinned and patted Hillary on the back. "Now you're talking. You've made me very proud, Hillary. You have winning in your blood, same as I have."

Hillary glanced at Cassie again and smiled smugly. "Thor and I will be blue-ribbon winners, I know we will."

"Would you like to ride Thor around some more, Hillary?" her mother asked. "We can come back for you."

"No, I'll ride him on Saturday at my group lesson," Hillary said. "Wait for me, okay?"

Hillary hurriedly slipped out of the saddle. "I'll put him in his stall now," she said, reins in hand. "Which stall will be his, Trisha?"

"I think the one across from Majesty would be fine," Trisha said.

"Great," said Hillary. "I'll unsaddle him and get him settled."

That was the first time Cassie had ever heard Hillary volunteer for any work herself. And it probably had a lot more to do with showing off her new horse to Cassie than helping out Trisha.

Trisha said, "Thank you, Hillary. Mr. and Mrs.

Craig, we can sign the contract in my office."

Cassie was standing in Majesty's stall, grooming him with a dandy brush, when Hillary led her new horse to the stall opposite.

"Oh, hello," Hillary said brightly, as though she had just noticed Cassie for the first time that day. "Have you seen my horse? His name is Thor."

"He's a beauty," Cassie said, continuing to brush Majesty.

Cassie had promised her parents—and herself—that she wouldn't waste any more time getting angry about Hillary Craig. After all, Majesty now was hers alone.

"Yes, he's gorgeous," Hillary said. "And the best thing about him is that since he's leased, I can ride whenever I want. I can ride him every day, if I feel like it." Hillary fiddled with Thor's mane with a curry comb.

Then she must have remembered that Cassie could ride Majesty whenever she wanted, too. She tossed the curry comb aside and stamped out of Thor's stall and up the alley.

By the time Saturday morning rolled around, Cassie and the Lipizzan were really getting to know each other. She had learned some of his funny little habits, like the way he stretched his neck out and sniffed her as she stepped through the stall door. Once Majesty was certain it was Cassie, he nickered a greeting deep in his throat.

Or the way he rubbed his forehead up and down on her shoulder after she pulled his bridle off. And the way he hated the sound of the fly-spray can. He always turned his ears straight back and stamped one foot as if to say, "Not in this stall!"

When they were in the ring, Majesty would let Cassie know when she was doing something that bothered him: either leaning too far forward in the saddle, or sitting a bit crooked, or pushing him off balance. The horse would curve his neck slightly, so one eye could peer in her direction. Cassie could almost hear him saying, "Hey! What's going on up there?"

Cassie figured Majesty had a right to ask. After all, he was the one with more experience. She had a lot more to learn from him than he did from her.

Cassie had already come to depend on the Lipizzan's intelligence and on his excellent attitude. Majesty went out of his way to do what she asked, from small things, like trotting slower or faster, to much bigger things, like jumping a three-foot fence.

Cassie couldn't have been happier than she was with the beautiful white horse.

But as soon as she saw Hillary on Saturday, she knew that things weren't going at all well for her and Thor.

Cassie had spent Friday night at Amy's. Mr. Lin drove them to Birchwood about half an hour before their Saturday group lesson. Cassie wanted to spend some time with Majesty in his stall. And she wanted him to get to know Amy, too.

Amy had come prepared with enough apple slices and carrots to feed Majesty and Freckles and three or four more horses. But on their way into the barn, Cassie and Amy happened to glance toward the outdoor rings. In the farther one, they saw a girl with reddish-brown hair riding a chestnut horse.

"It's Hillary on her new horse, Thor," Cassie said to Amy.

"Well, I don't think they're having any fun," Amy said.

Thor's head was raised high in the air, and Hillary was really bouncing around in the saddle.

"It looks as if they're having problems," Cassie agreed.

"Let's watch!" said Amy.

"Maybe we shouldn't," Cassie said. An audience was probably the last thing Hillary wanted right now.

"*She* watches *you*," Amy pointed out. "Come on."

So Cassie followed Amy over to the gazebo, and they sat down.

By this time, not only was Thor high-headed, he was dancing around. The more Hillary tugged on the reins, the more he fought the bit.

"She should loosen up on his mouth," Cassie said, remembering what Trisha had told her about Hillary's heavy hands on the reins. "He would stop fighting her then."

"I think she's scared of him," Amy said, adding, "That's a tall horse. Hillary has an awfully long way to fall."

Hillary did look panicky. And suddenly, to make matters worse, Thor lunged forward. Now he was trying to take the bit away from Hillary altogether.

Cassie didn't know what would have happened if an older girl, Jane Clark, hadn't ridden into the ring at that point. She took one look at what was going on between Hillary and Thor and moved her horse forward. She pressed Thor toward the fence, so he'd have to stop jumping around.

"Loosen up on the reins," Jane yelled to Hillary at the same time.

In a few seconds, Thor was standing still. Jane jumped off her horse and grabbed Thor's bridle so that Hillary could climb down.

When her feet touched the ground, Hillary almost collapsed. She really had been frightened.

"Let's leave before Hillary sees us," Cassie said to Amy. She was feeling sorry for the girl again. "There's no sense in making her more upset than she already is."

Where Is Hillary?

Hillary was mounted on Thor and ready to ride in the indoor ring when the group class began fifteen minutes later. She was brave. Cassie had to give her that.

Amy put it a different way, though. "I'd call it hard-headed and just plain dumb," Amy whispered to Cassie. "I'd never get on that horse again if I were Hillary!"

Whatever it was, Hillary took her turn in the middle of the ring, just like everyone else. Cassie and Amy knew that Thor had frightened her badly, but Hillary didn't say anything to Trisha about it. She squared her shoulders and started putting Thor through his paces as though she felt totally comfortable with him.

Of course, Trisha helped out by insisting that Hillary slow the horse down. "Keep him calm," Trisha told her. "Thor might get excitable if he gets too warmed up."

"'Excitable'?" Amy whispered to Cassie as they watched from the gate. "That's putting it mildly!"

"Maybe he'll behave himself if Hillary keeps him under control from the start," Cassie whispered back.

But she found herself holding her breath during most of Hillary's ride. For Cassie, Thor was a little like a firecracker with a long fuse. It might take a while, but it was almost certainly going to go off!

"Slow down, Hillary . . . halt," Trisha finally called out from the sidelines. "Good work."

Cassie saw Hillary's shoulders slump as she rode Thor toward the group at the gate. She'd been holding herself so tensely that her shoulders had been up around her ears.

"He's a beautiful horse," Sara said shyly to Hillary once she'd joined them. After all, Sara hadn't witnessed the commotion in the outdoor ring.

"Thanks," Hillary mumbled, her thoughts elsewhere. Then she snapped out of it and added quickly, "Isn't he great?" Looking over at Cassie on

Majesty, Hillary said, "Thor's the handsomest horse around and a registered Thoroughbred, too."

Of course, Hillary didn't realize that Cassie had seen her earlier struggle. And she was not going to admit that Thor was anything but super, especially not with Cassie and Majesty getting along so well.

Cassie took her turn next. She could hear Trisha talking to the others while she and Majesty moved around the ring.

"It's very important always to keep in contact with your horse's mouth and to keep the same *light* contact, no matter if he's walking, trotting, or cantering—or even jumping," Trisha was saying. "See how Cassie's arms follow the movements of Majesty's head? As his head moves up and down, so do her arms. She stays balanced in the middle of the saddle, and her hands keep in light contact with his mouth through the reins."

Cassie and the Lipizzan walked, trotted, and cantered in smaller and smaller circles to the right, and then to the left. Cassie used half-halts—almost invisible signals to the horse through her legs and hands—to let him know they would be shifting gears to a faster or slower speed. Majesty was so smooth that Cassie often felt as if she were riding in a dream.

When Cassie and Majesty had stopped and backed

up, ready to take their place beside the gate, Trisha said, "Well done, Cassie. You're getting better and better."

"Being able to ride as often as I like is making a big difference," Cassie said happily. "And Majesty teaches me something every time I get on him."

Then Trisha said to the class, "Think of your contact with your horse's mouth as a steady, warm handshake. Keep your fingers closed firmly around the reins, with your thumbs on top and pressing down. And keep your elbows relaxed, so you can go with the horse's motion." She added, "The worst thing you can do is loosen up on the reins, letting the horse go faster and faster until he gets away from you, then panic and yank on him."

Cassie glanced at Hillary. Trisha was describing exactly what had happened between Hillary and Thor in the outdoor ring.

Hillary must have realized it, too. She was concentrating so hard on what Trisha was saying that her lips moved as she repeated it to herself.

"Okay, that's all for today," Trisha said. "I'll see all of you next Saturday for our group lesson. I want everyone to start thinking about our first horse show, at Barker Farm in Port Pleasant. It's only three weeks away. And Cassie and Hillary: I'll see you tomorrow

afternoon at the usual time for your jumping classes."

"I can't wait to take Thor over the three-footers," Hillary said brightly.

"I think we'll start with some lower jumps first," Trisha said with a smile.

"I'm just glad I won't have to watch it," Amy whispered to Cassie. "I have a feeling that Hillary's going to be flying through the air without her horse!"

When Cassie arrived for her lesson the next day, she expected to find Hillary already hanging around the outdoor ring, waiting to see how well Cassie and Majesty were doing. Or waiting to catch Cassie messing up, which is how Amy would have put it.

But Hillary was nowhere in sight. And Cassie didn't mess up. She and Majesty sailed over every jump so beautifully that Trisha actually clapped!

Cassie was so caught up in her riding that she didn't give Hillary another thought until her class was over, and Trisha said, "I wonder where Hillary is. She should have been warming Thor up."

And suddenly Robert called from the barn, "Trisha! It's Mrs. Craig on the phone."

As Trisha hurried to take the call, Cassie led Majesty to the barn. Walking him toward his stall, Cassie paused when she overheard Trisha saying, "I'm sorry to hear that." Trisha went on, "I know that a stomach flu has been going around. That's all right, Mrs. Craig. I'll have Robert ride Thor, to give him some exercise. Yes, and I hope Hillary will be feeling better soon."

So Hillary wasn't at her jumping lesson because she was sick with the flu.

Cassie and Amy had made plans to go to the mall right after Cassie's lesson. Mrs. Lin and Amy stopped by the barn to pick her up.

"Any trouble with Hillary today?" Amy asked as Cassie slid into the back seat of the Lins' car.

"She didn't show up," Cassie said. "She has the flu."

"And its name is Thor," Amy added. "I bet she didn't want to ride him, and I don't blame her."

"Amy, I don't know where you get these ideas," Mrs. Lin said. "You barely know the girl, and you're already imagining what she's thinking."

Cassie shook her head. "I heard Trisha on the phone with Mrs. Craig. It sounded as if Hillary really is sick, Amy."

Amy rolled her eyes, but she didn't say anything else.

When they got to the mall, Mrs. Lin wanted to buy some towels at Lauren's Linens.

"Towels are so boring, Mom," Amy said. "Cassie

and I will look around, and meet you in . . ."

"In twenty minutes, in front of the fountain," Mrs. Lin said firmly. *"Twenty minutes, Amy."*

"Okay, Mom," Amy said, looking at her watch. "Where do you want to go, Cassie?"

"Boots and Saddles," Cassie replied immediately. The store sold everything a horsewoman might want: riding clothes, tack, trunks, grooming supplies. Cassie loved Boots and Saddles.

"Again?" Amy groaned, but she gave in. "Okay, eight minutes in Boots and Saddles, nine minutes in Dandelion looking at shorts and bathing suits, and three minutes buying some popcorn at the candy store. Let's hurry!"

The two of them raced up the middle aisle of the mall and burst through the door of Boots and Saddles.

"Hi, girls," said Linda, the salesperson. "We're having a sale on breeches and tights."

Cassie shook her head. "No, thanks. I want to buy a braiding kit."

She was planning ahead, to the first horse show, when she would be braiding Majesty's mane. The Lipizzan deserved his own supplies!

Because Cassie knew the store almost as well as she knew her own house, she found the braiding kit in less than three minutes. "Great. Let's look at the tights now," Amy said. "We have plenty of time."

The clothes were in the back part of the store, around a corner. Cassie and Amy were squeezing past a pile of hatboxes when Amy suddenly whispered, "Guess who's here. She doesn't look sick to me!"

It was Hillary, flipping through a rack of riding breeches. She looked healthy enough until she spotted Cassie and Amy. Then she started to look somewhat pale.

"Oh! Uh, hi," Hillary fumbled.

"Hi," said Cassie, and Amy just nodded.

"I didn't come to class today," Hillary began.

"I noticed," said Cassie.

"I wasn't feeling well. I had an awful headache." Hillary said.

"I heard it was the flu," Cassie said.

Hillary gulped. She looked as if she wanted to disappear. "Yes, well. That's what we thought at first."

"Are you feeling better now?" said Amy.

"Much," said Hillary. "I have to hurry. My mom is waiting."

"See you around," said Amy.

"Maybe I'll see you at the barn this week," said Cassie.

"Maybe," said Hillary. "By the way, you won't

mention this to Trisha, will you?" she added. "Running into me here at the mall, I mean. I really wouldn't want Trisha to think that I was, uh, goofing off or anything."

Cassie and Amy shook their heads, and Hillary rushed away.

Amy raised her eyebrows at Cassie.

"Okay, you were right," Cassie said to her friend. "Hillary didn't want to ride Thor."

"But if she doesn't ride him a lot, how can they ever get along any better?" Amy said.

"They can't," said Cassie. "I think Hillary chose the wrong horse for herself."

It made Cassie feel twice as lucky to have Majesty.

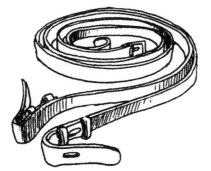

CHAPTER
NINE

Cassie to the Rescue

Cassie didn't see Hillary at the barn for the next few days, even though she biked over to Birchwood every morning herself. After she warmed Majesty up, Cassie rode him over a course of jumps that Trisha had helped her set up in one of the outdoor rings. The course included single fences and combinations. Combinations were two or more fences with two or fewer strides between them.

The Lipizzan was used to clearing much higher fences. He was perfect every time on the two-and-a-half footers that Cassie had him jumping. In fact, Cassie felt that she was much more likely to mess *him* up on a course than the other way around.

Cassie knew many of her faults. Sometimes she forgot herself and looked down at the jump as Majesty took off. That made her body snap too far forward and could throw Majesty off balance. Or she might be trying so hard to hold herself straight that she stiffened up during the jump, which could make her collapse forward on the landing.

Trisha had advised, "When you're jumping, imagine landing with your *feet* on the ground, not your *seat*. Above all, though, don't make lists of everything you think you should be doing. Try to relax, just feel the horse, and enjoy yourself."

So Cassie had plenty to work on. That was why she didn't notice Hillary and Thor in the other outdoor ring on Thursday morning until after she heard a shriek.

Cassie had almost reached the end of her jumping course, and she didn't let herself lose her concentration. She stared straight ahead and didn't shift in the saddle until Majesty had sailed over the last jump in the course, and she'd brought him gently to a halt.

Then Cassie stood up in her stirrups and peered over the fence toward the second ring.

At the far end of that ring, someone had set up three low fences in a line. At first Cassie didn't notice

Hillary, only Thor. He was standing near the last fence, wild-eyed, his head thrust high in the air. Then the horse whirled around, and Cassie realized that Hillary was clinging to his neck.

Hillary had lost her left stirrup. She was almost completely out of the saddle, her left leg clamped halfway up Thor's side. And with Thor as nervy as he was, anything might happen!

"Hang on, Hillary!" Cassie called out. "I'm coming."

She slid out of her own saddle. Normally a rider would never leave a horse alone in the ring with its bridle on, but this was an emergency.

Cassie quickly twisted her reins into a figure eight and slipped the outer loop around Majesty's neck. Now he couldn't step on the reins and hurt himself.

Then she raced through the gate of her ring, scaled the fence of the second ring, and walked quietly toward Thor. Cassie didn't run, because she didn't want to upset the horse any further, or he might start running himself.

Hillary must have grabbed hold of the right rein at that point, because Thor suddenly began to spin in a circle to the right.

As Cassie reached them, she ordered, "Turn the rein loose, Hillary," a lot more calmly than she felt.

Thor was big and strong—and almost out of

control. Cassie couldn't move closer to the horse without getting trampled unless he stopped spinning. And he wouldn't stop spinning unless Hillary let go of the right rein.

"I . . . I can't!" Hillary yelled. "I'll fall off!"

"I can't help you until you let go," Cassie said.

Hillary must have made herself drop the rein. Thor stopped whirling around. He straightened out and took notice of Cassie.

She stretched her hand out and spoke to him softly, "Whoa. Easy. Easy, boy."

Thor's ears pricked forward, so Cassie knew he was focusing on her.

"Easy," Cassie said again, moving closer to him.

Hillary was still hanging onto Thor's neck on the right side. Her left knee was hooked over the saddle.

"Good boy," Cassie said to the horse.

The fingers of Cassie's left hand closed on the headstall of his bridle, and she held Thor steady. With her right hand, Cassie reached out and grabbed Hillary's ankle and pulled down.

With Cassie's help, Hillary managed to wriggle her way back into the saddle.

Hillary sat there for a second, staring straight ahead while she tried to catch her breath. Her face was totally drained of color, and she was trembling.

Suddenly she pulled her right foot out of the stirrup, swung her leg over, and slid off Thor.

"Are you okay?" Cassie asked Hillary once she was safely on the ground.

At first, Hillary just nodded, still tongue-tied with fright. Finally she murmured, "I'm fine. Thank you."

Cassie handed Hillary Thor's reins. It wasn't really any of her business, but Cassie asked anyway. "Why don't you try another horse? If a leased horse doesn't work out, you can usually trade it in for one that . . ."

"No! I can win on Thor. I know I can!" Hillary exclaimed.

Then she gazed at Cassie through narrowed eyes. Did she really believe that Cassie was just trying to think of ways to beat her?

"We have a few kinks to work out, but I'm keeping this horse," Hillary said. "You can be sure of that!"

"A few kinks? More like a major disaster waiting to happen!" Cassie was thinking. But she shrugged and said, "I hope it works out for you and Thor. See you later."

As she started across the ring toward the gate, Hillary called after her, "You'd better not tell Trisha about this, either!"

Cassie walked Majesty around for a few minutes, cooling him down and cooling herself down, too. She had better things to do than tattle on Hillary. Then she led Majesty back to the barn and unsaddled him. She had just carried the saddle into the tack room when she heard an angry voice from inside the barn. A second later, Hillary stormed toward her.

"You had to do it, didn't you?" Hillary yelled. "You had to tell Trisha about Thor!"

As far as Cassie was concerned, Hillary was talking more nonsense! "I didn't say any . . . ," Cassie began.

But Hillary wouldn't listen. "Now I have to give him up. My stepfather is going to be so disappointed. I've let him down, and it's all thanks to you!" Hillary shouted. "You're a real creep, Cassie Sinclair!"

"Hillary, it's not what you think."

"I never had a chance around here," Hillary continued. "You're Trisha's favorite. Her precious Cassie can't do a thing wrong."

Cassie turned her back on Hillary. It was useless to argue with her. Besides, what Hillary said wasn't even true. Trisha didn't play favorites. She was fair to everyone.

Even though Cassie had turned her back, Hillary continued to rant. "She wouldn't let me ride Majesty, and now she won't let me ride Thor. And it's all your fault!"

Cassie spun around, her eyes flashing. "My fault?"

"Your fault!" Hillary repeated. "If I'd gotten Majesty to ride, the way I should have, none of this would have happened!"

"Do you know what?" Cassie said, sick of Hillary's attitude. "You're . . . you're just impossible!"

An Unexpected Visitor

"**A**nd then what?" Amy asked, when Cassie called to tell her about it later.

"I finished grooming Majesty, and Hillary stormed off in a huff," Cassie answered. "She's probably complaining to her parents right now. Hillary thinks everyone is out to get her, but the truth is she's her own worst enemy."

"Do you think she'll apologize to you?" Amy wanted to know.

"Hillary? You have to be kidding!" Cassie said. "Remember the good old days, Amy? Before Hillary Craig showed up, there was never this kind of tension at the stable. Now whenever I go there my stomach is completely tied up in knots."

"Maybe we should tell Trisha how we feel about Hillary," Amy said.

"What can Trisha do? Speak to Mr. and Mrs. Craig? They think Hillary is wonderful just the way she is. I tell you, Amy, I'd be really happy if I never had to see Hillary Craig again!" Cassie said. "And that's the truth!"

And for a few days, it seemed as though Cassie might get her wish.

On Friday morning, Cassie and Majesty had the outdoor rings to themselves. They were finishing a perfect ride around their jumping course when a white horse van rolled up to the barn. Cassie stopped Majesty beside the fence in time to see Robert leading Thor out of the barn. Trisha was following them.

She talked to the van driver. Then Robert loaded Thor into the white van and closed the tailgate. The van rolled back down the lane to the road.

"No more Thor," Cassie murmured to herself. But did that also mean *no more Hillary?*

Only Cassie, Amy, and Sara showed up for the Saturday group lesson.

"I'm dying to ask Trisha about Hillary," Amy whispered to Cassie while they waited for their turns. "But I don't have the nerve."

Cassie didn't have the nerve to ask, either. Not even when Hillary didn't come to her jumping class on Sunday.

By this time, Cassie wasn't sure exactly *how* she felt about it. She'd said to Amy that she'd be happy never to see Hillary again. But would she?

Cassie had to admit that having Hillary around had kept her on her toes. It had made Cassie try a little bit harder every time she rode.

And she felt just the teeniest bit bad for Hillary, too. Hillary was a good rider. It would be a shame if she gave it up completely.

Of course, Cassie wasn't spending all of her time thinking about Hillary Craig. Mostly she was thinking about getting ready for the first horse show, the one at Barker Farm, now only two weeks away.

Besides riding Majesty nearly every day, Cassie started doing exercises at home, such as lying on her back on the floor of the sunporch and doing scissor kicks in the air to strengthen the muscles in her back. Strong back muscles would help her to sit straighter in the saddle and to keep her balance better going over jumps.

Cassie was busy exercising when the doorbell rang at her house on Monday afternoon, the week after Hillary's mishap on Thor.

"Mom?" Cassie called out from the sunporch and kept touching her toes.

But Mrs. Sinclair was working at the computer in her home office.

The doorbell rang again.

"Coming!" Cassie yelled.

She hurried through the kitchen and living room and opened the front door. Hillary Craig stood on her front steps, looking down at her shoes.

"Hello," Hillary mumbled.

"Hello," Cassie said coolly. She couldn't imagine why Hillary was there.

Hillary cleared her throat. "Trisha said I had to apologize to you if I wanted to keep taking lessons at Birchwood," she mumbled at last. "So, I'm sorry for the way I've been acting."

Cassie nodded. That certainly explained Hillary's visit. And now that Hillary had done what Trisha had told her to do, Cassie fully expected her to leave.

But she didn't. Hillary went on, "I have some things to say myself, too." She stared down at the steps for a few seconds, then added: "You were right about Thor. Even though he *looked* great, he was too big and too high-strung for me. But it made me angry to have to admit it."

Cassie waited for her to continue.

"Trisha told me that you didn't say anything to her about Thor. It was Jane Clark," Hillary said.

"It's a good thing Jane did." Cassie said firmly. "You could have gotten hurt with that horse!"

"And you kept me from getting hurt that day," said Hillary, this time looking straight at Cassie. "I wanted to thank you again for that."

"Sure," said Cassie. She was starting to feel a little uncomfortable herself with all of these "thank you's," and "sorry's."

"How did you get here, anyway?" she asked Hillary, because there was no car waiting in the driveway. Cassie didn't see a bike leaning against the fence, either.

"My mom dropped me off on her way to the post office," Hillary said. "She'll be back for me in about ten minutes."

"Do you want to come in?" said Cassie.

"All right," Hillary said, and she followed Cassie into the house.

"Did I hear the bell?" Mrs. Sinclair was just walking into the living room. "Oh, hello."

"This is Hillary Craig, Mom," Cassie said, raising an eyebrow at her mother.

"Nice to meet you, Hillary," said Mrs. Sinclair. "Cassie, there are sodas in the refrigerator, and there is also a pitcher of freshly made iced tea."

"Tea would be nice," Hillary said politely.

Soon Hillary was sitting at the Sinclairs' kitchen table, drinking iced tea and munching on a cookie, as if she dropped by all the time. But she seemed to have run out of things to say.

So Cassie decided to take a turn at doing some of the talking.

"Will you be riding Bliss again?" she asked Hillary.

"I don't think so. I'm going to try out the bay horse, the one from last week," said Hillary. "He's not very pretty."

"Pretty isn't as important as steady," said Cassie, although she was lucky enough to have both in Majesty. "You know, I think we might be able to help each other with our riding."

"How?" Hillary asked, looking interested.

"When I'm practicing on Majesty, riding him over the jumps, I can't tell if I'm sitting quite right, or if I'm leaning too far forward, or if my legs are straight under me," Cassie said. "I could use a trainer. Somebody to tell me what I'm doing wrong, the way Trisha does during class."

"So if we ride at the same time during the week, we can take turns watching each other," Hillary said. She thought about it for a second and then said, "I think that's a good idea."

A car horn honked outside.

"That's my mom," Hillary said, standing up. "Thanks for the soda."

"Sure," said Cassie, standing up, too.

"I'm supposed to be getting the bay horse back tomorrow," Hillary told her. "Do you want to meet me at the barn on Wednesday morning to ride?"

"That's good for me," Cassie said. "I usually get there around nine o'clock."

Hillary nodded and said, "I'll see you at nine on Wednesday then."

Cassie walked Hillary to the front door and watched her hurry down the sidewalk to the waiting car. Cassie didn't think she and Hillary were necessarily going to be friends, at least not any time soon. But she did think the two of them could do each other some good now, instead of creating bad feelings.

When Amy heard about the arrangement Cassie had made with Hillary, she said, "But what if Hillary tries to mess you up? You know, like telling you that you're doing something wrong when you aren't. And ruining your concentration, or whatever."

"I don't think she will," Cassie said. "Because she doesn't want me to mess *her* up. Hillary is serious about her riding. And she now realizes that she can use extra help as much as I can."

"Hillary can use it a lot more, if you ask me!" Amy said, remembering the scene with Thor.

When Cassie rolled up to Birchwood on her bike on Wednesday morning at nine, Hillary was already waiting for her outside the tack room. The stocky bay horse was saddled, and Hillary was ready to go.

"This is Decker," she told Cassie. "He's a Quarter Horse and Thoroughbred mix."

"He seems really nice," Cassie said, scratching Decker's head under his forelock.

"He is nice. He didn't try to dump me off once yesterday," Hillary said, smiling a little. "I rode him all afternoon, and I think I can do pretty well on him."

Decker waited calmly while Cassie tacked up. Then the girls led their horses to one of the outdoor rings, where a line of low jumps was set up.

"You go first," Hillary said.

So Cassie pointed Majesty at the jumps, barely nudged him with her legs, and off they went. The Lipizzan sailed over the jumps as if they were ground poles. Once Cassie and Majesty had completed the course, they trotted back to Hillary and Decker. Cassie waited to hear what Hillary had to say.

"You looked great," Hillary told her.

"I know *Majesty* looked great," Cassie said. "He

always does. But what about me? Was I sitting just right? How were my feet?"

"I think you could bring your heels down more," Hillary said. "Especially when you're going over the jump. Heels down more, and toe out a little."

She seemed nervous about how Cassie might take it, but Cassie was pleased. "That's exactly the kind of thing I need to hear," she told Hillary.

Then it was Hillary's turn. Decker didn't have the stride that Majesty did. His legs were shorter, and so was his body. But he jumped neatly over the fences without flouncing or bouncing. And Hillary stayed centered in the saddle, her eyes straight ahead.

"How were we?" Hillary asked, after she'd trotted back to Cassie and Majesty.

Now Cassie felt a bit unsure about saying what she really thought about the ride. But she dove right in: "Well, I think you're a little heavy on the reins when you're going to a jump. And you're not really following his head with your hands once you've cleared the fence."

Cassie waited to see if Hillary would argue with her or get annoyed. Then they would be right back where they started.

But Hillary had listened to every word, and now she nodded. "Thanks," she said to Cassie. "That's just the kind of thing I need to know. Shall we do it again?"

"Let's," said Cassie.

She and Hillary didn't have to become best friends. After all, Cassie already *had* a best friend. But it was going to be great not having Hillary for an enemy.

The Horse Show

On the day of the horse show at Barker Farm, Trisha wanted all of the girls in the Saturday group to be at Birchwood Stable at six-thirty in the morning. The first classes at the show would be starting at nine o'clock. And it would take the girls quite some time to groom their horses, braid their horses' manes, and get them loaded into a van to travel to Barker Farm.

Cassie got to Birchwood at six that morning. She was so keyed up about riding Majesty in the show that she'd been ready to go since five-fifteen.

But Hillary was ahead of her. She was already leading Decker out to the grooming tree when Mr. Sinclair and Cassie pulled into the parking area that was located beside the barn.

"Hi!" Hillary called out as Cassie jumped out of the car.

"Hi!" Cassie called back. She grabbed her riding clothes out of the back seat: a black jacket, beige breeches, black boots, a white shirt with a white stock tie and gold pin, and black gloves. Her hat completed her outfit.

"Good luck, kid," Mr. Sinclair said to his daughter. "We'll see you at the show. We're rooting for you." He waved good-bye and drove away, yawning.

Cassie carried her clothes to Trisha's office, said hello to Trisha, and hurried to Majesty's stall. The Lipizzan had finished his breakfast and seemed to be waiting for her. Maybe he had sensed the excitement, because some of Trisha's other students were rushing here and there inside the barn, getting ready.

Cassie haltered Majesty and led him out to the grooming tree. She and Hillary had finished brushing their horses and were picking out their hooves when Amy and Sara arrived together by car with Sara's mom. Sara was so nervous about riding in public that her eyes looked ready to pop right out of her chalk-white face.

Not Amy. Amy was still only half-awake. She smiled sleepily at Cassie and said, "I don't know how you can move so fast at this time of day."

But with Cassie's help, Amy had Freckles groomed and braided and ready to be loaded into the van by seven-thirty. Then the girls changed into their riding clothes and piled into Trisha's station wagon along with two other kids. Thirty minutes later, they were pulling into the winding driveway of Barker Farm.

"Wow! So many people!" Amy said, staring out her window.

There were horse vans, horse trailers, cars, and trucks filling almost every inch of the large mowed field.

"Lots more than last year," Cassie agreed.

"And a big refreshment tent," Amy said. "I wonder if they'll have those incredible brownies again?"

Sara sighed and looked ready to faint. Food was the last thing on *her* mind!

"There's our van," Hillary said, pointing it out. "Decker's already unloaded."

Trisha drove the station wagon between two large trailers and pulled up beside the Birchwood horses.

"Here we are, girls," she said, opening her car door. "I'll pick up your numbers at the office. And remember, try to relax. Have some fun with this!"

Barker Farm had three outdoor rings, and at nine o'clock sharp, show classes started in two of them.

Little kids were riding in a line in the ring closest to the refreshment tent. In the middle ring, teenagers put their horses through the complicated movements of dressage.

Cassie would have liked to watch *everyone* doing *everything*. But she didn't have time.

Trisha came back with their numbers and pinned them to the backs of the girls' jackets. Cassie was "contestant number 38." Then Trisha walked the jumping course with Cassie and Hillary. It was set up in the third ring.

There were eight jumps arranged in a loose figure-eight pattern. Trisha helped Cassie and Hillary count how many strides their horses should be making before taking off over each of the jumps. Sometimes it was two strides; sometimes it was three or more.

After that, Cassie rode Majesty around in an open area to warm him up and loosen up his muscles so he'd be ready. The Lipizzan paid no attention to noisy kids, or dogs, or nickering horses, or the slamming of car doors and tailgates. He was all business, his ears turning back toward Cassie for any instructions she might have.

Amy and Freckles were walking around in a circle, taking in the sights. And now that Sara was mounted on Charlie, she'd gotten some of her color back. She even managed a smile at Cassie.

Cassie glanced over at Hillary and Decker. The bay horse was trotting along as calmly as if he were in the indoor ring at Birchwood. Cassie couldn't imagine *what* Thor would have been doing by now, but she was fairly certain that it wouldn't have been what Hillary wanted.

Then a voice on the loudspeaker announced the class that Amy and Sara would be riding in.

"Good luck!" Cassie and Hillary called out to both of them.

It seemed as though only seconds had passed before Amy was back, standing at the edge of the open space and waving a yellow ribbon at Cassie: "I won third!" she yelled. "And check out Sara!"

Sara was right behind her, proudly holding up a blue ribbon. "Way to go!" Cassie yelled back.

"Congratulations!" Hillary called to them.

In a few more minutes, the Beginning Equitation-Over-Fences class was announced. That was the class that Cassie and Hillary would be competing in.

The two girls looked at each other. "That's us," Cassie said, her heart pounding.

"Best of luck," Hillary said. And she sounded as if she meant it.

Cassie didn't watch the first two contestants jumping the course. She didn't try to spot her parents in the crowd, either. Instead, she tried to focus on relaxing by doing some deep breathing and walking Majesty slowly around.

Then the ring steward called out, "Number 15," Hillary's number.

Cassie moved Majesty closer to the ring. She couldn't see much of the course from where she was standing, but she did see Decker clearing the fifth and sixth fences like a pro. And Hillary followed his head with her hands on the way down, just as Cassie had told her to in practice.

When Hillary completed the course, the crowd around the ring broke into applause. As she rode Decker back through the gate, Mr. and Mrs. Craig hurried up to her. Mr. Craig gave Hillary a hug, and she looked ready to burst with pleased excitement.

Another girl rode through the course. Then the ring steward called Cassie's number.

"Show time," Cassie murmured to Majesty.

First she trotted him quietly into the ring and made a small, smooth circle. Then Cassie nudged Majesty into a canter and headed toward the first jump. It was a single pole, and Majesty cleared it effortlessly.

The Lipizzan turned to the left, and to the left again, and approached a combination fence, which was really two fences with two strides in between them. Cassie looked straight ahead and kept in touch with Majesty's mouth through the reins. They made perfect jumps over the combination.

The next fence was five strides away. Majesty felt to Cassie as though he might be moving a little too quickly, so she gave the slightest tug on the reins. Then he soared over the third fence, turned left, and turned left again to line up with the fourth fence, which was an oxer.

Oxers are wide jumps made with two separate fences and a little space in between them. For Cassie, an oxer was the scariest kind of jump, because she always felt that her horse might not make it across the open space to clear the second fence.

But she trusted Majesty to know what he was doing. All Cassie really had to worry about, she told herself, was sitting properly so that she wouldn't throw the Lipizzan off balance. And not looking down!

Cassie remembered her practices with Hillary and worked on keeping her heels down, her toes out, and her back straight, as she and Majesty took off over the wide jump. She tried to become a part of her horse.

And Majesty did a beautiful job, his head down, his knees up, his lower legs tight. His ears were pricked forward, his eyes already focusing on the next jump. And he cleared the oxer easily.

After the oxer, the rest of the course was a breeze. When Cassie cantered across the finish line, there was a roar from the crowd. She could pick out Amy's voice yelling, "Yay, Cassie!"

As soon as Cassie rode out of the gate, her parents rushed over to her.

"I've never been so proud in my life as when you sailed over that wide jump!" her dad said.

And her mom added, "I didn't know whether to close my eyes or keep them open, so I just crossed my fingers and held my breath."

"You were excellent!" Amy said when she joined them. "Good work, Majesty," she added, patting the horse's neck. And Majesty bobbed his head up and down as if he were agreeing with her.

The last girl rode, and the class was over. It took the judge a few minutes to check her scores and hand the results to the ring steward.

Cassie glanced around for Hillary and spotted her with Decker, standing at the far side of the ring with the Craigs. Hillary saw Cassie and held one hand up in the air with her fingers crossed.

"Sixth place goes to number 23!" the ring steward called out.

A girl on a tall gray gelding rode into the ring to pick up her green ribbon.

The ring steward called out the number for the fifth-place winner, then fourth, then third. Cassie was beginning to worry, especially when he got to second place and announced, "The second place ribbon goes to . . . number 15!"

"That's Hillary," Cassie said to her parents and Amy. And her heart sank, because she couldn't imagine doing better than second place!

Hillary had a wide smile on her face as the steward fastened a red ribbon to Decker's headstall. Her parents were beaming, too.

The ring steward paused for a minute to allow Hillary to ride out of the ring. Then he called out, "The blue ribbon for first place for this event goes to . . ." He looked down at the paper he was holding, and continued, "contestant number . . . 38!"

Cassie almost couldn't believe her ears!

"That's you, Cassie!" Amy squealed.

"Congratulations, sweetie!" said Mrs. Sinclair.

"Get in there, honey," said Mr. Sinclair, giving her a pat on the knee.

As she rode Majesty toward the gate, Cassie saw

Hillary waiting beside it for her.

"You made a great ride. You deserve first!" Hillary said.

"Thanks," Cassie said, smiling at her.

But Cassie knew exactly who deserved the blue: Majesty, her Lipizzan!

FACTS
ABOUT THE BREED

You probably know a lot about Lipizzan horses from reading this book. Here are some more interesting facts about this special breed.

∩ Lipizzans generally stand between 14.2 and 16.1 hands high. Instead of using feet and inches, all horses are measured in hands. A hand is equal to four inches.

∩ Lipizzans get their name from a town in the former Yugoslavia. In Lipizza (or Lipica), Austria's Archduke Charles II bred the first Lipizzans from horses that he had imported from Spain.

∩ The most famous Lipizzans are the performing stallions of Vienna's Spanish Riding School. The school is called

"Spanish" in honor of the horses that the Archduke first brought from that country in 1580.

∩ Since 1735, the Spanish School has had its own imposing building in downtown Vienna. The school is housed in part of the Hofburg Palace. Even the stables at the school look like part of a palace. The horses eat from red marble mangers.

∩ Traditionally, the training of a Lipizzan begins late. The horses of the Spanish School are allowed to frolic in the pastures until they are four years old.

∩ A young Lipizzan first learns to work on a lunge line, a long rein that allows the horse to move around the trainer in a large circle. Then the horse learns to perform the *piaffe*, a delicate prancing trot that is done in place, and also a *pirouette*, like a ballerina.

∩ Talented horses go on to learn the "airs above the ground." In the *levade*, the horse bends his hind legs and raises his chest and forelegs off the ground so that he looks like a marble statue about to leap into action.

∩ Next comes the *courbette*. Starting in the *levade* position, the horse jumps forward on his hind legs and lands on his hind legs. All the while, his forelegs are kept neatly tucked under the chest. The strongest horses can perform ten of these difficult jumps in a row.

∩ In the *croupade*, the horse leaps into the air and tucks all four feet underneath him.

∩ The *ballotade*, like the *croupade*, is executed by jumping into the air. In this move, however, the horse turns his hind feet up so the viewer can see the bottoms of his gleaming hooves.

∩ The *capriole* is probably the most spectacular of the "high-school movements." Like the winged Pegasus of the Greek myth, the horse leaps into the air. At the very height of his jump, he kicks out his hind legs and truly looks as if he can fly. The horse does land, though, and on all four feet.

∩ While Lipizzans are slow to mature, they live a long time. Some of the stallions performing with the Spanish School are more than 20 years old.

∩ Lipizzans are great performers and are also becoming popular private horses. Many Lipizzan owners practice dressage or drive small carriages. Others find that the Lipizzan's sensible temperament and great loyalty make these alabaster beauties superior riding horses.

PRETTY LADY OF SARATOGA

The story of a spirited Thoroughbred, a determined girl, and the race of a lifetime

Written by Deborah Felder
Illustrated by Sandy Rabinowitz
Cover Illustration by Christa Keiffer
Developed by Nancy Hall, Inc.

CONTENTS

Pretty Lady

On a sunny June morning in 1925, Polly
Canfield, a pretty girl with blue eyes and golden hair,
was leaning over a fence at Canfield Farm.

On the other side of the fence, in a field, horses
ran, frolicked, or grazed contentedly. From time to
time, the grazing horses raised their heads and
touched noses with their neighbors in a friendly way.

But one horse, a filly, stood alone in the middle of
the field. She didn't run or buck playfully like the
others.

The horse was a three-year-old chestnut
Thoroughbred named Pretty Lady. Looking at her
made Polly sigh. She knew the reason the filly had

lost her spirit, and it made her both angry and sad.

Just then, Polly heard the sound of a car behind her. She turned to see a snappy roadster drive up the lane and stop a few feet away from the fence. A man and a woman got out of the car.

The man was wearing a cream-colored linen suit and a straw hat with a flat brim. The woman was dressed in a white linen skirt and a long, white blouse. She wore a small, round hat that covered most of her bobbed hair, white gloves, and a long strand of pearls. She carried a blue silk parasol.

I bet they're tourists, Polly thought as the man and woman walked toward her.

Canfield Farm was located just a few miles outside Saratoga Springs, New York. Every summer hundreds of people flocked to Saratoga to watch the horse races. This early in the summer, Saratoga was just beginning to become crowded with tourists, but it would become even more so when the races began in August.

Polly wasn't surprised to see tourists at Canfield Farm. Her father, Bill Canfield, stabled and trained racehorses, and ever since she was a little girl, she had seen summer visitors strolling down the lane from time to time to watch the horses in the field.

"Hi, kiddo," the man said, grinning at Polly in a

friendly way. "We're looking for Bill Canfield. Is he here?"

"He's at the racetrack right now," Polly told the man. "I'm Polly Canfield. Maybe I can help you. Do you want to see one of the horses?"

The man nodded. "My wife and I are thinking of buying a colt named Whirlwind," he said. "I heard he's being stabled here and that Bill Canfield is training him."

"That's right," Polly said. She turned and pointed to a brown colt with a white blaze. The colt was running and bucking in a separate paddock. "That's Whirlwind over there."

The woman suddenly pointed her parasol at Pretty Lady. "Hey, take a look at that filly," she said to her husband. "She's a real beaut!"

"She's the cat's meow, all right," her husband agreed.

The couple's admiration of the filly pleased Polly. "She's the most beautiful Thoroughbred in Saratoga," Polly told them proudly. "Her name is Pretty Lady."

"Pretty Lady," the woman murmured. "I think I remember that name. Wasn't Pretty Lady the filly who showed such great form on the racetrack last summer? People said that she was a sure bet to win the Travers Stakes or the Saratoga Cup this year."

"Pretty Lady is the same filly," Polly told the woman. "But I'm not sure she's going to be racing this year."

"Why not?" the man asked.

"It's a very sad story," Polly replied. "Before Pretty Lady came here, she'd been stabled somewhere else. It was a big stable and, according to Dad, not a very good one. The owner didn't pay his hands well, and he hired whomever he could find."

"Anyway," she went on, "The groom who was in charge of Pretty Lady treated her roughly. When he rode her, she balked, and he whipped her to make her go. After awhile, she became sour and sulky. Now she won't let anyone ride her."

"Gee, that's too bad," the man said, shaking his head. "She sure is a pretty filly."

"Well, who cares about a horse that can't race, anyway," the woman said in a bored voice. She turned and stepped over to the paddock, followed by her husband and Polly. "Now, what about Whirlwind? What's the price tag on him?"

"I'm not sure," Polly told the woman in a polite but stiff tone. "You'll have to ask Dad."

"We'll do that," the man said. "Tell your father we'll be back another time, will you, kiddo?"

The man took his wife's arm, and together they

walked back to their car. Polly watched them drive away. Then she turned to look at Pretty Lady again.

"Poor Pretty Lady," she said with a sigh. "It seems like nobody cares about you anymore, just because you're not going to race."

The filly stopped grazing, looked up at a horsefly buzzing around her, and shook her head. In the sun, her silken mane flashed reddish-gold with the movement of her head.

Polly was glad that Pretty Lady had finally found a good home at Canfield Farm. She loved helping her father take care of the filly and the other horses every morning before school and in the evenings.

Now that school was out for the summer, Polly planned to spend all her time with Pretty Lady. More than anything in the world, she wanted to make friends with the nervous Thoroughbred.

From the moment Pretty Lady arrived at the farm, she had refused to let Sam, the Canfields' groom, anywhere near her. Only Bill Canfield had been able to handle her. He treated her gently and expertly, but lately he had been too busy with the other horses in his care to spend time trying to cure Pretty Lady of her skittishness.

As the weeks went by, Pretty Lady had become used to seeing Polly in the field and at her stall. She had begun to shy away less and less whenever Polly approached her. But she remained skittish, and so far, she had shied away every time Polly had tried to touch her.

Polly knew that if she could convince Pretty Lady to let her stroke her, it would be an important step in winning her trust.

Polly saw Pretty Lady head over to a nearby section of the fence, and she went over to where the horse was standing. She held out her hand to the filly. Just as she usually did, Pretty Lady snorted, tossed her head, and nervously backed away.

In the past, whenever the filly had shied away, Polly had left her alone. But as she stood watching the horse run across the field, Polly decided that today would be different. Today she was determined to gain Pretty Lady's trust.

CHAPTER
TWO

Bad News

Polly waited until she saw Pretty Lady station herself at another section of the fence. Then, walking as slowly and quietly as she could, she circled the fence toward the filly.

As Polly moved closer, she talked to the filly in a soothing tone. At the same time, she reached into her pocket and took out a lump of sugar.

"Hello, girl," Polly murmured. "Don't be afraid. No one is going to hurt you."

Pretty Lady pricked up her ears at the sound of Polly's voice. Slowly, Polly reached over the fence and held out the lump of sugar. The filly stood very still for several moments, watching Polly.

Polly waited patiently, her hand stretched out toward Pretty Lady. Finally, with a sudden movement, the horse stepped up to the fence, lowered her delicate neck, and sniffed at the sugar. Daintily, she picked it up with her teeth.

While the filly ate, Polly reached over and touched her velvety neck. To her delight, Pretty Lady didn't shy. She stood still and let Polly stroke her. She seemed more relaxed than ever before.

"I guess I was acting nervous, and that made you nervous, too," Polly whispered to the filly as she continued to stroke her. "Everyone has the wrong idea about you, girl. I bet that all you need is some retraining, and you'll be ready to race again."

Polly remembered the first time she had seen Pretty Lady in action. Late last summer Polly had gone to a race with her father to watch one of the colts he had trained. But she could not take her eyes off the beautiful filly blazing down the track, edging past the other horses length by length. Pretty Lady had won that race with ease, and Polly was certain that with the right training she could win again.

Polly smiled as she pictured the scene in her mind. "I can just see you standing in the winner's circle with the flowered horseshoe around your beautiful neck," she said to Pretty Lady.

Suddenly, Polly's daydream was interrupted by the sound of a truck. She turned and saw her father driving the Canfields' horse truck up the lane toward the stable.

"Here comes Dad, bringing Challenger back from his workout," Polly said. "I'd better go and help him get the horse out of the truck and into his stall."

She smiled at Pretty Lady. "I'm glad we've become friends at last," she whispered. "I'll come back to visit you later, okay, girl?"

Pretty Lady nickered. Then she tossed her head proudly and trotted away from the fence. It was almost as if she were saying, "Maybe I'll let you visit me again, and maybe I won't."

Polly hurried over to the stable yard, where her father had parked. Bill Canfield stepped out of the cab and smiled at his daughter. He was a good-natured man in his early thirties, with blue eyes and golden hair, the same color as Polly's.

Bill Canfield took off his cap and wiped the sweat from his brow with the back of his hand. "Whew!" he said. "It sure is hot today. And it was even hotter standing in the sun at the track, watching Challenger's workout."

"Challenger must be hot, too," Polly said. "Do you want me to rub him down?"

"I rubbed him down at the track," her father said. "But you can help me get him out of the truck." He walked to the back of the truck and unfolded the ramp that was attached to the edge.

Inside the truck, Challenger stood in one of the stalls. He was a black colt with white stockings. To keep him from lurching around inside the truck, he had been hitched up to ropes attached to each side of the front of his stall.

Polly snapped the lead line onto Challenger's halter, while her father undid the ropes. Challenger began to move back and forth in anticipation of being freed, but Polly held onto his lead line. With her other hand, she patted his neck.

"Easy, boy," she said. "You'll be out of here in a minute."

After her father had finished untying the ropes, Polly took over. "Okay, boy, back up now," she said to the colt. Challenger snorted and tried to toss his head. But Polly kept a firm hold on the colt's lead line. At the same time, she slowly backed the colt out of the stall and down the ramp.

"You did a good job getting Challenger out of the truck, Polly," Bill Canfield said as he walked with her over to the colt's stall. "He's feeling pretty frisky today. I clocked him at an even forty-seven seconds. His owner is thinking of entering him in the Travers Stakes."

Polly knew that the Travers was the oldest stakes race for three-year-old horses in America. It had been run in Saratoga since 1864. A horse that won the Travers Stakes was really special.

Bill Canfield's mention of the Travers Stakes reminded Polly of her hopes for Pretty Lady. "That's swell, Dad," Polly said. "But I bet Pretty Lady could run even faster than Challenger if she had the chance. When is Mr. Harrington going to let you train her?"

James Harrington was Pretty Lady's owner. He was a rich newspaper tycoon who lived nearby on his estate. At the moment, though, he was vacationing in Europe.

Polly's father hesitated at the door to Challenger's stall. Then he turned to his daughter and said, "I'm afraid I have some bad news, Polly. Mr. Harrington sent me a telegram yesterday from London. He doesn't think Pretty Lady has it in her to win any more races. He plans to turn her into a broodmare and use her for breeding. A groom is coming here tomorrow morning to take her to the stables he's had built on his estate."

Polly stood there, unable to believe what her father had just told her.

Bill Canfield gave his daughter a sympathetic look. "I'm sorry, Polly," he said, putting his arm around her shoulders. Then he took Challenger's lead line from Polly's hand and walked the colt into his stall.

Polly felt terrible. Now Pretty Lady would never be given a chance to prove herself as a racehorse. And, even worse, after tomorrow, Pretty Lady would be gone from Canfield Farm forever.

CHAPTER THREE

"End of Discussion"

 Before dinner, Polly and her father went out to the field to bring the horses back to the stable. When Pretty Lady and Whirlwind were the only two horses left outside, Polly said, "Please let me take Pretty Lady in, Dad. I want to spend as much time with her as I can before she goes away."

Bill Canfield turned and looked at his daughter with a surprised expression. "Are you sure?" he asked. "You know how skittish she can be."

"I think she's beginning to trust me," Polly insisted. "She let me stroke her today."

Before her father could object again, Polly walked slowly toward Pretty Lady. She talked to the filly in a soothing tone as she had done earlier, being careful to act relaxed.

When she reached Pretty Lady, she stood in front of the filly for a moment without moving a muscle. "You and I are friends, girl, remember?" she said softly.

Pretty Lady gave a snort, but once again she did not shy away from Polly's touch.

"Good girl," Polly whispered as she hitched Pretty Lady's lead line to her halter and began to lead the filly toward her father.

Bill Canfield gave a low whistle. "Well, what do you know," he said, shaking his head. "You really have a way with her, Polly."

He glanced down at his watch. "We'd better get Pretty Lady and Whirlwind settled down for the night,"

he said. "Your mother will be calling us in for dinner soon."

Polly led Pretty Lady out the gate. As she did every evening, the filly snorted nervously and pulled back when she saw the stable. She had a long memory, and the sight of the stable reminded her of the groom who had treated her so roughly. Polly soothed her with encouraging words and gentle pats, and she finally convinced Pretty Lady to step into her stall.

Despite Pretty Lady's behavior, Polly didn't feel discouraged. After what had happened between them earlier, she was sure that, with time and patience, Pretty Lady could be cured of her skittishness and retrained for racing.

"I just wish you could stay here and let Dad and me prove it," Polly said to the filly.

Just then, she heard her mother call her to dinner. Polly took one last look at Pretty Lady, who was busy nuzzling the hay net that hung from the wall. Then she closed the door of the stall and hurried over to the house.

Polly ran up the porch steps and pulled open the screen door. The door creaked as it opened and creaked again as it closed behind her. Much of the old farmhouse creaked or always seemed to be in need of repair. But it was a comfortable, friendly house, and Polly loved it.

Polly washed her hands and hurried into the dining room, where her father was ladling out servings of chicken and dumplings.

"Your father has just told me that Pretty Lady is moving to the Harringtons' stable tomorrow," Laura Canfield said. "It's too bad. She showed so much promise as a racehorse last summer. But I guess she's too skittish to race any more."

"All Pretty Lady needs is time and a patient, gentle hand," Polly insisted. "She needs you, Dad. After all, you're the best horse trainer in Saratoga."

Bill Canfield smiled at his daughter. "I'm glad you think I'm the best," he said. "But Mr. Harrington has made his decision. Now let's have dinner."

"You could talk to him about Pretty Lady," Polly said desperately. "Talk to him and try to convince him to give Pretty Lady one more chance. Please?"

Polly's father put down his fork. "I understand how sad you feel at losing Pretty Lady," he told his daughter, "but you have to understand: No matter how attached we become to the horses we stable and train here, horseracing is a business. If a Thoroughbred isn't performing, it will be sold or retired. End of discussion."

"End of Discussion"

Polly looked down at her plate in despair.
Tomorrow Pretty Lady would be gone from Canfield
Farm. For the rest of her days, she would be a
broodmare. She would never have another chance to
win a race. And there was nothing Polly could do
about it.

CHAPTER FOUR

A Secret Visit

The next morning, after Polly had helped her father feed and water the horses, she headed over to Pretty Lady's stall to turn her out into the field. As Polly was hooking the filly's lead line onto her halter, her father said, "Leave Pretty Lady in her stall. The Harringtons' groom will be arriving any minute, so there's no point in turning her out."

"I guess I'd better say goodbye to you now, then," Polly said to the filly. As she reached up and stroked Pretty Lady, her eyes filled with tears. "Goodbye, girl," she whispered in a trembling voice. "I'll miss you."

All too soon, Polly heard a truck driving up the lane. The driver, a short, gray-haired man, stepped over to Polly and her father and took off his cap. He had a pleasant, smiling face that was seamed with lines from spending many years out in the sun.

"The name's Joe McCall," he said to Polly's father. "Mr. Harrington's groom. You must be Mr. Canfield."

After the two men had shaken hands, Bill Canfield introduced Polly. Joe gave a friendly nod in Polly's direction. Then he looked over at Pretty Lady, and his face lit up with admiration. "So this is the boss's new filly," he said. "She sure is a beauty."

"Yes, she is," Bill Canfield agreed as he opened the door to Pretty Lady's stall. "But she was treated badly at another stable, and she became sour."

Joe nodded. "I know the story," he said. "It's a crying shame what some people do to horses." He reached out a hand to take Pretty Lady's lead line from Polly. Polly hesitated for a moment. Then she reluctantly handed the lead line to Joe and stepped aside so that he could lead the filly out of her stall.

Pretty Lady snorted nervously and began to pull back.

"Don't tug too hard on her line," Polly told Joe anxiously.

"Polly has grown very attached to Pretty Lady," Bill Canfield explained. "And . . ."

"And it's hard for her to see the filly go," Joe

145

finished. He gave Polly an understanding smile. "Don't worry, Miss," he said kindly. "I've worked with horses ever since I was a boy, and I know how to treat them. I promise to take good care of Pretty Lady. She'll have a good home."

Pretty Lady already has a good home *here*, Polly thought as she watched Joe soothe the filly and lead her up the ramp into the truck. Moments later, Polly looked on sadly as Joe drove Pretty Lady away from Canfield Farm.

Bill Canfield put his arm around his daughter's shoulders. "If you want, you can help me to train the new filly who arrived yesterday. Her name is Morning Mist. She's a little wild, and I could use your help."

"Okay, Dad," Polly said, nodding. Maybe training a new horse will help me to take my mind off Pretty Lady, she thought.

But it didn't. A little while later, as Polly stood in the center of the training ring holding the lunge rein and watching Morning Mist move in a circle around her, she couldn't help but think of Pretty Lady. She wished there were a way to see Pretty Lady and make sure she was all right.

Just then, Morning Mist tossed back her head, and Polly felt her begin to pull away. "Polly, please pay attention," her father said. "You're letting the lunge rein go slack. Tighten it up a little."

"Sorry, Dad," Polly said, pulling up on the lunge rein. Polly tried to concentrate, but her thoughts kept drifting back to Pretty Lady. She knew there was no chance that she would ever see the filly again.

Or was there? As Polly held the lunge rein and watched Morning Mist trot around the ring, she remembered that Mr. Harrington was away in Europe. She knew he had a teenage son, but he was in New York City for the summer, working as a copyboy at one of the family's newspapers. With both the Harringtons gone from the estate, she might be able to sneak in to see Pretty Lady. The more Polly thought about her idea, the better she liked it.

Later, as she was sitting at the table with her parents eating lunch, she turned to her father. "Do you need me to help you in the stable this afternoon, Dad?" she asked.

"I'll be at the track for the afternoon," her father replied, spooning a second helping of potato salad onto his plate. "So, I don't need you. I can't speak for your mother, though."

"You deserve a break, Polly," Laura Canfield said. "After all, you should be able to enjoy your summer vacation."

That was all Polly needed to hear. She hastily

swallowed the last bite of her sandwich. "May I be excused?" she asked.

"Of course," her mother said. "Have a good time."

If my plan to see Pretty Lady works, I'll have a very good time, Polly thought as she hurried out the door. As always, the screen door creaked when it was opened. "I really must oil those doors when I have the time," Polly heard her father say as the door shut behind her.

Polly ran to her bicycle, which was propped up against the side of the house. She knew that the Harringtons' estate was about a mile and a half beyond town, in an area with fields and rolling hills. Her father once had pointed out the estate to her when they passed it on their way to the racetrack. Unfortunately, all she had been able to see was a long, tree-lined drive and a gate in the high, brick wall that surrounded the property.

When Polly reached the end of town, she pedaled along a quiet country road. After pedaling for several minutes, she came to the long drive of the Harringtons' estate. She rode down the drive until she reached the wrought-iron gate at the end. The drive continued past the gate and ended in a circle in front of a large, rambling, three-story clapboard house. Polly thought that her parents' little farmhouse with its small porch could have fit easily into one side of the Harringtons' mansion.

I wonder how it feels to be rich and live in a mansion like this, Polly thought as she gazed at the house beyond the gate. I bet the screen doors in this house don't creak and squeak. I bet the Harringtons have a whole army of servants to make sure everything in their house works perfectly!

She peered through the gate, trying to see where the stable was, but the large house took up her whole view. She thought for a moment, then decided to go left and follow the narrow path that ran between the woods and the high, brick wall. Polly circled the wall until she came to what she guessed was the back of the house. There the wall suddenly sloped up into an open, vine-covered archway. As Polly neared the archway, she heard a horse neigh. Polly recognized the neigh at once. It belonged to Pretty Lady.

Polly wheeled her bike through the archway and found herself in a big field. In a fenced-in area of the field, Pretty Lady fretted. She trotted nervously around the field, whinnying for the horses she had left behind at the farm.

Polly looked around anxiously to see if Joe McCall or anyone else was in sight, but except for the filly, the field seemed to be deserted. With a sigh of relief, Polly walked to the fence and, with one last look around, climbed over it.

Pretty Lady, worn out from trotting, had stopped near a section of the fence. Polly approached her, moving slowly so as not to frighten her. "Hello, girl," she said as she neared the filly. "Don't be scared. It's just me."

She stepped up to Pretty Lady and stood in front of her for a moment without moving. The filly snorted and tossed her head. She watched Polly with her usual wary look, but she did not shy away. Polly reached up and stroked her neck.

"Good girl," Polly said quietly. "You remembered that we're friends."

Polly continued to stroke Pretty Lady. She was concentrating so hard on keeping the filly calm that she was startled to hear a voice suddenly shout out, "Hey, you! What do you think you're doing with that horse?" In the next instant, a handsome, dark-haired teenage boy in knickers, boots, and a white shirt jumped down from the fence into the paddock.

The filly was startled, too. She gave a loud, high whinny and reared up. Then she turned and took off at top speed across the field, straight for the opposite fence.

Polly gasped in fear. It looked as if Pretty Lady was going to try to jump the high fence!

The Stable Boy

Pretty Lady approached the fence at a gallop. Then a few feet short of the fence the filly stopped, turned, and cantered away, snorting.

Polly whirled around and faced the boy, her eyes blazing with anger. "For crying out loud! How could you do such a thing to a horse like Pretty Lady?" she demanded. "You saw how carefully I was handling her, didn't you? For a stable hand, you obviously don't know the first thing about horses!"

"Oh, yeah?" the boy said angrily. "Well, I want to know who you are and why you're trespassing on private property!"

Polly felt the anger slide out of her. She realized

she was trespassing, and now she would have to explain herself.

"My name is Polly Canfield," she told the boy. "Pretty Lady used to be stabled at my place. Until today, that is. My father's a trainer, you see." She swallowed hard. "I know I'm trespassing, but I really had to see Pretty Lady again. We were just starting to become friends before she had to go away to live here."

The boy's expression softened as he listened to Polly. "Gee, that's tough," he said in a sympathetic tone. "I know how I'd feel if I lost a horse I cared about." He paused for a moment. "My name's Mike, by the way."

Polly nodded and turned her attention back to Pretty Lady. The filly was standing across the field looking over the fence. Mike followed Polly's gaze.

"She's one of the niftiest Thoroughbreds I've ever seen," Mike said admiringly. "And one of the fastest, too. I've never seen a filly move as speedily as she just did."

They watched Pretty Lady in silence for a moment. Then Mike turned to Polly. "Say, I'm sorry I shouted at you before," he said. "I guess I got a little carried away when I saw a trespasser on the property. How did you get in here, anyway?"

Polly pointed to the brick wall. "I came in through the archway in the wall," she explained. "I didn't see anyone around, so I thought it would be safe to visit Pretty Lady."

"I'm really sorry I spooked her," Mike said. "I just arrived here this afternoon, and I haven't had a chance to meet the horses yet. I didn't realize Pretty Lady would react like that. What has made her so nervous, anyway?"

Polly told him about Pretty Lady's promising career, the bad stable, and the groom's rough handling of the filly. When she described some of the bad treatment Pretty Lady had received, she saw Mike's face darken with anger.

Polly felt glad that Mike shared her outrage at what had happened to Pretty Lady.

She looked across the field at the filly. Pretty Lady was still standing by the fence. Every so often, she tossed her head and snorted nervously. "Pretty Lady is still jittery," Polly said. "I can tell."

"It's time to bring her in," Mike said. He climbed over the fence and ran off toward a long, white building. A few moments later he was back, holding Pretty Lady's halter. He started toward the filly.

"Wait a minute," Polly said quickly.

Mike stopped, turned, and gave her a questioning

look. "What's the matter?" he asked.

"I think you should let me bring her in," Polly said. "You might be the stable boy here, but I know Pretty Lady better than you do. She trusts me."

An amused smile crossed Mike's face.

I bet he thinks I can't do it, Polly thought. "What's so funny?" she asked him in a huffy tone.

"Oh, nothing," Mike replied. "It's just that I . . ." He paused for a moment. Then he shook his head and said, "Never mind." He gestured toward Pretty Lady. "Go ahead, see if you can get her. For a kid, you seem pretty sure of yourself."

"I'm not a kid," Polly said hotly. "I'm twelve going on thirteen. How old are *you*, anyway?"

"I turned fifteen last month," Mike replied.

"Oh," Polly said. "Well, I don't care if you are older than I am. Like I told you, I know Pretty Lady. You don't. Just watch me bring her in." She took the halter from him. Then, without another word, she turned and walked off across the field toward the filly.

In her determination to show Mike that she knew how to handle Pretty Lady, she forgot to approach the filly slowly and quietly. As soon as Pretty Lady saw Polly coming, she shook her head and backed away.

Polly slowed her stride and carefully moved toward Pretty Lady again. This time she managed to step up to the filly. "That's right, girl," she said gently. "You know you can trust me."

She reached out her hand toward Pretty Lady. As soon as the filly felt the touch of Polly's hand, her nostrils flared and she pinned back her ears. Then she tossed her head, turned, and twisted away. Polly ran in front of her to block her retreat, but Pretty Lady turned away from her again.

"Come on, girl," Polly said desperately. "Stop acting so skittish. We're supposed to be friends, remember?"

She approached Pretty Lady, and once again the filly twisted away. Try as she might, Polly could not convince Pretty Lady to settle down. Finally, Polly gave up.

Discouraged, she walked back to Mike. He was standing with his back against the fence, his arms folded across his chest. There was a thoughtful look in his eyes and a smile on his handsome face.

He'd better not laugh at me, Polly thought furiously. He'd better not say I'm just a kid who doesn't know how to handle a skittish horse.

But Mike didn't say a word to Polly. Instead, he took the halter from her, moved away from the fence, and walked toward Pretty Lady.

"All right, girl," Polly heard him say in a soothing

murmur as he walked. "No one's going to hurt you. Calm down."

As Polly watched Mike, she was surprised to see that he had closed one of his eyes. What's he doing that for? Polly wondered.

She also noticed that Pretty Lady did not shy when she saw the stable boy approach her. To Polly's amazement, the filly stood completely still and let Mike step right up to her and slip on her halter.

It won't last, Polly thought smugly. In another minute, Pretty Lady will twist out of his grasp and run away from him, just like she ran away from me.

But Polly was wrong. Several minutes passed, and Pretty Lady still stood calmly in the same spot. Even when Mike released his hold on her halter, Pretty Lady continued to stand quietly and let him stroke her.

Polly couldn't stand it any longer. She had to know what Mike had done to make Pretty Lady calm down like that. She started to head toward them. At the same time, Mike walked toward her, leading Pretty Lady by the halter. The filly jerked her head up and down several times, but she followed him obediently without trying to pull away.

"How did you do that?" Polly asked Mike, when he and the filly had reached her. "Was it some kind of trick?"

"That's exactly what it was," Mike said with a grin. "It's the one-eye trick. I learned it from my grandfather, my father's father. He was a horse trainer in Ireland and a good one, too. He taught me everything he knew about horses."

Polly took advantage of the fact that Pretty Lady was standing close to her, and she gently stroked the filly's neck. "Tell me more about the one-eye trick."

"Why don't I explain it while we walk Pretty Lady over to the stable," Mike suggested. "She's had enough excitement for one day. Besides," he added with a smile, "I bet you want to see our stable to make sure that Pretty Lady is living in comfort."

Polly noticed that Mike had a very nice smile that lit up his whole face. She smiled back at him and nodded. "You're right," she said eagerly. "I would like to see where Pretty Lady is living."

Polly walked next to Pretty Lady as Mike led the filly through the gate. "The one-eye trick is pretty simple," Mike continued, as they approached the stable. "You walk toward the horse slowly but confidently, but with one eye closed. The horse is caught off guard and doesn't have time to react. It can be a good way to calm down a nervous horse, like Pretty Lady."

They had reached the long, freshly painted white

building. A string of stalls stretched from one end of
the stable to the other, similar to the stalls at Canfield
Farm.

"The stable is brand new," Mike told her. "Right
now we have only five horses, but by next summer,
every stall should be filled." He led Pretty Lady over to
an end stall. Polly opened the door so that Mike could
walk the filly inside. She glanced into the stall and
saw that there was fresh straw on the floor, a water
pail, and a hay net. Everything looked neat, clean, and
comfortable.

Once inside, Pretty Lady turned and poked her
head over the top of the Dutch door. Mike pulled a
lump of sugar from his pocket and gave it to the filly,
along with a pat on her neck. Pretty Lady ate the
sugar lump daintily. Polly saw how gentle Mike was
with Pretty Lady and how the filly was beginning to
trust him. Her neck was arched and her ears were
pricked forward, which meant she was feeling relaxed
and friendly.

"Well, I guess I'd better go home now," Polly said
reluctantly. "It's getting late. Anyway, you probably
have work to do."

"I'll take extra-good care of Pretty Lady," Mike
promised her. "And you can visit her any time you
want. But next time, come to the gate, ring the bell,

and I'll let you in. There are two bells on the wall by the gate. The bottom bell rings in the stable."

Polly nodded. "I'll remember," she said. "And thanks, Mike." A doorbell that rings in the stable! she thought. The Harringtons really must be rich if they have something like that!

She reached up to give Pretty Lady a loving pat. "Goodbye, girl," she whispered. "I'll see you again soon."

As she was riding home on her bike, Polly decided that Mike was a very nice boy. She remembered how gentle he was with Pretty Lady, and she felt reassured that he would keep his promise to treat the filly with extra-special care. And best of all, she could visit Pretty Lady every day if she wanted to!

Everything would be just about perfect, Polly thought, if only Mr. Harrington could be convinced to give Pretty Lady another chance to race.

New Plans

The next time Polly went to see Pretty Lady, she rang the bottom bell by the front gate, as Mike had suggested. She waited for several moments, but Mike did not appear. Just as she was beginning to worry that he either hadn't heard the bell ring in the stable or wasn't on the estate, she saw him hurrying toward her.

"I'm glad you decided to come back to visit Pretty Lady," Mike said with a smile as he walked up to the gate. "She's waiting for you." He reached into the pocket of his knickers and pulled out a set of keys. He selected a large key from the ring, unlocked the gate, and pulled it open.

I'm glad that I'm a guest on the estate today and not a trespasser, Polly thought, as she stepped through the gate. Even if I am just a guest of the Harringtons' stable boy.

"I'm sorry I took so long to get here," Mike said, closing the gate behind her. "I was using the phone in the stable office to call the vet. One of the mares has developed a bad case of colic. Joe's with her now."

"Gee, you have a phone in the stable office," Polly said with awe.

Mike looked at her in surprise. "Doesn't your father have a phone in his office?" he asked.

"Dad doesn't even have an office," Polly replied with a laugh. "When he needs to write bills or pay them, he uses the kitchen table as a desk.

The only phone we have is in the hallway. We aren't rich, like the Harringtons."

They were walking around the raked gravel drive in front of the house. Polly gazed around her in awe. Now that she was closer to the house, Polly could see more clearly how beautiful the mansion and the carefully landscaped grounds around it really were.

The front door of the house was made of polished oak, and there was a gleaming brass knocker in the center of it. There were flower boxes and brightly striped awnings at each of the mansion's windows, and expensive-looking white wicker sofas, chairs, and tables on the verandas.

When Polly and Mike reached the back of the house, Polly saw a huge stone patio with wide steps that led down to a marble fountain. The fountain had three levels. Water flowed in a stream from the top level to a fish pond at the bottom of the fountain. On another part of the lawn was a swimming pool surrounded by a tiled patio.

Polly gazed around her with shining eyes. "The Harringtons' estate is so beautiful," she said with a sigh as they walked through a tall hedge that separated the back lawn from the field and the stable. "It must be wonderful to be rich. I bet that Mr. Harrington's son gets anything he wants."

Mike shrugged. "Being rich isn't so swell, I bet," he said. "I'd rather work with horses any day than be rich."

Polly noticed a bitter tone in Mike's voice, and she wondered why it was there. Maybe deep down he wished that he were rich, too.

"Well, I think it would be nifty to work with horses and be rich," Polly said. "But I know what you mean. Anyway, I bet Mr. Harrington's son is really spoiled."

Just then, Polly spotted Pretty Lady standing in the fenced-in field, and her eyes lit up with pleasure.

"I have to go back to the stable now to wait for the vet to arrive," Mike told her. "But I'll come over as soon as he's finished treating the mare. Do you mind?"

Polly shook her head. She didn't mind at all. She felt glad at the chance to have Pretty Lady all to herself. Mike smiled at her and hurried off toward the stable. At the same time, Polly eagerly headed toward the field.

Pretty Lady had been drinking from a small pond in the middle of the field. Now she wandered over to a corner section of the fence near the gate. Polly circled the fence to where Pretty Lady was standing and stepped up to the filly. When Pretty Lady saw Polly, she nickered softly.

"Hello, girl," Polly said. "I see you're feeling friendlier today." She carefully climbed up onto the bottom rung of the fence, slowly reached out her hand, and gently stroked the filly's neck. "I guess you're getting used to your new home."

The thought that Pretty Lady liked living here as much as she had liked living at Canfield Farm made Polly feel a little sad. But she noticed that the filly looked healthy, well-groomed, and relaxed, and she had to admit that Mike had kept his promise to look after her.

I still wish she were living with us, Polly thought. But she seems happy and contented, and that's what matters.

As she stroked Pretty Lady, Polly noticed a cavesson, lunge line, and lunge whip near the gate. Impulsively, she decided to see how Pretty Lady would respond to the lunge line. Polly knew that if she were training the filly, she would start with lunging exercises to teach her to obey human commands again. The exercises would also help to calm and strengthen Pretty Lady and to make her more supple.

Polly patted the filly and said, "Don't go away, girl. I'll be right back." She walked over to the gate, picked up the tack, and slowly approached Pretty Lady. When she reached the filly, she slipped the cavesson over her head and clipped the lunge line onto the metal ring in the center of the cavesson.

"Good girl," Polly said in an approving tone. She patted the filly. "Now that didn't hurt a bit, did it?"

Pretty Lady shook her head and gave a snort. She

didn't seem to mind wearing the cavesson, but her behavior showed Polly that she was beginning to feel restless.

"First, we'll try a walk," Polly said to the filly. She held the lunge line in her left hand and pulled gently on it. Pretty Lady snorted and tried to jerk away from Polly's grasp. Polly tugged the line again. This time the filly did not pull back. Instead, she stood stubbornly where she was. Try as she might, Polly could not get her to budge. It was as if Pretty Lady were made of stone.

Polly loosened her grip on the lunge line and began to stroke the filly's neck. "Please take a walk with me, girl," she said softly. "Just a short walk, okay?"

Polly patiently continued to stroke Pretty Lady and to talk to her in soothing tones. At the same time, she pulled gently on the lunge line. Finally, to Polly's relief, the filly moved forward. Polly led Pretty Lady into the center of a small ring she had noticed earlier and walked her around in a circle. After they had completed the circle, Polly stopped and said, "Halt." The filly stopped moving.

I knew she would remember how to respond to commands, Polly thought excitedly.

She smiled at Pretty Lady. "Good girl," she said. "I

knew you could do it. Now, let's try it again."

This time, as Polly circled the ring with Pretty Lady, she let the lunge line out slowly, until she was standing several feet away from Pretty Lady, and the filly was moving counterclockwise around her.

Polly knew that using the lunge whip would scare Pretty Lady. Instead she relied on her voice and the firm but gentle repetition of the commands, "Walk" and "Halt," to make the filly obey her.

At first, Pretty Lady responded to Polly's commands, but she soon felt the freedom of being held so loosely on the lunge line, and she turned away from Polly and quickly doubled back to the outside of the circle.

Just then, Polly spotted Mike walking toward the ring. All of a sudden, she felt uneasy about what she had done. She realized that Mike might very well be angry with her for taking Pretty Lady out of the field and using the lunging tack without permission.

Polly pulled on the lunge line and told the filly to halt. Pretty Lady snorted and stopped in her tracks. Polly quickly unclipped the lunge line and removed the cavesson. The filly shook her head and then immediately trotted away to the other side of the ring. Polly turned to face Mike, who was entering the ring.

"I saw the tack, and I thought I'd see if Pretty

Lady would respond to some lunging exercises," Polly explained in a rush as Mike stepped over to her. "I think that she could be a winner again. All she needs is a gentle hand and some retraining."

She stopped and waited anxiously for Mike to reply. To her relief, he smiled at her and said, "I agree. Yesterday, when I saw Pretty Lady galloping across the field, I felt that she had the mark of a true champion."

Without thinking, Polly and Mike had begun to walk together across the ring to where Pretty Lady was standing. When they reached the filly, Mike picked up the lunge line and cavesson Polly had left on the ground.

All of a sudden, Polly stared at Mike, her eyes wide. "That tack," she said. *"You're* the one who left it there!"

Mike nodded. "I was going to try some lunging exercises with Pretty Lady today, too," he admitted. He hesitated for a moment. Then he said almost shyly, "See, my dream has always been to become a professional horse trainer, like my grandfather. And I want to train Thoroughbred racehorses, like he did. When you told me about Pretty Lady, I thought that she was getting a raw deal," Mike continued. "She deserves a second chance to race, and I want to give her that chance. My plan is to train her and then convince Mr. Harrington to enter her in the Travers Stakes."

"Gee, Mike, that's swell," Polly said, looking at him with shining eyes. "We can work together!"

"Well, I don't know about that," Mike said with a frown. "Training Pretty Lady to race in the Travers Stakes means a lot to me. What do you know about training horses? You're just a kid."

Polly turned to him, her face flushed with anger. "For crying out loud, stop calling me a *kid*!" she said hotly. "Anyway, I bet I know just as much as you do about training horses. My father is a professional trainer, and he's taught me, just as your grandfather taught you."

Mike studied her thoughtfully. Then he shook his head. "I don't know, Polly," he said doubtfully. "I saw you earlier with Pretty Lady. It looked like you were having a hard time controlling her."

"But that's just because it was her first time on the lunge," Polly argued.

"Maybe that's true," Mike admitted. "But for now, I'm going to train her myself." He walked back to Pretty Lady and slipped on her cavesson.

Polly felt her eyes fill with tears of frustration as she watched Mike clip the lunge line onto Pretty Lady's cavesson. It was my idea to train Pretty Lady in the first place! she thought angrily. And now Mike is taking over. He's just a stable boy, but he acts as if Pretty Lady belongs to him.

Polly brushed the tears from her eyes, turned, and began to march out of the ring. When she reached the gate, she stopped in her tracks. She was still angry at Mike, but she was also curious to see what kind of a trainer he was and how well Pretty Lady would obey his commands.

Polly climbed up onto the fence and sat on the top rail. She watched as Mike let out the lunge line and said in an encouraging tone, "Okay, girl, walk now." Pretty Lady shook her head, snorted, and stayed where she was. Mike repeated the command. This time, Pretty Lady stepped forward. Then she turned toward Mike and walked in the opposite direction from where he wanted her to go.

Polly stifled a giggle. "You'll never get her to obey you that way," she called out.

"Huh?" Mike said, turning toward her. "What do you mean?"

"Here," Polly said, climbing down from the fence and walking over to him. "Give me the lunge line, and I'll show you."

She held out her hand. Mike hesitated for a moment. Then he shrugged and gave it to her. "Pretty

Lady is skittish, remember?" she said to him as she looped up the lunge line and held it so that she was standing close to the filly. "She'll act up if you let her. You can't give her freedom on the lunge right at the beginning, and you can't hurry her. You have to remind her of what she's supposed to do first."

Polly led Pretty Lady around in a small, counterclockwise circle. She talked to the filly in soothing tones as they walked. After Polly and Pretty Lady had completed two circles, Polly let out the lunge line. Soon she was standing in the center of the ring, and Pretty Lady was circling around her. Polly was pleased to see how well Pretty Lady responded to her calm but firm commands to walk and halt.

Smiling, she turned to look at Mike. "Well?" she asked, trying hard not to sound smug. "How did I do?"

Mike shook his head with admiration. "I thought you were spouting a lot of banana oil before, when you told me you knew how to train horses," he told her. "But you really showed me up just now."

He walked over to Polly and held out his hand. "I guess that means we're going to be partners after all," he said.

Polly shook Mike's hand. "I guess it does," she replied. "When do you want to meet again?" she asked eagerly.

"The sooner the better," Mike replied. "How about tomorrow afternoon, after lunch?"

Polly nodded in agreement. "That would be perfect," she said, adding, "Maybe we should take Pretty Lady back to the field now. She'd probably like some freedom after all that hard work."

"Would you mind doing it?" Mike asked. "I'd like to check on the colicky mare."

"I don't mind," Polly said with a smile. She led the filly out of the ring.

When she reached the field, she led Pretty Lady through the gate. She unclipped the lunge line and slipped off the cavesson.

"Congratulations, girl," she whispered. "You just took the first step into the winner's circle!"

CHAPTER
SEVEN

Becoming a Team

Every afternoon Polly and Mike worked hard to train Pretty Lady. They kept her on the lunge, and slowly but surely, they convinced her to trot and canter, as well as to walk, around the ring. One day Polly held the lunge line and gave the commands; the next day, Mike did. Polly was glad they were taking turns and working as a team. At first she had been a little worried that Mike would try to take over because he was older than she was.

Now that Pretty Lady was in training, Polly and Mike kept her apart from the other horses. She was turned out for only a few hours each day. As the weeks went by, Pretty Lady became calmer, stronger, and more supple. But the filly could still be difficult at times. One hot July afternoon, as Polly was holding two lunge reins and walking behind Pretty Lady while the filly circled the ring, she heard a low rumble of thunder in the distance. Without thinking, Polly looked up at the sky and saw dark clouds beginning to form.

Suddenly, she felt Pretty Lady turn sharply to the left and saw her move her hindquarters to the right. "Polly, you're holding her inside line too tightly," she heard Mike say. "You're throwing her off balance."

"Sorry," Polly said, immediately slackening the inside line so that it was the same length as the outside line. But Pretty Lady had been distracted by Polly's mistake. She gave a snort, shook her head, and stopped halfway around the circle.

"Walk, girl," Polly ordered. Pretty Lady refused to budge.

Mike stepped over to Pretty Lady. "What's wrong?" he asked the filly softly as he stroked her. "I made a mistake with the lunge line yesterday, and you didn't let it bother you."

Just then there was another low rumble of thunder. Pretty Lady whinnied. "Is the thunder making you nervous?" Mike asked.

Polly smiled as she watched the stable boy soothe

Pretty Lady. At first, all Mike had seemed to care about was training the filly to be a prizewinning racehorse. But as the weeks went on, Polly noticed a change in the way Mike handled Pretty Lady. Slowly he seemed to be learning to like the filly for herself, not just because she might win an important race. Polly was glad that he liked Pretty Lady almost as much as she herself did.

It thundered again, and the wind picked up. Polly felt a few drops of rain. "It's going to rain hard any minute," Polly said. "We should take Pretty Lady back to the stable until the storm is over."

Mike nodded and led the filly out of the ring. Pretty Lady balked once, then followed him. Polly could tell from the way she snorted and tossed her head that Pretty Lady was feeling nervous.

As they walked toward the stable, Polly glanced at the field and saw Joe McCall bringing in the Thoroughbred mare who had been sick with colic a few weeks ago. The Harringtons' three other horses still grazed and didn't seem to be at all nervous at the approaching storm, but Polly knew that they would have to be brought to shelter. She looked at Mike and was surprised that he made no move to help Joe.

"Shouldn't you help Joe bring in the horses?" Polly asked Mike. "Isn't that part of your job?"

"My job?" Mike said, looking at her with a puzzled expression. "Oh, yes . . . sure, that's my job."

He handed Pretty Lady's lunge reins to Polly and hurried off toward the field. Polly looked after him and shook her head. "I guess Mike likes you so much, he's forgotten about the other horses around here," she said to Pretty Lady as she continued walking the filly back to the stable.

The rain began to pour just as Polly led Pretty Lady into her stall. Polly could tell from the filly's relaxed behavior that she was relieved to be safe inside. Polly checked her water supply, then stepped out of the stall and stood under the overhang, waiting for the storm to end.

A moment later, she saw Mike walk toward the stable, leading a dark bay mare. Behind him was Joe with a dappled gray mare. It continued to thunder, and Polly could hear the rain beat down on the roof of the stable.

"Thanks for your help, Mr. Mike," she heard Joe say as he passed Mike on his way to the gray mare's stall. "I'll go and get the other mare." Polly noticed the respectful tone in Joe's voice, and she wondered at it. She also didn't understand why Joe had called his stable boy "Mister." Maybe it was some kind of joke between them.

After several minutes, Mike came out of the bay mare's stall and joined Polly under the overhang. "What a storm," he said as a gust of wind blew a sheet of rain into their faces. "It's a good thing we got the horses in when we did. And ourselves, too. I remember being in the middle of Central Park in New York City once, when a storm like this began. The guy I was riding with wouldn't go back to the stable. He nearly got both of us struck by lightning."

This was the first time Mike had ever talked about himself. Polly suddenly realized that even though she had been working with him for three weeks, she really knew very little about him. They had been so busy training Pretty Lady, they hadn't had a chance to talk about themselves. Polly didn't know who Mike's family was or where he came from. She didn't even know the Harringtons' stable boy's last name.

"New York City? Is that where you lived before you came to Saratoga?" she asked Mike.

Mike nodded. Polly waited for him to say more, but he didn't. So she asked, "Do you have any brothers or sisters?"

"No," Mike said briefly. "I'm an only child."

"I am, too," Polly said. "Most of the time I like it that way. But sometimes I wish I had a brother or a sister. Then Mother and Dad wouldn't expect so much from me. Sometimes they treat me like an adult. But other times, they act as if I'm too young to make my own decisions."

Mike looked at her with interest. Then he stared at the rain and said, "I think I know what you mean."

Polly wondered why he sounded so sad. "Did your parents mind when you decided to come to Saratoga to work?" she asked.

"They didn't say anything about it," Mike said. "They couldn't." Before Polly could say anything else, he added quickly, "The rain's stopped, but the ground will be too wet to take Pretty Lady out for more lunge work. Why don't we just call it a day until tomorrow?"

"Sure," Polly said. She sensed that Mike didn't want to talk about his parents, though she didn't understand why.

As Polly rode home, she went over in her mind the conversation with Mike. Maybe he didn't have a family anymore. Maybe they had died and now he was an orphan. She decided that she would never ask him about his parents again. She was sure that it hurt Mike too much to talk about them.

The First Ride

One afternoon in late July, after Mike had let Polly in through the front gate, he said to her, "The Travers Stakes is just a few weeks away, and Mr. Harrington is due back any day. That means we don't have much time left. Pretty Lady's been making such good progress on the lunge. Maybe we should try and saddle her."

Polly's eyes lit up. For several days now, she had been thinking the same thing. "That's a swell idea," she said eagerly. "First we should lunge her with the riding tack. Then, if she lets us ride her, we can start working on her speed."

They stopped at the tack room at the end of the

stable to get the lunging tack. Then they picked out a bridle, a saddle, and a saddle pad. Polly also took a martingale off one of the hooks on the wall. "We'll need this to keep Pretty Lady from tossing her head up during the ride," Polly said.

They carried the tack over to the small ring and then went over to the field to get Pretty Lady. "Let's keep her as calm as possible," Polly suggested as they approached the filly. "She's been pretty relaxed lately, but we don't know how she's going to react to the bridle and the saddle."

Slowly they stepped over to Pretty Lady. Polly slipped the lunging cavesson over her head. "So far, so good," Polly whispered to Mike as the filly obediently followed her on the lunge line.

After Polly had led Pretty Lady into the ring, Mike brought the bridle over to the filly. "You remember this," he said as he placed the bit in her mouth. Pretty Lady jerked her head up as she felt the bit go in, but she didn't shy away, and Mike was able to slip the bridle over her head. Polly snapped on the lunge line and held it firmly as Mike placed the martingale around the filly's neck.

Next Mike placed the saddle pad on Pretty Lady's back. "Here comes the tricky part," he murmured as he picked up the saddle. He brought the saddle over to the filly and lifted it up to put it on her back. Pretty Lady snorted and pranced back and forth. Mike lowered the saddle and held it until the filly had stopped prancing.

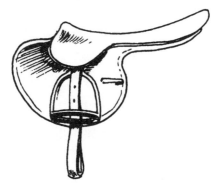

Polly stroked the filly. As soon as she touched Pretty Lady, she felt the filly tremble. "No one's going to hurt you, girl," Polly said softly. "I promise."

As Polly stroked Pretty Lady, Mike lifted up the saddle again. This time, Pretty Lady stood still while he placed it on her back. He slid the end of the martingale onto the girth strap, buckled the girth, and stood up. Pretty Lady snorted and shook her head several times.

Using the lunge line, Polly walked Pretty Lady around the ring. Then she let out the line and lunged the filly counterclockwise around her.

"I think she's gotten used to wearing the riding tack," Polly said, after the filly had circled several times. "Now we should lunge her with a rider. It's been a long time since she's had the weight of a rider on her back, and she needs to get used to it again."

"Okay, Pretty Lady," Mike said, stepping up to the filly. "Let's see if you'll agree to let me sit on your back."

Polly bent over and laced her fingers together to give Mike a leg up. Mike put his foot into Polly's hands and hoisted himself up onto Pretty Lady's back. As soon as the filly felt Mike's weight on her back, she whinnied and pranced nervously. Polly quickly stepped away.

Pretty Lady whinnied again and reared, throwing Mike to the ground. Polly rushed over to him. "Are you all right?" she asked anxiously.

Mike sat up and slowly shook his head. "I'm fine," he said a bit breathlessly. "I just had the wind knocked out of me."

"Let me try," Polly said, handing him the lunge line. Mike gave her a leg up, and she hoisted herself into the saddle.

Pretty Lady pranced again, but Mike kept a firm hold on the lunge line, and the filly was unable to rear.

"Calm down, now, girl," Polly said. She continued to talk to Pretty Lady quietly, and the filly finally stood still.

"I'm going to lunge her," Mike said. Polly nodded and held onto the reins as Mike let out the lunge line.

"Walk on, girl," Mike commanded. The filly shook her head and refused to go forward. Oh, no, Polly thought. She's balking again.

"Walk on," Mike repeated calmly but firmly. This time, Pretty Lady stepped forward. Polly glanced over at Mike, and they smiled at each other. Polly was sure he was thinking the same thing she was. If Pretty Lady had gotten over her habit of balking under saddle, it meant that their training was really working.

"Would you like to take over?" Mike asked after awhile.

"Very much," Polly said, nodding. She held the reins firmly and used her hands and her voice to command Pretty Lady to circle several times around Mike. Then Mike unclipped the lunge line, and Polly said, "Halt."

The filly stopped. Polly touched her boots to the filly's sides and clicked her tongue against the roof of her mouth. Pretty Lady hesitated for a moment, and Polly repeated the signals. The filly started forward.

After Polly had commanded Pretty Lady to walk and trot around the ring several times, she urged the filly into a canter. Pretty Lady moved into the faster gait with high-spirited ease. Polly sensed that the filly wanted to go even faster, so she called out to Mike, "I want to take her for a run."

"Are you sure?" Mike asked.

"I'm sure," Polly replied with a confident smile. She gripped the reins and guided Pretty Lady out of the ring. When they had cantered past the fenced-in field, Polly urged the filly into a gallop. Pretty Lady was only too happy to obey.

Polly felt wonderful galloping across the field. She had ridden Thoroughbreds before, to exercise them, but none of them had been as fast as Pretty Lady. Polly could have galloped forever, but she knew she shouldn't tire the filly out.

"Whoa, girl," she called as she pulled on the reins. At first the high-spirited filly refused to stop, but Polly continued to pull on the reins, and the filly finally slowed to a canter.

"Right now, you need a rubdown and a drink of water," Polly told Pretty Lady as she guided the filly toward the stable at a walk.

"Mike and I were right about you all along, girl," she said softly. "I can't wait to show you to Mr. Harrington. After he sees how fast you are, I just know he'll want to enter you in the Travers Stakes!"

A Party

For the next few weeks, Polly and Mike took turns riding Pretty Lady. Soon they were galloping the filly on the estate's practice track, using a stopwatch to mark her time. They conditioned her legs with long gallops and began to ask her for bursts of speed as she rounded the track. Polly and Mike knew that the filly would need to speed up quickly at the start of the race.

One day, as Polly and Mike were examining Pretty Lady's legs for signs of swelling, Polly said, "It's so quiet here. I'm worried that Pretty Lady will become nervous again when we take her to the track. There will be a lot of noise and people around."

Mike nodded and thought for a minute. "I'll be right back," he said, running off toward the stable office. Several moments later, he was back, lugging a phonograph.

"This belongs to Joe," Mike said with a grin. "We can use it to see how Pretty Lady reacts to the sound."

Mike cranked up the phonograph and started to play a record, a loud, boisterous marching tune.

Pretty Lady snorted and shook her head, but she didn't skitter.

"I don't think she likes the music very much," Polly said with a laugh.

"As long as the sound doesn't bother her, that's all that matters," Mike said, smiling.

Every day after that, Mike played the phonograph during Pretty Lady's workout. The filly soon became accustomed to the sound of Joe's records as she galloped around the track.

As Pretty Lady's workouts continued, her time improved. Polly and Mike were pleased with the filly's progress, but they also began to feel that she needed a break from her training.

"Why don't we take Pretty Lady for a longer ride today?" Mike suggested late one afternoon, after Polly had galloped Pretty Lady around the track. "There's a big field on the other side of the estate. I rode the bay mare over there this morning."

"Swell," Polly said. She gave the filly a pat, adding, "I bet Pretty Lady would like a nice, long, easy ride, wouldn't you, girl?" The filly tossed her head and neighed. Polly was sure she was eager to be off.

They decided that Mike would ride Pretty Lady to the field, and Polly would ride the gray mare. On the way back, they would switch.

They quickly saddled up the two horses and set off. As they cantered across the Harringtons' field, Polly couldn't help but notice the difference between the horse she was riding and Pretty Lady. The gray mare was sweet-tempered and speedy, but she wasn't half as fast as the filly, or as exciting to ride.

Soon they were cantering across the next field side by side. "It's beautiful here," Polly said, gazing around at the brightly colored wildflowers that covered the field.

Mike motioned toward a gently sloping hill up ahead. "On the other side of that hill is a pond. We can rest the horses there before we ride back."

Polly nodded and urged the mare on. As she began to climb the hill, Mike and Pretty Lady passed her. Mike grinned at Polly over his shoulder. What a couple of showoffs, Polly thought, smiling.

After Polly had ridden down the other side of the hill, she brought the mare to a halt in front of a small pond ringed with fir trees. Mike had already dismounted, and Polly did the same.

"You and Pretty Lady were cantering faster than we were. I couldn't keep up," Polly said to Mike as she slipped the reins over the mare's head. Together, she and Mike led the horses down to the edge of the pond for a drink. Pretty Lady and the mare both slurped up the clear water noisily.

"Pretty Lady was born to go fast," Mike said. "That's why she's going to win the Travers Stakes."

Polly looked over at him. "Winning the race

means a lot to you, doesn't it?" she asked. "I remember you saying that the day we started to train Pretty Lady together."

Mike nodded. "It *is* important to me," he admitted. "If she wins, I'll be closer to my dream of becoming a professional horse trainer."

"Oh," Polly said in a low tone. "I guess you wish you had trained Pretty Lady alone. Then you could take all the credit when she wins the race."

Mike smiled and shook his head. "No, Polly, you're wrong," he said. "I thought that at first, but I realized very soon that I couldn't train Pretty Lady without you. We'll both share the credit when she wins. We're a team, remember?"

Polly and Mike stood together in comfortable silence for a moment, looking out across the pond. Suddenly, Polly noticed that the sun was getting lower in the sky. "Say, we'd better start back before it gets dark," she said to Mike.

They quickly led the horses away from the water. Polly mounted Pretty Lady and urged her back up the hill. Mike, on the gray mare, followed behind. As Polly guided Pretty Lady toward the field, she felt how responsive the filly was to her slightest command. A month ago, she was a sour horse, Polly thought as she urged the filly into a gallop. Now she's confident and high-spirited, just as she should be.

The sun was setting by the time Polly and Mike reached the Harringtons' field. They slowed the horses to a walk, and as they came closer to the house, Polly was surprised to hear the sounds of a jazz band coming from the patio. She stopped Pretty Lady and looked toward the house. Expensive-looking cars were driving up to the front of the house. Men in tuxedos and women in stylish evening dresses climbed out of the cars.

Polly looked at the patio and saw that it was lit by strings of multicolored Chinese lanterns. A crowd of men and women milled around the patio and stood by the big fountain on the back lawn, talking and laughing. Through the crowd servants with trays passed, offering food and drinks.

The band began to play a Charleston. Many couples immediately stopped talking and laughing and began to dance. Polly watched the beads on the women's dresses glitter in the lantern light. The silky ostrich feathers waved in their hair as they moved their arms and legs to the rhythm of the dance.

"Gee," Polly said in an awed tone as she gazed with wide, admiring eyes at the scene before her. "I knew people gave ritzy parties like this in Saratoga, but I've never actually seen one until now."

She turned to Mike. "The party must mean that Mr. Harrington has come home," she said excitedly. "Now you can tell him about Pretty Lady."

When Mike didn't reply, Polly looked at him more closely. She was surprised to see that he was pale and that he had a grim expression on his face. She was even more surprised when he said urgently, "We have to get the horses back to the stable right now, Polly. Before Mr. Harrington sees us."

Quickly Mike dismounted, slipped the reins over the gray mare's head, and began to lead her away.

Polly stared at Mike for a moment with a puzzled expression. Then she climbed off Pretty Lady and followed him with the filly. They led the horses around the edge of the crowd toward the stable. As they came closer to the party, Polly hoped Pretty Lady would stay calm with all the people and noise around her.

To Polly's relief, the filly followed her quietly. Then, just as they were passing the fountain, Polly saw a woman with bright red lips look over at them. "Ooh!" the woman squealed with delight when she noticed Pretty Lady. "What a nifty-looking horse!" She motioned to a few of her friends, who were standing nearby. "Come on over, everybody, and see the pretty horse!"

A Party

Before Polly could lead Pretty Lady away, the woman and her friends rushed up to the filly and began to pat her. Pretty Lady snorted and nervously backed away.

"Please don't crowd her," Polly begged the woman and her friends as she struggled to control the skittish filly. "Can't you see that you're making her nervous?"

But they didn't pay any attention to Polly's plea. They went on patting Pretty Lady and exclaiming over her beauty. Their continual fussing made the filly more and more nervous. She jerked up her head and started to rear. Polly gripped the reins tightly and managed to turn the filly away from the woman and her friends. She talked to Pretty Lady in soothing tones and kept a firm, close hold on the reins as she led the frightened filly toward the stable.

"Well, how do you like that!" she heard one of the women say indignantly. "What's wrong with that horse, anyway?"

An Unpleasant Meeting

When Polly led Pretty Lady into her stall and removed her saddle and bridle, she could see that the filly was still nervous. Pretty Lady snorted and shook her head and pranced back and forth in the stall. "I'm sorry those people scared you like that, girl," Polly said softly.

Polly knew Pretty Lady needed a rubdown after her trip to the field, but the filly was acting so skittish that she decided to leave her alone for a while.

She stepped out of the stall and saw Mike coming toward her from the gray mare's stall. "What took you so long?" he asked in a worried tone. "You didn't run into Mr. Harrington, did you?"

"No," Polly said. She explained to him what had happened. "Pretty Lady is still skittish," she finished. "I certainly hope we can calm her down by the time Mr. Harrington sees her." She paused for a moment. Then she said, "I don't understand something, Mike. Why didn't you want Mr. Harrington to see us?"

"I didn't want to interrupt the Harringtons' swanky party, that's all," Mike muttered.

"Oh," Polly said with a nod.

But then she remembered the grim expression on Mike's face and how pale he had looked back by the house. She began to wonder if there were other reasons he had wanted to avoid Mr. Harrington.

"Say, you are going to tell Mr. Harrington about Pretty Lady, aren't you?" Polly wanted to know. "I mean, you're not losing your nerve or your faith in Pretty Lady, are you?"

Mike shook his head and sighed. "No, Polly, I believe in Pretty Lady more than anything in the world," he said. "I promise I'll talk to Mr. Harrington as soon as I feel I can."

Polly saw a small truck driving up to the stable. "That's Joe," Mike told her. "I told him you needed a ride home. He's already put your bike in the truck." Without another word, he turned and went into Pretty Lady's stall.

Polly glanced into the stall and noticed a troubled look in Mike's brown eyes as he began to give Pretty Lady her rubdown. Something is bothering Mike, she thought as she stepped into the truck. I wish I knew what it was.

The next afternoon, when Polly arrived at the front gate of the Harringtons' estate, she rang the stable bell as usual. She waited for a while, and when Mike did not appear, she wheeled her bicycle around to the back of the estate and stepped through the archway, as she had done the first day she had come to visit Pretty Lady.

When she reached the field, she saw the filly grazing. But there was no sign of Mike anywhere.

"Do you know where Mike is?" she asked Joe, who was passing by.

"No, I don't, Miss," Joe replied. "Haven't seen him all day." He gave her a friendly nod and headed toward the stable.

When Pretty Lady saw Polly coming toward her, she nickered softly. "How are you today, girl?" Polly asked as she approached the filly.

As she stroked Pretty Lady, she wondered what had happened to Mike. He hadn't been acting like his usual cheerful self. She thought about how well she and Mike worked together as a team. She also realized what a good friend he had become.

Just then, she spotted a tall, well-dressed man walking toward the field. With him was a bald, heavyset man in a rumpled suit and a boater hat.

The men went over and stood before Polly. "My name is James Harrington," the tall man said in a brisk, businesslike tone. "Who are you and what are you doing here?"

Polly looked up at Mr. Harrington. "I'm Polly Canfield, a friend of Mike, the stable boy."

Mr. Harrington shook his head. "I don't know to whom you're referring," he said curtly. "No one by that name works for me."

As Polly blinked at him in disbelief, he took the reins from her hands and said in the same curt tone, "This horse is a valuable piece of property, young lady. She is not a pet. Now, run along home, like a good girl."

Polly took a few steps back, her face burning with embarrassment.

Mr. Harrington turned to the heavyset man. "You can look her over now, Mr. Baker," he said.

Polly watched as Mr. Baker stepped up to Pretty Lady and examined her teeth. Then he expertly ran his hand along her body and down her legs.

He turned to Mr. Harrington. "She'll do," he said.

"Here's what I'm willing to pay." He named a price.

"That seems fair," Mr. Harrington said, nodding. "But I'll have to think about it. I may be receiving other offers."

Polly stared in horror as she realized what was happening. Mr. Harrington was planning to sell Pretty Lady! She looked at the filly and tears filled her eyes. Then Polly turned and ran.

Polly Takes Charge

P olly, her head down, ran as fast as she could. She didn't know where she was going, and she didn't care. All of sudden, she bumped headfirst into someone. She looked up and saw Mike.

"What is it, Polly?" he asked anxiously. "What's wrong?"

Polly stared at him for a few seconds. Then she demanded angrily, "Who are you, Mike?"

When Mike didn't reply, Polly said hotly, "I just met Mr. Harrington, so I know you're not his stable boy. I want to know who you really are and why you've been lying to me."

Mike looked away from Polly.

"Your name probably isn't even Mike!" Polly added disgustedly.

He turned back to her and said quietly, "My name *is* Mike, Polly. It's short for Michael. Michael Harrington."

Polly clenched her fists in anger. "You're lying again!" she cried. "Michael Harrington is in New York City. He's working as a copyboy on his father's newspaper."

"No, Polly," Mike said, shaking his head. "I was supposed to work there after school got out, but I came to Saratoga instead. See, my father wants me to learn about newspapers, so that I can work in the family business some day. That's *his* dream. I came here to start pursuing *my* dream—to be a professional horse trainer."

Mike hesitated for a moment. Then he said in a desperate tone, "I thought if I could prove to Dad that I could train a winning horse, he'd let me choose my own career. But all that doesn't matter now," he added bitterly. "When Dad found out I wasn't working at the newspaper, he ordered me to go to New York City."

Polly saw the anguished look on Mike's face, and deep down she couldn't help feeling sorry for him. But she was too angry to admit it. "You should have told me the truth instead of lying to me," she said. "I thought we were friends. Didn't you trust me?"

"I never told you I was a stable boy," Mike reminded her. "You assumed I was."

"That doesn't matter," Polly said stubbornly. "You still should have told me who you really were."

"I *was* going to tell you," Mike insisted desperately. "But the more we worked together with Pretty Lady, the harder it became. See, I really liked the way you treated me—like I was a regular guy instead of some spoiled rich kid. That's what you said about the Harringtons' kid the day we began to train Pretty Lady, remember? I was afraid that if I told you I was Mr. Harrington's son, you wouldn't want to be my friend."

"If you think that, then you're hopeless!" Polly told him. "I like you because you're *Mike*. I don't care if you're a stable boy or a rich kid. Just like I love Pretty Lady for herself, not just because she might win an important race."

"You're right," Mike admitted. "I see that now. I'm sorry for not being honest with you, Polly. If I could make it up to you somehow, I would. But it's too late for that. I have to leave for New York tomorrow morning."

Without another word, he turned and walked toward the house.

Polly had never felt so miserable in her whole life. Mike was leaving, and Pretty Lady was never going to get the chance to race. Polly might never see either one of them again.

Before she left forever, Polly wanted to see Pretty Lady one last time. She walked back to the field and, stepping up to the filly, buried her face in her mane. Pretty Lady nickered softly. Then she turned her head and nuzzled Polly's shoulder. Despite her unhappiness, Polly couldn't help noticing that it was the first time Pretty Lady had done that. Somehow, the filly's friendly nuzzle made Polly feel worse than ever.

"Oh, Pretty Lady," she whispered. "I just lost a good friend, and now I'm going to lose you, too. I don't want either you or Mike to go away, but what can I do to stop it?"

As Polly stood there, she began to think hard about what to do next. After several moments, she made up her mind. She gave the filly a last, loving pat, turned, and strode over to the house. She stepped up to the front door, a determined expression on her face, and rapped the brass knocker several times.

The door opened, and a man in a butler's uniform appeared before her. "Yes?" the butler said stiffly.

"I would like to see Mr. Harrington, please," Polly told him, adding quickly, "I'm a friend of his son, Mike."

The butler nodded and closed the door. Polly bit her lip and waited for his return. A few moments later, he reappeared. "Mr. Harrington will see you," he said.

Polly followed the butler across the tiled entrance hall, past a long staircase with wide steps and highly polished oak banisters. The butler stopped at a door, opened it, and ushered Polly into a wood-paneled library. Then he closed the door silently behind her, leaving Polly alone with Mike's father.

Mr. Harrington sat behind an oak desk, studying a page from his newspaper. Polly stepped toward the desk and stood before him.

Mr. Harrington put down the newspaper and looked at Polly. Before he could ask her what she wanted, she said boldly, "Mr. Harrington, I don't think you're being fair to Mike or to Pretty Lady. Both of

them deserve a chance to prove themselves. I think you should give them that chance."

Mike's father raised his eyebrows in surprise, but he didn't say anything.

Polly took a deep breath and continued. "Mike and I have been training Pretty Lady for weeks," she said. "She's a different horse now. I know she can win the Travers Stakes." Polly stared into Mr. Harrington's stern eyes. "Mike has worked so hard. Please let him show you what a swell job he's done."

After Polly had finished speaking, Mr. Harrington remained silent. Polly waited anxiously for his reply. After several moments, he nodded gravely at her. "Thank you for being so honest with me, young lady," he said.

He stood up from his desk, turned, and pulled a satin bell rope attached to the wall behind him. A moment later, the door to the library opened, and the Harringtons' butler stepped into the room.

"Hobson, would you show Miss Canfield out, please?" Mr. Harrington said.

"Very good, Sir," the butler replied, holding the door open for Polly.

Polly stared at Mr. Harrington. He picked up the newspaper and began studying it again. "But, Mr. Harrington, you haven't told me what— " she began.

"Thank you, Miss Canfield," he said, looking up briefly. Then he went back to his reading.

Polly turned and slowly left the room. "This way, Miss," the butler said as he led her across the tiled entrance hall to the front door.

Polly walked out of the house, feeling worse than before. She had let Mike and Pretty Lady down, and now she was going to lose the two of them forever.

Mr. Harrington Decides

T he next morning, Polly tried to keep herself busy by helping her father with the horses. But all she could think about were Mike and Pretty Lady, and how she would never see them again.

Because it was a hot, sticky day, Polly went back to the house for a glass of lemonade after she had finished her chores. She had just stepped into the front hall, when the phone rang.

It was Hobson, the Harringtons' butler, asking her to call on Mr. Harrington at her earliest convenience.

Polly didn't reply for a moment or two. She felt completely baffled by Mr. Harrington's request.

"May I tell Mr. Harrington that you will call, Miss

Canfield?" the butler asked politely.

"I'll come over right away," Polly said.

Why does Mike's father want to see me? she wondered as she pedaled toward the Harringtons' estate. Maybe Pretty Lady is sick or injured, she thought anxiously. She thought of other possibilities, but none of them made sense. When she reached Mike's house, she was just as puzzled as she had been earlier.

She got off her bicycle, stepped toward the front gate, and pressed the top bell. A few moments later, she saw Hobson, the butler, walking toward her from the house. "Good morning, Miss," he said as he opened the gate. "Mr. Harrington is waiting for you in the library."

Polly followed the butler into the house and back to the library. When she stepped into the room, she was surprised to see that Mike stood in front of his father's desk. Mr. Harrington sat behind the desk, studying some papers in a folder. Polly walked across the room, stood next to Mike, and gave him a questioning look. Mike shrugged, as if to say, "I don't know any more about this than you do."

Mr. Harrington closed the folder and looked first at Polly and then at Mike. "Yesterday, Miss Canfield told me that you have both spent a great deal of time training Pretty Lady to race again," he said to his son in his usual brisk manner. "Is this true?"

"Yes, Father," Mike said. "I wanted to prove to you—"

Mr. Harrington held up his hand. "Let's stick with the subject of Pretty Lady for now," he said quietly.

He turned to Polly. "Last night, I thought about what you said to me, young lady," he told her. "I would like to know if you truly believe Pretty Lady has a chance of winning a race like the Travers Stakes."

Polly felt a glimmer of hope at Mr. Harrington's words. "We really do think she can win, Mr. Harrington," she said eagerly.

She and Mike took turns explaining to him how they had trained the filly on the lunge and how fast she was when they rode her.

"Pretty Lady can still be skittish now and then," Polly said, finally. She told Mr. Harrington what had happened two nights earlier, when the party guests had pestered the filly.

"But that could have happened to just about any high-strung Thoroughbred," Mike was quick to point out, after Polly had finished. "Honestly, Pretty Lady isn't sour toward humans anymore. She obeys and trusts people who treat her right. You should see how high-spirited she is and how fast she can run!"

Mr. Harrington nodded. "I intend to do just that," he said. "I plan to give Pretty Lady a workout on the track. If the filly runs as fast as you and Polly say she does, I'll consider entering her in the Stakes."

Polly and Mike looked at each other joyfully. "Gee, that's swell, Mr. Harrington," Polly said, her eyes shining. "Thank you!"

At the Track

A few mornings later, Polly sat in the back seat of the Harringtons' Cadillac with Mike and his father, as the Harringtons' chauffeur drove them to the racetrack for Pretty Lady's workout. Ahead of them Joe drove the filly in the family's horse truck.

Polly was eager to get to the racetrack to see Pretty Lady work out, but at the same time, she was excited to be riding in a chauffeured motorcar.

"I feel as if I were rich, too, riding in this fancy car," Polly said to Mike with a happy sigh as she settled back comfortably against the upholstered seat.

When Mike didn't reply, Polly saw that he was nervously fingering the stopwatch in his hands.

"Don't worry," she whispered. "Pretty Lady will run at top speed today. I know she will!"

Mike nodded and smiled, but he continued to turn the stopwatch over and over in his hands.

A few moments later, they drove up to the fence that surrounded the oval-shaped racetrack. Polly looked out the window and saw that they were near the grandstand. If everything goes the way we planned, she thought, in two weeks we'll be sitting up there cheering for Pretty Lady in the Travers Stakes.

The chauffeur got out of the car and opened the door on Polly's side. Polly stepped out, followed by Mike and his father.

Mr. Harrington led the way to the truck, where Joe guided Pretty Lady down the back ramp. Polly saw the filly shake her head up and down several times, but she willingly followed Joe's lead.

"She's in high spirits this morning, Sir," Joe said to Mr. Harrington as he saddled her. "But she's given me no trouble so far."

Just then, a short, slim man in a polo shirt, knickers, riding boots, and a cap walk toward them. The man stepped up to Mike's father and took off his cap. "Well, Mr. Harrington, I'm here, just as you asked," he said with a smile. "Now, where's this filly you want me to ride?"

"Thank you for coming on such short notice, Danny," Mr. Harrington said. Then he turned to Polly and Mike. "This is Danny Peterson," he told them. "One of the finest jockeys around. I've hired him to be my personal jockey. Pretty Lady will be the first horse he races for me. If," he added, "I decide to enter her in the Travers."

He led Danny over to Pretty Lady. Polly and Mike followed behind. Danny mounted Pretty Lady and guided her through an opening in the fence onto the track. He warmed her up by taking her on a slow circuit around the track. Then he urged her into a gallop. Mike pressed the button on the stopwatch and timed them, as Danny and Pretty Lady breezed along the track. After Danny had ridden her for a quarter of a mile, Mike checked the stopwatch.

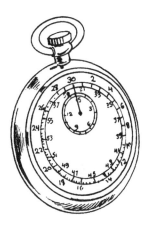

"Well?" Mr. Harrington said, turning to his son.

Mike smiled broadly at his father. "Twenty-three seconds," he said proudly. "And Danny wasn't even riding her at blazing speed, the way he would in the race."

"And Pretty Lady's time is even faster than Challenger's," Polly said with delight. "I knew she could do it!"

Mr. Harrington looked pleased as he waved at Danny to keep going. The jockey and Pretty Lady continued to breeze down the track in quarter–mile sections. Mike clocked her speed at each quarter mile. When the jockey had finished the full mile–and–a–quarter circuit that marked the length of the Travers Stakes race, he slowed the filly down and rode her over to Polly, Mike, and Mr. Harrington.

"This filly of yours is a real pleasure to ride," Danny said. "She sure shows speed, and she's responsive. How come you've been keeping her under wraps all year?"

Mr. Harrington smiled at Polly and Mike. "I've made up my mind. I'm entering Pretty Lady in the Travers Stakes."

Polly and Mike looked at each other, their faces lit up with joy. "That's swell, Mr, Harrington," Polly said. "I just knew you'd change your mind about Pretty Lady once you saw her on the track."

"Well, young lady," Mike's father said with a twinkle in his eye. "It looks as if you were right."

"And They're Off!"

Every morning after that, Polly and Mike went over to the track to watch Danny exercise Pretty Lady. Their training of Pretty Lady was over, but they enjoyed seeing her improve under Danny's care.

A few days before the race, Polly and Mike sat in the Harringtons' stable office, looking at the local newspaper. They studied the paper each day to see which horses were running in the Travers Stakes and which horses had dropped out. Polly knew from her father that Mr. Sinclair had entered Challenger.

"Look," Mike said suddenly. "This article about the Travers says that more owners have pulled their horses out of the race."

Polly took the newspaper from him and read out loud, "Many in Saratoga's racing world believe it is the presence of a speedy Thoroughbred named Challenger, and that steady prizewinner, Lucky Star, that has convinced the rest of the owners to withdraw their horses from the Travers. Now the only entries are Challenger, Lucky Star, and a long shot named Pretty Lady, owned by Mr. James Harrington. This reporter wonders: Will Mr. Harrington pull his filly out of the race, too?"

Polly put the paper down. "Of course, Pretty Lady is going to stay in the race," she said indignantly. Then she looked at Mike, her eyes wide. "This means that the Travers Stakes will be only a three-horse race, Mike!"

"I know," Mike said with a worried expression. "It's exciting, but it also means that everyone will be watching Pretty Lady to see how she competes against the two fastest horses in Saratoga."

"Pretty Lady is faster than Challenger, and I bet she can beat Lucky Star, too," Polly said confidently. "Trust me."

"I do," Mike said. "And I trust Pretty Lady, too. I know that she'll run on Saturday like she's never run before."

When the afternoon of the Travers Stakes finally

arrived, Polly felt almost as skittish as Pretty Lady had once been as she drove over to the racetrack with her parents. Sam, the Canfields' groom, had left in the horse truck with Challenger earlier.

"Stop fidgeting so much," Laura Canfield told her daughter gently. "We'll be there soon."

"Polly can't help it, dear," Bill Canfield said to his wife with a chuckle. "After all, it's not every day our daughter has the chance to race a horse against one that has been trained by her own father."

"Will you be angry if Pretty Lady wins instead of Challenger, Dad?" Polly asked.

"I'll be disappointed," Bill Canfield admitted. "But I'll be very proud of you. Your happiness is more important to me than whether or not Challenger wins today."

"Thanks for being such a good sport, Dad," Polly said, adding with a grin, "especially since you know that Pretty Lady is going to win the race."

Her father laughed. "Well, we'll see about that," he said good-naturedly. "You never know what can happen in a horse race!"

A few moments later, Bill Canfield pulled into the racetrack parking area. Polly and her parents got out of the car and walked over to the paddock, the closed-in area where the horses were saddled.

As Polly approached the paddock, she glanced at the grandstand and saw that it was crowded with people. Another crowd of spectators lined the fence that surrounded the racetrack. Still more spectators filled the grassy, fenced-in oval inside the track. There were three high poles in the grassy area, with signs attached to them. The signs displayed the names of the jockeys and the horses they were riding today. Polly knew that, after the race, another sign would announce the names of the winning horse and jockey. When Polly and her parents reached the paddock, Polly saw Mr. Harrington, Mike, and Danny Peterson standing by Pretty Lady. The jockey looked wonderful in his blue-and-white silk racing uniform.

Polly introduced her parents to Mike and his father. Then Bill Canfield said, "I'm afraid you'll have to excuse me, Mr. Harrington. I need to speak to Challenger's owner and to his jockey."

"I understand," Mr. Harrington said graciously. "Good luck to you, Mr. Canfield."

"The same to you, Sir," Polly's father said. He smiled at his daughter and gave her a wink. Then he walked off toward Challenger.

"It's a quarter to three," Mike said, glancing at his watch. "Fifteen minutes until post time."

Danny Peterson nodded, swung himself onto

Pretty Lady's back, and placed his feet into the short stirrups of the racing saddle. The filly began to prance back and forth, but Polly could tell from the forward position of her ears and the rippling muscles of her body that she was feeling high-spirited rather than nervous.

"She's ready to go," Danny said, echoing Polly's thoughts.

She and Mike stepped up to Pretty Lady. "Fly like the wind, girl," Mike said, giving the filly a pat.

Polly put her arms around Pretty Lady and kissed her silky neck. "Good luck, girl," she whispered. "We'll be cheering for you."

Just then, they heard the bugle call that told the horses and their jockeys it was time to parade to the starting line. Polly and Mike stepped back and watched with pride as Pretty Lady joined Challenger and Lucky Star in the parade from the paddock to the starting line. As the three horses approached the barriers that marked the start of the race, Polly and Mike could hear wild cheers and loud applause coming from the grandstand.

"We'd better find our seats, quick," Polly said to Mike. "The race will begin any minute!"

The two of them hurried out of the paddock and toward the grandstand. "There's my father and your parents," Mike said, pointing to a row in the grandstand that was right in front of the starting line. They rushed up the steps and found two empty seats next to Mike's father.

Polly turned to face the track and saw that the three horses were lined up behind the starting post, with Pretty Lady in the center. A hush came over the crowd. Polly crossed her fingers and waited.

A moment later, the starter dropped the flag. The horses sprinted forward, and at the same time, the crowd in the grandstand yelled, "And they're off!"

The race was on!

The Race

olly and Mike watched breathlessly as
Challenger, Pretty Lady, and Lucky Star pounded
along the track neck and neck. The filly gained speed
and edged past Lucky Star at the turn. Rounding the
bend, she broke free from the two horses.

"Go, Pretty Lady, go!" Polly yelled.

Pretty Lady stayed in front down the length of the
straightaway. Then Challenger started to pick up
speed, and Pretty Lady began to fall behind him.
Seconds later, Lucky Star gained on both of them. But
Pretty Lady, urged on by Danny, broke free again,
passed both horses around the next bend, and
breezed down the straightaway. Polly and Mike

cheered wildly for her, almost as if they hoped that she could hear them.

Pretty Lady fell back, surged ahead, fell back, and gained again.

Then it happened. At the last turn before the final approach to the finish line, Pretty Lady stumbled.

The crowd gasped in unison.

Challenger and Lucky Star sped by Pretty Lady. To Polly and Mike's relief, Danny quickly steadied her. He urged the filly back to top speed, and soon she was edging past Lucky Star. But as she approached the finish line, she was almost a full length behind Challenger.

"I can't watch," Polly said with a groan. She covered her eyes with her hands and waited for the race to be over.

"Look, Polly, look!" she heard Mike yell suddenly. "I can't believe what's happening!"

Polly took her hands away from her eyes just in time to see Pretty Lady sprint forward. The crowd rose to its feet as she went neck and neck with Challenger and then passed him. With a good foot to spare between her and the colt, Pretty Lady dashed across the finish line first.

The crowd roared with excitement. "She did it!" Polly cried as she and Mike hugged each other. "I

knew she could win, and she did!"

Mike grinned at her and then turned to shake hands with his father. "Come on," Mike said, after Polly had hugged her parents. "Let's get down to the winner's circle."

Polly and Mike hurried out of the grandstand, followed by Polly's parents and Mr. Harrington. They reached the enclosure near the track where the awards were given at the same time as a crowd of newspaper reporters and photographers.

A moment later, Danny rode into the winner's circle and brought Pretty Lady to a halt. The Canfields and the Harringtons rushed toward them.

Polly stroked Pretty Lady. "You won, girl!" she said excitedly. "I'm so proud of you!"

"Congratulations, Danny," Mr. Harrington said, shaking the jockey's hand. "You did a fine job out there today. But then, you had a fine horse to ride."

"I'd say so," Danny replied, reaching over to pat Pretty Lady.

Just then, an official of the racetrack approached them, holding a wreath of flowers. Polly watched, her eyes shining with joy, as the official placed the horseshoe-shaped wreath around Pretty Lady's neck.

The official cleared his throat. "And now," he said, "I would like to award this check and trophy to you,

Mr. Harrington, as the owner of this year's Travers Stakes winner, Pretty Lady."

Polly felt as though she would burst with pride.

"What do you plan to do with the money, Mr. Harrington?" one of the reporters asked.

"I'm donating it to Pretty Lady's trainers, Polly Canfield and my son, Mike," he replied. "Without their faith in Pretty Lady, we wouldn't be standing in the winner's circle today."

Polly felt pleased and proud. She looked at Mike. From the way he was smiling, she was sure he felt the same way.

After the reporters and photographers had left the enclosure, Danny climbed off Pretty Lady's back and carefully removed the wreath from her neck. The filly snorted and tossed her head in a spirited manner.

"She wants to have another breeze around that track," Mike said with a laugh.

Mr. Harrington turned to his son and smiled. "She'll have that chance again soon," he said. "But she wouldn't have had any chance at all, if you hadn't believed in her or in yourself. You've proved to me that you have the makings of a fine horse trainer, just like your grandfather. If that's the career you want, son, I won't stand in your way."

"Thank you, Father," Mike said.

Then Mr. Harrington turned to Polly, his eyes twinkling. "I have you to thank, young lady, for helping me understand about Mike and Pretty Lady," he said. "I want you to know that I've decided not to sell Pretty Lady, and I hope that you'll feel free to visit her as often as you'd like."

"Thank you, Mr. Harrington," Polly said, smiling back at him.

That night, there was a victory party for Pretty Lady at the Harringtons' mansion. Polly felt a twinge of excitement as she stepped onto the patio behind the house with her parents. She felt grown up and stylish in her pretty new dress, and she was glad that she had let her mother curl her short hair with a curling iron.

Polly gazed at the glittering scene around her. "Everything looks exactly like it did that other night," she said to Mike when he came up to her. "Only this time, I'm not just watching the party. I'm a guest!"

Suddenly, she noticed that Mike's hair was slicked back and that he was wearing a tuxedo. She had never seen him so dressed up before. "You look nice," she said. "You don't look the way you usually do, like— "

"Like a stable boy?" Mike asked with a grin.

"Right!" Polly said, laughing.

Just then, the band struck up a Charleston. "Come on," Polly said eagerly, grabbing Mike's hand. "Let's dance!"

Together they headed for the center of the patio and began to dance to the music. They grinned at each other as they crossed their hands over their knees in the style of the popular dance.

"That was fun," Polly said, when the dance was over. She and Mike walked toward the big fountain. Polly looked at the beautiful mansion silhouetted against the moonlight and the stylishly dressed guests laughing, talking, and dancing. She sighed happily and thought that she had never been to such a wonderful party before in her whole life.

But she couldn't forget who had helped to make all this possible. She excused herself and began to walk away.

"Where are you going?" Mike asked in surprise.

"I have to see someone," Polly said to him over her shoulder as she hurried away. "I'll be right back!"

She ran across the lawn, through the hedge, and to the stable.

Pretty Lady was looking out the top door of her stall. When she sensed Polly's presence, she nickered softly. Polly stepped up to her and stroked her neck gently. "You won the Travers Stakes today, girl!" she said softly to the filly. "I knew all the time that you could do it."

Pretty Lady tossed her head and whinnied as if to say that *she* had known all along that she could do it, too.

FACTS
ABOUT THE BREED

You probably know a lot about Thoroughbreds from reading this book. Here are some more interesting facts about this swift-footed breed.

∩ Thoroughbreds generally stand between 15.3 and 16.2 hands. Instead of using feet and inches, all horses are measured in hands and inches. A hand is equal to four inches.

∩ Thoroughbreds are usually brown, bay (brown with black mane, tail, and lower leg), chestnut (reddish brown all over), black, or gray.

∩ Thoroughbreds, like Arabians, have thin skin. Often the veins in the head are visible beneath the skin.

∩ Thoroughbreds are the fastest horses in the world. Some can run faster than 50 miles an hour.

∩ While Thoroughbreds have great courage, stamina, and athletic ability, they can be nervous, high strung, and temperamental.

∩ All Thoroughbred horses that race receive their very own registration number. When the horse is two years old, this number is tattooed on the inside of its upper lip so that the horse can always be positively identified.

∩ The first digit of the registration number is actually a letter. Every horse born in the same year gets a registration number that starts with the same letter. For example, horses born in 1992 have registration numbers starting with a V. Those born in 1993 got numbers starting with W and so on through the alphabet. If you were a Thoroughbred, what letter would your registration number start with?

∩ The Thoroughbred was first developed in England in the seventeenth and eighteenth centuries. Three Arabian horses are regarded as the founding sires, or fathers, of the Thoroughbred breed—the Byerly Turk, the Darley Arabian, and the Godolphin Arabian. These three stallions were bred to the native race horses to produce the Thoroughbred.

∩ Thoroughbreds are popular all over the world. There are major Thoroughbred racing and breeding centers in England, Ireland, the United States, and France. Excellent Thoroughbreds are also raised in Australia, New Zealand, and Italy.

∩ Horse racing has been popular in England for hundreds of years. After regaining the throne in 1660, Charles II did much to promote racing, known as the sport of kings. Charles II encouraged the common people to attend races and even rode in them himself.

∩ The most famous Thoroughbred race in the United States is the Kentucky Derby. Run every year in the beginning of May since 1875, the 1 1/4-mile long Derby is a race for three-year-olds.

∩ Three races—the Kentucky Derby, the Preakness Stakes, and the Belmont Stakes—make up the Triple Crown, racing's most glamorous prize.

∩ Only eleven horses have won the Triple Crown—Sir Barton in 1919, Gallant Fox in 1930, Omaha in 1935, War Admiral in 1937, Whirlaway in 1941, Count Fleet in 1943, Assault in 1946, Citation in 1948, Secretariat in 1973, Seattle Slew in 1977, and Affirmed in 1978.

∩ Man O'War was one of the most famous Thoroughbred race horses ever. Also known as "Big Red," he was beaten in a race only once and that was when he was just two years old. He died in 1947, and more than one thousand people went to his funeral. He is buried in the Kentucky Horse Park near Lexington, Kentucky, where a statue in his likeness stands proudly as a tribute to the horse.

∩ Citation was another very famous Thoroughbred. Foaled in 1945, Citation was the first race horse to win a million dollars. Citation was so fast that when he ran the Preakness Stakes as a three year old, he ran alone. No other horse dared to challenge him!

∩ Secretariat, the Triple Crown winner in 1973, still holds the speed record for both the Kentucky Derby and the Belmont Stakes.

∩ Thoroughbreds have played an important role in the development of other breeds of horses. In 1756, Janus, a chestnut Thoroughbred stallion, was brought to Virginia from England. Janus, a grandson of the Godolphin Arabian, was bred to the local racing mares and became one of the foundation sires of the American Quarter Horse.

♘ Besides serving as race horses, Thoroughbreds also excel as hunters, polo ponies, steeplechasers, and in the dressage ring.

THE
STALLION OF
BOX CANYON

*The story of a wild Mustang and
the girl who wins his trust*

Written by **Jahnna N. Malcolm**
Illustrated by **Sandy Rabinowitz**
Cover Illustration by **Christa Keiffer**
Developed by Nancy Hall, Inc.

CONTENTS

CHAPTER ONE

Abby the Orphan

Abigail Armstrong watched the huge black steam engine pull into the station, and her knees went weak. In a few minutes, she would be on that train, saying good-bye to Davenport, Iowa, and heading out for the Territory of Wyoming.

"Say, ain't that Abby Armstrong?" a scruffy boy in patched wool pants and yellowing cotton shirt called from the door of the depot.

Abby didn't need to look. She knew who it was. Thirteen-year-old Budge Jenkins, the town bully. Next to Budge stood her cousin, Luke, a gaunt boy of fourteen.

"Yep. That's Abby, all right. Pa's shipping her off today," Luke explained in his irritatingly nasal voice.

Abby could feel her cheeks heat up as the two boys discussed her. She clutched her small canvas bag with all of her belongings close to her chest and tilted her chin up defiantly.

"You'd think an orphan like her would be grateful your Pa took her in," Budge said, moving across the train platform toward Abby.

"Them's Pa's words exactly," Luke replied, keeping in step with Budge. "But she's pig-headed. Refused to wear the clothes my sisters give her. Wouldn't help Ma with the chores. Spent all day climbing trees in the apple orchard."

"Whoo-ee!" Budge whistled. "That musta made your ma mad."

"Madder than a cat caught in a briar patch. 'Course Ma never liked Abby's parents. They thought they was better'n all of us, just cause Abby's Pa was a newspaper man. Well, look what happened to 'em."

"What?" Budge asked.

"Diphtheria. Took Aunt Emily, Uncle Will, and the baby, just like that." Luke snapped his fingers. "They was dead in seven days."

Budge snorted. "I guess that showed 'em!"

Abby dropped her canvas bag and spun to face the two boys. Her green eyes flashed angrily, and her tangled yellow hair whipped across her face.

"Lucas Armstrong and Budge Jenkins, you shut your mouths!" she shouted. "My mama and papa were great people. They had more smarts in their little fingers than you two have in your entire bodies. And if you say one more bad word about them, I swear I'll . . . I'll . . ."

"You'll what?" Budge asked, shoving his pimply face close to hers.

Even though Abby was small for an eleven-year-old, she was tough. She had to be. After a year of being passed from one household to another, she had developed a very thick skin. And hard knuckles.

"I'll clobber you," she whispered directly into Budge's face. And she meant it!

Budge's eyes widened, and he took a step backwards, bumping into Luke. "That girl's a wildcat!" he sputtered.

Luke backed up, too. "That's why they're shipping her off to the Wild West. It's the only place left that'll take her!"

Abby's face was now a blazing crimson color. She raised one fist and was just about to sock Luke in the nose, when a man from the Rock Island Railroad stepped out of the depot.

"Will all of the orphans line up by the luggage car?" he called. "All of you from the Children's Aid

Society and the Juvenile Asylum, line up over there."

Luke grinned. "That's you, Abigail."

Abby was indignant. "It most certainly is not! I don't know any of those children!"

But the conductor thought differently. He spied the tag pinned to Abby's shabby dress.

"You there." He squinted one eye to read the words on her tag out loud. "Number 52. Bound for Laramie. Line up with the others."

"But I'm not one of them!" Abby knew very well who those *others* were. They were part of the Orphan Train system that took abandoned children off the streets of New York and Boston and shipped them west. She had *not* been abandoned! Her parents had died.

"All children traveling alone, move over there!" The conductor pointed impatiently at a group of children huddled together by the luggage car. All of them wore tags, and all looked worn out from their trip from the East.

Abby wasn't about to ride in the luggage car. She glared at the conductor and barked, "I won't!"

"Oh, yes, you will," a woman's voice trilled from beside Abby. It was her Aunt Esther. She gripped Abby by the arm and squeezed tightly. "You'll do whatever that good man says."

"Ow!" Abby tried to wrench her arm loose. "That hurts!"

Aunt Esther and her best friend, Mrs. Hickman, had come to the station to make sure Abby got on the train. They looked like two plump partridges in their best "go-to-meeting" clothes and feathered hats.

Aunt Esther dragged Abby to the group of children clustered around the luggage car, handed Abby her ticket, and barked, "Now stay put!"

Then Aunt Esther stepped back to join Mrs. Hickman. She pulled a handkerchief out of the base of her sleeve and dabbed dramatically at the corners of her eyes.

"Now don't you start feeling bad, Esther," Mrs. Hickman clucked, patting her on the arm. "Your house was overcrowded, and this child was just another mouth to feed." She pursed her lips and added, "You did your best, Esther, no one can say otherwise."

"When her ma and pa passed away," Aunt Esther explained, "I knew we had to take her in. It was the right thing to do."

"And you did just that," Mrs. Hickman reminded her. "And don't forget, you weren't the only one to have trouble with her. Remember the Lloyd family in Ames? They took her into their home, and what did she do? Run away."

Aunt Esther nodded grimly. "Impossible. That's the word they used to describe her. *Im*-possible."

Abby remembered the Lloyds. They *did* take her in. But only because they wanted to loot her family's home. They took the piano, her mother's walnut china cupboard and dining set, her father's books and clothes, and almost every piece of jewelry that her mother owned.

The one thing they didn't get was the necklace Abby's mother was wearing when she died. It was an odd pendant—half a heart, strung on a gold chain— but it was her mother's favorite.

Abby patted her canvas suitcase. The necklace, along with the blue ribbons from her brother's booties and a tintype of her father, were inside. Those few treasures were all that Abby had left of her family as she headed off to live with her mother's sister, Mary, on a ranch.

While Aunt Esther and Mrs. Hickman gossiped and the train was readied for departure, Abby hopped onto the edge of the wooden luggage cart and waited with the other orphan children.

She still didn't feel she was one of them. She knew who her parents were. Just to reassure herself, Abby felt in her bag once again for her treasures. Her hand touched the cool frame of the tintype.

She pulled it out and, carefully balancing it in her lap, stared down at the picture. It had been taken on her tenth birthday. Her father, a handsome man with dark brown eyes and a fine moustache, held the reins of a shaggy-maned pony. Astride the pony was a pretty little girl with sausage curls and two big bows

in her hair, and a grin that stretched from ear to ear.

Abby smiled. That had been a wonderful birthday. Her parents had surprised her with a brown–and–white pinto named Toby. Even her baby brother, Benjamin, had joined in the celebration by burying his face in the cherry pie her mother had baked for the occasion.

Abby's smile slowly faded. It was barely a month after her birthday party that the sickness came.

Little Ben was the first to go. Then Papa. And last, Mama. She lay in bed, burning with fever and gasping for breath for two nights and days. Then it was over. Abby's entire family—wiped out in a week.

Abby squinted up at the white puffs of smoke spewing from the train's engine, trying to remember if she'd ever been happy since.

Whoo-oo!

The train whistle blew its lonesome call, and Abby leapt to her feet. She joined the line of orphans waiting to climb up the steps into the train.

To her relief, she discovered the children didn't have to ride in the luggage car, after all. They were in a real passenger car with windows. It wasn't as fancy as the Pullman cars near the rear of the train, but at least it had seats. Flat wooden benches lined either side of the aisle.

Abby found a place by the window near the back of the car, hoping to catch Aunt Esther's eye so she could wave good-bye. But her aunt was too busy gossiping with Mrs. Hickman to notice Abby had left the platform.

"All aboard!" the conductor called.

Aunt Esther looked up in surprise and searched the windows for Abby.

Abby pressed her hand against the glass, but Aunt Esther didn't see her.

With a jerk and a hiss of brakes the train rolled forward. As the train chugged out of the station, Abby watched the figures of her aunt and Mrs. Hickman slide by the window. "Good-bye, Iowa," Abby whispered.

The rhythm of the wheels quickened as the train gathered speed.

One of the kids across the aisle cupped his hands around his mouth and announced, "Next stop, the wild, Wild West!"

Westward Ho!

Abby wiped a grimy smudge off her cheek and stared out the stagecoach window.

Days of constant jostling on the hard wooden benches of the Rock Island and Union Pacific railroads had worn her out. The trains ran in a straight line across treeless plains, then pierced a spine of rugged mountains into the Wyoming Territory.

At Laramie she had been put on a stagecoach that bounced north along the edge of the Laramie River.

A balding circuit preacher sat across from Abby, speaking to the young woman beside him. She was to be the new school marm in Rock River. Abby sensed that the woman felt as frightened and alone as she did.

Beside Abby sat a heavy man with a red face and thick jowls. He chewed tobacco, and every so often he spat a thin stream of brown juice into a tin cup. Abby tried to lean as far away from him as possible.

The Laramie River wound through the valley in great undulating curves. On the horizon huge, craggy mountains towered above the valley floor, their snowy peaks shrouded in thick white clouds.

"So wild and beautiful!" Abby whispered.

At the same time a tiny voice inside her warned, Don't get too attached. Every time you do, it gets taken away from you.

When the stagecoach finally rumbled into Medicine Bow, Abby sat up in her seat, peering anxiously out the window. She was covered from head to toe in black soot and red dust from the long journey. Her mouth was dry and gritty, and every muscle in her body ached. But still she was excited.

This little town, which consisted of one rickety wooden building and a few tents, would be her new home.

Abby spied a family standing in front of the wooden building. The man was tall and handsome.

He wore blue Union pants with a broad yellow stripe down the sides, a vest over his collarless white shirt, and tooled leather boots that stretched to his knees. Around his neck was a bright blue bandanna.

Beside him stood a blonde woman in a twill skirt, gingham blouse, broad-brimmed leather hat, and boots just like the man's. A round-faced girl with brown braids in a cotton print shirtdress was hopping up and down next to the couple.

"That must be them!" Abby whispered. "Captain Joe, Aunt Mary, and Cousin Elizabeth."

All three of them were grinning and waving merrily. They looked genuinely happy to see her.

Abby would have loved to jump down from the coach and leap right into Aunt Mary's open arms. But that little voice—the one deep inside her—said, Don't do it. You can't trust them. You can't trust anybody.

Instead, Abby stood stiffly by the coach as the family rushed over to greet her.

"Oh, Abigail!" Aunt Mary cried, scooping her up in her arms and hugging her tight. "Am I glad to see you! I've dreamed about this day." Aunt Mary's voice caught in her throat as tears streamed down her cheeks. "Forgive me, honey," she whispered. "You look so much like your mother, it's almost too much to bear."

"Let me hug my cousin!" Elizabeth cried. "It's my turn." She spun Abby around to face her.

Although Elizabeth was the same age as Abby, she was two full inches taller. She had warm, brown eyes, freckles that dotted her tanned cheeks, and a big friendly smile. Her hug nearly took Abby's breath away.

"I'm so excited I could spit," Elizabeth said. "Mama and I fixed up a bed for you in my room. We put a quilt on it that my mama and your mama stitched when they were little girls."

Abby's heart leapt up. How wonderful! Something still remained that her mother had touched, other than the gold necklace with the broken heart.

Captain Joe was the last to greet her. He took off his hat and smiled warmly at her. Abby gazed up at him in wonder. She didn't think she'd ever seen such a handsome moustache. It was waxed and curled up into a perfect handlebar. His face was deeply tanned, which made his blue eyes look even brighter.

"Welcome to Wyoming, Abigail," Captain Joe rumbled in a voice so deep Abby could almost feel the ground vibrate beneath her boots. "The Carter family is pleased to have you join us at the Double Diamond Ranch."

As the family led her to the buckboard wagon

that would carry them out to the ranch, she glanced back over her shoulder at the stagecoach.

Don't get too comfortable, the little voice inside her warned. It won't be long before you're back on that stagecoach.

The Double Diamond

*D*ing-a-ling-a-ling!

The clang of the cook's triangle shattered the morning stillness, and Abby sat up in her bed with a start.

Sunlight poured through the bedroom window onto the patchwork quilt covering her bed. She quickly checked the other bed to see if her cousin Elizabeth was still asleep.

Elizabeth was gone. Her bed was made, and her nightgown was neatly folded and placed on top of her pillow.

"What time is it?" Abby said out loud, rubbing the sleep from her eyes.

Elizabeth ducked her head into the room. "Time to get up, sleepyhead. Cook's got breakfast on the table, and he sure gets riled if the food gets cold."

Abby threw back the covers and looked down at herself. She was wearing a pretty white muslin nightgown with lace at the cuffs. "Where did I get this?"

"It used to be one of mine," Elizabeth explained. "I'm happy it fits you."

"Oh," Abby mumbled. After her arrival at the ranch the night before, she'd taken a hot bath in a washtub in the kitchen, nibbled on a sourdough biscuit, and collapsed into bed. She couldn't even remember putting on the nightgown.

"So what do you think of our room?" Elizabeth asked, gesturing to the jar of wildflowers she'd placed on the knotty pine dresser that stood across from their beds.

Abby blinked several times as she looked around the room. It was a cheery place, with whitewashed walls and polished wooden floorboards. The dresser, bedsteads, and chair were rough-hewn. But there were accents everywhere of things that clearly came from back east.

Four gilt-framed colored illustrations of birds hung on the wall. A lace doily was draped over the simple wooden table between their beds. And several postcards of scenes from Chicago framed the mirror above the dresser.

Abby loved it, but she couldn't bring herself to tell Elizabeth that. She just shrugged and said, "It's fine, I guess."

Elizabeth sat on the bed across from Abby. "I was afraid you wouldn't like it. That you'd be homesick."

"Homesick?" Abby cocked her head. "For what?"

The last three places she'd stayed, Abby had either slept on the floor in a borrowed blanket or been forced to curl up at the end of someone's bed. How could she be homesick for that?

"For, um, your own room," Elizabeth stammered. "You know, with Aunt Emily and Uncle—"

Abby cut her cousin off with a sharp wave of her hand. "That was long ago," she said stiffly. "I barely remember it."

"Oh." Elizabeth stood up awkwardly. "Well, I guess I'll let you get dressed. Hurry and join us for breakfast. After we eat, I'll show you around the ranch."

Abby took her time getting dressed. She didn't want to appear too eager to please. She knew from experience that as soon as she acted like she really wanted something, it was taken away from her.

By the time she made an appearance in the dining room, the table was deserted. A single plate with silverware and a glass were all that remained on the table.

Aunt Mary swept in from the kitchen, a long white apron over her red-and-white gingham smock. "There you are!" she greeted Abby. "We were afraid you were going to skip breakfast altogether."

"No, ma'am," Abby said. "I had some trouble finding my clothes."

Aunt Mary's hand flew to her mouth. "Oh, I'm sorry. While you were asleep, I took your traveling clothes to wash them. I forgot to have Elizabeth tell you that I'd left another set of clothes for you on the chair." She gestured at Abby's navy blue-and-white polka dot dress, with matching blue cotton leggings and leather boots, and smiled. "But I see you found them. Do they fit?"

Abby nodded. "Yes, ma'am." Not only did they fit perfectly—they were almost like new. Something she hadn't experienced in a long time. But she didn't tell Aunt Mary that.

Aunt Mary studied Abby's face. Finally she said, "Well, let's get some food in you. Take a seat."

Breakfast was delicious: a plate of steaming hotcakes with huckleberry syrup, three strips of bacon, and a big glass of milk.

"Elizabeth wants to show you around the ranch," Aunt Mary said, as she cleared Abby's plate. "She's in the henhouse, gathering eggs. Why don't you join her?"

Abby stepped onto the front porch of the family ranch house, expecting to find the chicken coop right outside. But she was surprised to discover that the Double Diamond Ranch was far larger than any farm she had ever seen in Iowa.

Open range stretched eastward as far as the eye could see. The prairie was dotted with clusters of cattle. Surrounding the western side of the range were huge red cliffs. They looked like a layer cake.

The ranch house was a rambling two-story

building made of smooth ponderosa pine logs that were each at least a foot thick. The smaller outbuildings looked like echoes of the main house, each a little log cabin with its own cedar shake or sod roof.

"Hey, lil' lady, you look lost!" a voice drawled from behind her.

Abby spun around. Standing before her was a scrawny, bowlegged man dressed in woolly chaps, pointed boots, and a huge hat with a broad brim. His face looked like wrinkled leather. And when he grinned, Abby saw that he only had one front tooth.

"I'm looking for the place where you keep chickens," she explained.

The man squinted one eye shut. "You must be that little girl come from back east."

Abby tilted up her chin. "I'm Abigail Armstrong. But most folks call me Abby."

"That suits me just fine, Miss Abby." The little man tipped his hat toward her. "Pleased to meet you. I'm Big Tim. And I believe I saw Miss Elizabeth out by the henhouse. Which would be that-a-way." Big Tim gestured to a small shed with a sloping roof about a hundred yard to Abby's right.

Abby hesitated. She didn't know if she was ready to be with Elizabeth, just yet. She wanted to investigate her new surroundings by herself first.

"What's that over there?" Abby pointed to a fenced-in area in the distance. A green swath of pasture spread out from beneath the fence poles and rails until it met a flowing stream lined with cottonwoods and weeping willows.

"That's the horse corral," Big Tim explained. "And to the north there is the cookshack, bunkhouse, blacksmith shop, and storage sheds."

A wisp of smoke puffed out of the stovepipe of the cookshack's sod roof. Abby decided to start her exploration there.

She bid farewell to Big Tim and hurried toward the little log hut. Along the way, she bumped into the ranch foreman, Waddy Hancock.

Waddy was just the opposite of Big Tim. He was huge—tall, barrel-chested, with a red beard that exploded out of his chin in all directions.

"I take it you're Miss Abby," Waddy declared, tipping his low-crowned hat, which had a brim even wider than Big Tim's. "Welcome to the Double Diamond."

Waddy clapped his hat back on his head and sauntered off toward the barn. With each long stride, his leather chaps flapped and spurs jingled.

Then a boy about the same age as Abby's cousin Luke trotted by on a black-and-white pinto. His chaps were streaked with trail dust, and so was the big yellow bandanna draped over his plaid shirt. "Name's Curly," the boy called out as he passed by.

"Nice to meet you," she said. "I'm Abby."

"I know. Missed you at breakfast."

Abby turned in a circle as she watched Curly lope toward the horse corral. "Sorry," she called. "I guess I overslept."

When she poked her head in the open doorway of the cookshack, she was instantly hit with the savory aroma of bubbling stew.

Then a terrifying voice roared, "Who dares enter my domain without knocking?"

Just-Me-Abigail

"It's just me, Abigail," Abby cried, quickly stepping back outside.

"Just-Me-Abigail?" A tall black man loomed in the doorway, clutching a long wooden ladle in his right hand and a cast-iron pot lid in his left. He was dressed like a cowboy except, instead of chaps, he wore an apron around his waist. "What kind of tom-fool name is that for a person?"

"I just wondered who lived here. So I peeked inside," she quickly explained. "I didn't mean to trespass, or anything."

The cook had a long thin face. A bowler perched on the top of his head. He stared at Abby with his dark eyes for quite awhile. She held her breath, not knowing whether to run or stay.

"Well, Just-Me-Abigail, I'm making up a mess of Anything'll-Do-Stew." His mouth creased into a grin. "Care to have a taste?"

Abby wasn't too sure. With a name like Anything'll-Do, the stew sounded like it could be made out of lizard and frog guts. "Um, what kind of meat's in there?" she asked, timidly.

Luckily the cook wasn't insulted. No doubt he thought she was asking for the recipe. "You take two pounds lean beef shank, half a calf heart, one set sweetbreads, salt and pepper, and my secret ingredient." He dipped the ladle into the bubbling stew and held it up for her to taste. "Louisiana hot sauce."

Abby took a sip. It was warm and spicy. "Whew!" she gasped. "That really is tasty!"

The cook grinned and put the lid back on the pot. "It'll clear your sinuses, I promise you." Then he wiped one hand on his apron and stuck it towards her. "My name's Silas Morehouse. I served with Captain Joe in the Union Army—we stood together at Antietam—and he invited me to come work at the Double Diamond."

Abby shook the cook's hand. "I'm Captain Joe's niece, Abigail."

Silas nodded gravely. "We're all mighty glad you're here. Mighty glad."

This caught Abby by surprise. "Really?"

"Oh my, yes." Silas pulled an apple out of a basket in the corner and tossed it to her. "It's hard on a ranchin' family that's got but one child. A ranch this size needs a big family to work it. That's why we're all so glad you're here. It'll be good to have another hard worker around the place."

Abby thanked Silas for the apple and wandered outside. His last words worried her.

Before Abby had left Iowa, Aunt Esther had mentioned something nasty about being shipped west to do hard labor. And on the train, many of the orphans had worried about the same thing.

Could this be true about her? Had the Carters brought her here just to be a ranch hand?

Abby suddenly felt the urge to run. Away from the ranch. And away from the Carters. She needed time to think.

Looking around, she spied the towering red rock cliff that sheltered the ranch on the north side and bolted toward it. She raced through the tall grass, until she reached the base of the bluff.

"This must be Box Canyon," she said out loud as she looked into a cleft in the rocks that led into a deep, narrow canyon. She'd heard her uncle talking about it on the long wagon ride to the ranch.

The rippling stream that bordered the pasture ran down the center of Box Canyon. To her right, an almost dry creek bed angled away from the stream, falling abruptly into a steep gully just below the cliff.

The entire field was covered in cornflowers and Indian paintbrush. Abby picked a bouquet of blue cornflowers, then made a place for herself in the tall grass. She closed her eyes and, tilting her head back, basked in the morning sun. One of her hands was pressed against the ground. And that's where she felt the rumbling.

It was tiny at first. Barely perceptible. But then it got bigger.

Abby's eyes popped open. Her arm was shaking. The rumbling grew louder, sounding more like thunder. Abby leapt to her feet. Her whole body was trembling.

"What's happening?" she cried out loud.

"Don't panic, Abby!" a girl's voice called from behind her.

It was Elizabeth.

Abby stumbled toward her cousin.

Elizabeth pulled Abby closer toward the cliff. "Stay close to the wall," she shouted over the thundering noise.

"But what's going on?" Abby pleaded, pressing her body against the rock wall. "What's that noise?" Elizabeth pointed to the mouth of the canyon. "It's the wild horses!"

The Wild Mustangs

"**M**ustangs!"

Elizabeth's cry was drowned out by the herd of horses thundering out of the canyon.

"Oh, my gosh!" Abby gasped at the magnificent sight. There were white horses and roans, sorrels and bays. She even spied two pintos and a palomino. They raced around the pasture, tossing their manes and kicking out their back legs.

"There have to be at least twenty of 'em," Elizabeth shouted, keeping her body pressed flat against the base of the cliff. She pointed to the lead horse, a dappled grey stallion with white mane and tail. "Looks like the General has picked up a few more mares during this past winter."

The General, whose flanks and shoulders were covered with scars, galloped around the herd of mares and colts, gathering them together in a tight circle.

"Are these all yours?" Abby cried.

Elizabeth chuckled, stepping away from the cliff. "No! These mustangs are wild. They don't belong to anybody but themselves."

Abby watched as one horse—a dun-colored stallion with a black mane and black socks—danced away from the group. His nimble steps reminded Abby of the jig danced by performers in traveling minstrel shows. "Look at that one go!" she cried, clapping her hands. He looks like one of the buckdancers that used to come through Ames, Abby thought.

"He must be almost three years old," Elizabeth remarked. "Pretty soon the General is going to kick him out of the herd."

"Kick him out!" Abby gasped in dismay. "But why?"

Elizabeth shrugged. "There's usually only one stallion in the family band. There are a lot of mares, and some colts, but only one leader."

"But what will happen to him?" Abby asked,

watching the General nip at Buckdancer's flank to push him back toward the herd.

"He'll go find his own family. Sometimes a few of the young stallions get together and form a bachelor band. They travel around together, looking for their own mares."

"It must be fun to have a herd like this living on your ranch," Abby said.

Elizabeth grimaced. "Fun for them, maybe. But not for Papa. He can't stand the wild horses. Calls 'em broomtails."

Abby was shocked. "But how could Captain Joe not like them?"

"They eat the food our cattle need." Elizabeth pointed to the pasture in front of them. "Sometimes they even eat the apples off Mama's tree. For most of the year, we hardly ever see the Mustangs. Then in spring they come in from the canyons. They're usually half-starved from the long winter. But boy, are they tough! They've survived cougars, wolves, and freezing cold blizzards."

Abby looked at the Mustangs with even more admiration. These tough little fellows with their sleek coats and wild manes had to have some kind of fierce will to endure all of those hardships.

"Nobody takes care of them," Elizabeth continued.

"They take care of themselves."

Abby watched as Buckdancer continued to prance, both ears pricked forward and his mane flying in the wind. He looked so spirited and free. She tossed her own hair. "I wish I could be like them," she said, half to Elizabeth but mostly to herself.

"Really?" Elizabeth cocked her head. "But they're so wild."

Abby suddenly remembered the words of Budge Jenkins and her cousin, Lucas. "That girl's a wildcat. That's why they're shipping her off to the Wild West. It's the only place left that'll take her!"

That's right, Abby thought to herself. I am wild. I'm just like those Mustangs. I can take care of myself.

Secret Visits

A week later, Abby was hastily smoothing the quilt over her bed when Elizabeth stuck her head through the door.

"Mama wants to see you after you eat your breakfast," she announced.

"You don't have to yell at me," Abby snapped.

Elizabeth cocked her head. "I wasn't yelling, Abby. I was just delivering Mama's message."

Abby was feeling guilty about lazing in bed while everyone else did their morning chores. She was sure that Elizabeth resented her, and this made her grumpy.

Abby punched the pillow with her fist. "Tell Aunt Mary I'm hurrying as fast as I can."

Elizabeth nodded stiffly and left the room.

Abby wanted to run after Elizabeth and apologize for her behavior, but the little voice inside her stopped her. And instead of hurrying, Abby took a long time getting dressed.

A half hour later, Abby sauntered downstairs and paused at the bottom step. Carefully she leaned around the bannister and peered into the dining room. Usually the table was cleared, with only her table setting remaining. But today it was different. Her plate and silverware were gone.

Abby hurried toward the kitchen.

Aunt Mary was just finishing the morning dishes when Abby came in. She glanced over her shoulder and said, "Good morning, Abigail. There's a bowl of new potatoes on the table. Silas needs them peeled and delivered to the cookshack right away."

"What?" Abby was surprised. She was being told to work. Not asked. *Told.*

Aunt Mary picked up a towel and began drying the dishes. "Sourdough biscuits are in the breadbox. You can put honey or preserves on them, if you're hungry."

Aunt Mary was now telling her to get her own

breakfast! "I don't understand," Abby cried, putting her hands on her hips. "Did I do something wrong?"

Aunt Mary finished her dishes and hung the towel on the back of a kitchen chair to dry. "Of course not," she said as she picked up a broom and dustpan from the corner. "But Silas never waits breakfast. He only did that as a special favor while you were getting used to living here. But a week has passed."

"A whole week?" Abby said. It felt like she'd just arrived.

"We gave you that time to get settled in," Aunt Mary explained, as she swept the kitchen floor. "But now it's time for you to get on our schedule. Breakfast is at 6:30 sharp. After that, you're to help clear the dishes and wash up. Then you can get started on your job assignments."

"Job?" Abby repeated.

"Well, yes." Aunt Mary brushed the dirt into the dustpan and straightened up. "This is a working ranch. And every hand has to pull her own weight."

Abby felt her heart sink. She'd always had to do chores. At home, and when she was living with the Lloyds and her cousins. But this was different. This sounded like she was going to have to work for her keep.

It's just as I suspected, she thought, narrowing

her eyes at her aunt. *They don't want another daughter. They want a servant.*

Abby's tasks weren't difficult, but they took all morning to finish. Everyday as soon as she cleaned the breakfast dishes, she went straight to the cookshack to help Silas prepare for lunch. She hauled endless buckets of water from the pump to cisterns in the cookshack and bunkhouse. Then she helped in the barn, mucking out stalls and bringing hay down from the loft.

Elizabeth flew through her chores and often offered to help Abby with hers, but Abby always refused. *If I can't do the work alone,* she told herself, *they'll ship me away.*

For a whole week, Abby toiled away silently. In the hour or two after lunch, she'd slip off to the bluff, hoping to catch sight of the Mustangs.

On Monday, she finally saw them as they thundered down the canyon toward the open prairie. Unfortunately, the lead stallion spotted her. Before she could duck behind a rock, he had signaled the rest of the horses that it wasn't safe.

The General faced Abby, his head high and ears pricked forward, while the mares and colts left the pasture.

Abby froze.

The General snorted several times at her. It was as if he were saying, "You stay away from my family!"

"Don't worry, General," she whispered. "I won't do you any harm."

She watched as another horse paused at the mouth of the canyon. It was the young stallion with the black socks and black mane. She remembered him prancing in the pasture a few weeks before. He'd reminded her of a buckdancer from a traveling minstrel show.

The General turned. He took several steps toward the young stallion, then spun back, ready to face any surprise attack. Buckdancer mirrored the General's every move, tossing his head and snorting his own warning at Abby.

The two horses did it again, trotting toward the canyon and turning back abruptly.

Abby didn't move. She barely breathed.

Finally, at the mouth of the canyon, the General and Buckdancer reared up on their hind legs and slashed the air with their forelegs. Then they were gone.

Abby exhaled loudly at the impressive performance. Though she'd only seen the horses twice, she'd already noticed that they seemed to obey some strict rules.

The General always led the way into the pasture. First in line behind him was the palomino mare. Abby decided that she had to be the lead mare because whenever the General sounded the alarm, the palomino led the escape. And the other horses always followed in the exact order that they'd come in.

I guess they really are like a band, she thought with a smile. But instead of one that marches, this band gallops.

Abby the Outcast

Whm Abby returned to the ranch, she was surprised to see a covered wagon loaded down with supplies in front of the house. A team of draft mules had been unhitched and were standing calmly nearby as a redheaded girl looped feedbags over their heads.

A man and a woman sat chatting with Aunt Mary and Captain Joe on the front porch, while five children all under the age of ten raced around the wagon shrieking with laughter.

Elizabeth perched on the wagon, smiling at the little ones. When she spied Abby, Elizabeth sprang to her feet and raced to meet her.

"The Stoffards are here!" Elizabeth cried. "Isn't

that wonderful? They've got six kids and are so much fun."

"Are they neighbors?" Abby asked, watching the three littlest ones attempt cartwheels across the dirt road.

"You might say so. They live about fifty miles west of here. We hardly get to see them but twice a year. That's when they do their spring and fall supply run to Laramie." She gestured for the redheaded girl to join them. "This is Mabel Stoffard. She's twelve."

"Pleased to meet ya." Mabel stuck out her hand. Abby shook it, but didn't say anything. She was suddenly tongue-tied.

"Mabel's family is going to have supper with us," Elizabeth explained.

Abby tried to force a smile.

There was a thunk and then a cry from the vicinity of the wagon. Mabel looked over in dismay. "Eben's hurt himself, again. I had better go help."

As Mabel hurried to help her little brother, Elizabeth grabbed Abby's arm and pulled her toward the other children. "Come on and play. It'll be fun."

Abby dug her heels into the dirt. "I need to clean up first and finish the rest of my chores."

"Oh, pshaw!" Elizabeth waved one hand. "The chores can wait. We have guests!"

Abby didn't know what was making her so hesitant. Maybe the thought of meeting so many strangers at once. Or just that word—*guests.*

While she was at the Lloyds' or her Aunt Esther's house, *guests* meant that Abby wasn't wanted. She would be sent to sleep and eat in the shed to make room for them. It was a time when both houses made it clear that she was *not* considered part of their family.

"I'll go clean up and be right back," Abby said, anxious to get away.

Back in her room, Abby made an attempt to freshen up. Some weeds were caught in her tangled blonde hair, and she had a smudge of dirt on one cheek. She wiped the dirt from her face, but couldn't get her brush through the tangle in her hair. Finally she slammed the brush down on the dresser.

"It's no use," she told her reflection. "I don't belong with them. I'll just hide out in the barn until they leave."

Abby snuck out the back door and scurried along in the shadows of the sheds, until she reached the barn. She climbed the wooden ladder into the hayloft and hid in the far corner.

One of the barn cats had dropped a litter a few weeks before. A tiny black and white kitten wriggled its way into her lap, mewing loudly.

"What's the matter, little one?" she whispered to the kitten. "Did your mama go off and leave you all alone?" She stroked the top of the tiny cat's head. "I know just how you feel."

Suddenly the barn door swung open, and light poured onto the hay below. Abby kept perfectly still.

"Bet you can't catch me!" a boy bellowed as he raced into the barn. He was pursued by four other children.

It was the Stoffard kids.

"Let's jump out of the hayloft," the boy cried, charging for the ladder.

His younger brother, Eben, was right behind him. "Me first. It's my turn."

"No, it's my turn," the littlest girl cried. "Ain't that right, Mabel?"

Mabel stepped through the barn door and leaned against the wall, coughing. "Now, don't you kids quarrel," she rasped. "I don't feel so good. My throat burns, and I've got a headache."

"Why don't you sit over there?" Elizabeth pointed to a milking stool by the barn wall. "I'll fetch you a drink of water."

Mabel winced. "Water won't help, Elizabeth. It hurts to swallow."

By now, four of the Stoffard children had made it

into the loft. But luckily for Abby, they didn't notice her huddled in the corner.

The oldest boy, a redhead with freckles, called down to the floor below. "Say, what happened to that Abigail girl? I thought she was going to play with us."

"I'm not sure where she went," Elizabeth replied. "But she's a little, um, shy."

"Shy?" Mabel coughed. "Stuck up, more'n likely. She wouldn't even say boo to me. I bet she thinks she's too good to play with us."

"Now, Mabel, be fair," Elizabeth cut in. "I know Abby can be on the difficult side. I mean, we've all tried to break through the ice, but Mama says we have to remember Abby's an orphan. She lost her entire family a year ago."

"Then what's she doin' acting so uppity?" Mabel replied. "You'd think she'd be grateful you took her in."

Abby hung her head. It was humiliating to hear herself being talked about this way.

"I don't think Abby thinks of it like that," Elizabeth replied. "We are family, after all."

"Humph!" Mabel folded her arms and leaned back against the barn wall. "My ma said she has plenty of relatives, but no one will have her. If Captain Joe hadn't offered to take her in, she'd be stuck in the poorhouse, or in an orphan asylum."

Abby couldn't bear to hear another word. She set the kitten in the hay and crawled on her hands and knees toward a ladder on the wall. But as she neared the ladder, her foot knocked down a clump of hay.

"Who's there?" Elizabeth demanded, squinting up at the hayloft.

Abby leaned into the light. "It's me. Abigail."

Elizabeth's hand flew to her mouth. "Oh, Abby! Have you been there all the time?"

Abby didn't reply. She bolted down the ladder and out the rear door of the barn. Elizabeth was right behind her.

"Abby, stop, please!"

Elizabeth chased after Abby, catching up with her at the horse corral.

"Please Abby, let me talk to you," Elizabeth huffed, out of breath.

Abby was so upset, her face had turned a bright shade of purple. "I heard every word you and your snooty friend said," she cried.

"We didn't mean to hurt your feel—"

Abby wouldn't let Elizabeth finish. She was too angry. "You think I like being stranded on this dismal old ranch in the middle of nowhere with no friends?"

Elizabeth blinked in surprise. Finally she said,

stiffly, "If you made the least bit of effort to be nice, Abigail Armstrong, you'd make friends."

"Nice! Why should I be nice to a snob like Mabel?" Abby shot back.

Now it was Elizabeth's turn to get angry. "Mabel is *not* a snob," she said between gritted teeth. "You're the one who thinks you're better than everyone else. Lying in bed till all hours of the morning, acting shocked whenever you're asked to help out . . ."

"That was the first week," Abby protested. "I'm doing my work."

"And acting like it's killing you." Elizabeth spat her words at Abby. "You're slow as molasses with chores you don't like, and you have never once said a kind word to me."

"What?" Abby gasped.

Elizabeth's face was now as purple as Abby's. "We've all bent over backwards to be nice to you, but you don't deserve it." She put her hands on her hips. "You're rude, and unpleasant, and just plain mean."

Her words cut through Abby like a knife.

"Well, maybe I'll just leave!" Abby sputtered, fighting back tears.

"Go ahead," Elizabeth said. "See if I care!" With that she spun on her heel and marched back to the barn.

Abby turned and fled. Tears clouded her vision as she stumbled blindly away from the ranch.

Had she really been so hateful to all of them? The thought was almost too much to bear.

Behind her she could hear the *ding-a-ling-a-ling* of the cook's triangle, calling everyone to supper.

Abby hesitated for a fraction of a second. She knew she should go back, but how could she? Silas and Curly and even Big Tim must have been talking about her. She couldn't bear to face them or her aunt and uncle. Abby decided to keep running.

Her feet led her to the mouth of Box Canyon. She collapsed on her knees at the base of the bluff and buried her head in her hands.

No sooner had her knees hit the ground than she heard movement behind her.

Abby froze, straining to listen. She heard labored breathing.

She didn't dare look. What if it were a cougar, or a wolf? What would she do then? She squeezed her eyes closed, listening to her heart pound in her chest.

Another sound—the clatter of rocks! Abby's hands were now shaking. Whatever it was, it was going to get her. She knew it would!

Crrrack!

That sound was like a twig breaking. It was

followed by more rocks. But the sound wasn't coming any closer.

Should she look? Abby didn't know if she could. Every part of her was quivering. She had to!

Finally, Abby mustered every ounce of courage she had inside and slowly turned to look.

"Oh, my word!" she gasped in astonishment.

Buckdancer Is Hurt!

There, in the dried-up gully, six feet below Abby, was a Mustang. It was the young stallion with the dun-colored coat and black stockings, and he was hurt!

He limped in a circle around the creek bed, looking up at her. Each time he placed his weight on his left front leg, he reared his head back and snorted loudly.

Abby moved to the edge of the gully, and the Mustang skittered backwards. He whinnied shrilly.

He's trying to signal the General to come for him, Abby thought.

In the distance, she heard an answering whinny echo from the canyon, but no horse appeared.

He must have fallen and hurt himself, Abby thought, peering down.

This was the horse she'd seen dancing in the field so wild and free, like one of the buckdancers from the traveling minstrel shows. Now the Mustang looked dazed and confused. He limped frantically around the rocky creek bed, searching for a way to escape or a place to hide.

Abby inched toward the edge of the gully. "Don't worry, fella," she whispered. "I'm not going to hurt you."

The horse turned to face her, his sides heaving in and out like a blacksmith's bellows.

"Oh, my gosh!" Abby gasped, as she saw his wounds for the first time.

He had several gashes on his belly and a bleeding cut across his nose. A slash above his front knee oozed blood. The knee was so swollen he could barely put any weight on it.

Could a fall do this much damage? she wondered. Abby looked around the edge of the gully for the place where he must have fallen.

She found what she was looking for ten feet away at the base of a boulder.

The body of a bobcat lay bloodied and lifeless half-hidden by the tall weeds. The ground near the body was torn up in great big clods, and there was a gash in the edge of the gully where the Mustang must have fallen in.

"I'll bet you were battling this wildcat and the ground gave way beneath you, throwing you into this creek bed," she murmured.

The Mustang hobbled away from Abby. "You must be in such pain," she whispered. "Poor Buckdancer."

The horse's head flew up.

"Buckdancer," she repeated softly.

He didn't move, but continued to stare at her.

"Good Buckdancer," Abby cooed. "That's a good boy."

Abby knew if she went any closer, or made any sudden moves, the Mustang might panic and hurt himself even more. So she knelt at the edge of the gully, keeping her distance from him.

"It's all right," she murmured. "It's only me, little old Abby. I'd never think of hurting you."

Abby tried to keep her voice low and soothing. Buckdancer listened with his ears pricked forward.

"You're hurt, but you're going to get better," she told him. "You'll see."

She kept talking for nearly half an hour. Her back

and knees ached with the strain of sitting so still. She longed to shift her position, but she knew that might frighten the young stallion.

A melody came into her head. It was a song her mother used to sing to her when she was upset or hurt.

"Hush, little baby, don't say a word,
Mama's going to buy you a mockingbird.
If that mockingbird don't sing,
Mama's going to buy you a diamond ring . . ."

The more she sang, the more Buckdancer seemed to relax. His breathing eased and his nostrils no longer flared.

Abby studied his wounds carefully as she sang. She knew the gashes on his nose and belly would probably heal quickly. The blood was already scabbing over.

It was his leg that worried her. Was the knee swollen because of the wound above it? Or had he broken his leg in the fall? If it was a break, the Mustang was done for. He'd never be able to climb out of that gully.

In the week she'd been at the Double Diamond, she'd seen Waddy Hancock doctor a few horses. One horse had injured himself on the corral gate, giving himself a big gash on his shoulder. Waddy had been able to stitch up the gash in no time.

Another horse had strained a tendon. His leg had
swollen up like Buckdancer's. Waddy had slathered
the leg in plain old mud, explaining to Abby that the
coolness of it would take down the swelling. Then
later, Waddy covered the leg in a warm poultice he'd
made out of bran.

"If I could just get back to the barn, maybe I could
find some bandages and salve for your wounds," she
whispered to the horse. "And I could grab a bucket
and make up a bran poultice for your leg."

It was growing late. The sun was just about to set
behind the bluff, and Abby knew she had better get
back soon. Supper was long over, and the Carters
would probably be coming to look for her.

She didn't want to leave the wounded Mustang,
but she knew she had to.

"Water," she said to the horse, inching back from
the edge of the gully. "You'll need water to help you
through the night. And in the morning, I'll bring food."

She hurried toward the stream that ran out of
Box Canyon into the pasture. "Now if I could just find
something to put it in."

Abby was in luck. She found a wide metal pan
sticking out of the weeds. It was covered with rust
but seemed sound enough. Abby wondered if the pan

had been used by a prospector, then abandoned and left to rust when he headed north to Virginia City in the Territory of Montana.

Abby filled the pan as full as she could, then carefully carried it to the gully. It was only six feet to the bottom. If Buckdancer hadn't been wounded, he could have leapt that distance in a single bound. But it was hard for Abby to climb down while balancing a pan of water.

She decided to go the same route the Mustang had taken. Stepping gingerly over the body of the dead bobcat, Abby sat on her bottom and slowly slid down the side of the rocky creek bed.

Buckdancer backed as far away from her as he could limp.

"Stay calm, fella," she whispered, keeping her voice soothing. "I'm going to set this water here for you to drink. Then I'll be on my way."

She very carefully placed the pan between two rocks, so it wouldn't tip over.

"Here, boy," Abby called. "Here's some water. Come take a drink."

Then she scrambled up the side of the gully. The last thing Abby did before leaving was to move the body of the dead bobcat as far away from the gully as possible. She didn't want the smell of it to attract any other predators. Then she raced back to the edge of the gully.

"You take care of yourself, Buckdancer," Abby called softly. "Drink that water and keep out of sight. I'll be back for you in the morning."

Doctor Abigail

"**A**bigail!" Captain Joe boomed from the head of the breakfast table the next morning. "On this ranch, you let us know where you're going before you leave the premises."

His voice was as stern as his stony face.

Abby felt her cheeks instantly blaze pink.

Being lectured by Captain Joe was particularly embarrassing because the Stoffards had stayed overnight and had joined the family at the breakfast table.

Luckily Mabel wasn't there. She hadn't felt well and had asked if she could sleep late. But Elizabeth was sitting right across from Abby, glaring at her.

"This is still the Wild West," Captain Joe continued. "If anything ever happened to you in those canyons, we might never find you. Do you understand me?"

Abby nodded as she stared down at her plate of biscuits and sausage gravy.

"After we're done eating, help your Aunt Mary with the dishes and then get on over to the cookshack. Silas is preparing a big lunch basket for the Stoffards' trip home. Bring it back to the wagon."

"Yes, sir," Abby mumbled.

She had meant to tell Captain Joe or Waddy about Buckdancer, in the hope that they'd go help the injured horse. But something made her change her mind. The Captain appeared to be in a foul mood. And why would he help a "broomtail?" He'd probably shoot it.

Abby never looked up at the Stoffards. She ate her breakfast quickly and hurried off to help in the kitchen. The sooner she got through with her chores, the sooner she could get back to the cliff to help Buckdancer.

But things didn't work out the way she'd hoped.

After she hauled the picnic basket to the Stoffard's wagon, Aunt Mary caught hold of her arm. "Spring roundup starts in three days."

"What's that?" Abby asked.

"It's the time when we round up the cattle on the entire ranch, cut out the calves, and brand them."

"We have to do that?" Abby gasped.

"No, we don't," Aunt Mary chuckled. "But our cowboys do. We just go with them to the branding camp to help kick things off."

Abby frowned in confusion.

"Now don't look so downfaced, child." Aunt Mary swatted playfully at Abby's shoulder. "Roundup is about the most exciting event of the year in Medicine Bow. We like to celebrate it with plenty of food and lots of singing. It's sort of a going–away party for all the cowboys who'll be out rounding up our cattle."

"How many do they have to round up?" Abby asked.

"Last count we had over three thousand head of cattle."

Abby whistled softly between her teeth. Roundup would take a long time.

"We've got to start our baking now," Aunt Mary continued. "Silas is stocking supplies for the chuck wagon. Waddy and the boys are getting their tack and gear ready. And we're baking bread, biscuits, and pies to take along on the trail."

Abby's heart sank. She'd promised Buckdancer she'd be back that morning. Now it looked like she'd have to break her promise to the Mustang.

Abby made one more attempt to get back to the wounded horse that day. After supper, she helped with the dishes as usual, volunteering to dry so that she'd be the last person in the kitchen. But as she stepped out the back door, Abby bumped into Captain Joe smoking his pipe on the back porch.

"You're not planning to leave the grounds, are you?" he asked, eyeing the canvas bag tucked under her arm. She'd planned to use it to carry her supplies from the barn.

"No, Captain Joe. 'Course not."

He pointed to the sky with the stem of his pipe. "It's getting dark. And those clouds say it may rain. That's a dangerous time for anyone to be wandering around these canyons. You don't want to be caught in a flash flood."

Abby knew he was right, but her heart ached for the poor Mustang trapped in the gully.

"Now you go on back inside," Captain Joe said. "I hear Curly's offered to pick a few tunes for us on his guitar."

Reluctantly, Abby went back in the house.

That night she could barely sleep. She tossed and turned in her bed, while visions of the Mustang passed through her dreams. Around 3 A.M., she abruptly sat up, certain she'd heard Buckdancer whinny.

I don't care what Captain Joe says, she thought as she threw back the covers, I've got to help Buckdancer.

She touched her throat. It hurt. And her head ached. But she was bound and determined to get to that Mustang.

Abby felt in the darkness for her clothes. Then she dressed quietly, being careful not to wake Elizabeth. She carried her shoes in her hand and tiptoed downstairs. It was still pitch black outside, but she was able to find a lantern in the kitchen and light it.

Abby grabbed several apples from a bowl in the kitchen and stuffed some greens from the root cellar into her canvas bag.

She left the house and slowly made her way to the barn, terrified that she might trip on a bucket or step on a stick and wake the Captain or one of the ranch hands.

Abby filled the rest of the bag with bandages and other supplies that she'd found in the tack room. Then she grabbed a bucket that was near one of the troughs. The last thing she did was fill a flour sack with bran.

Abby hauled the lantern, heavy bucket, bandages, and bran across the open pasture, stopping at the stream for water. As she neared the canyon, the first rays of dawn were just lighting the eastern sky.

"Please be alive, Buckdancer, please!" she murmured over and over to herself. "Please be alive!"

Near the mouth of Box Canyon, Abby paused. She strained to hear some sign of life in the gully below. But all was quiet.

Not a whinny. Not even the barest rustle of movement.

She squeezed her eyes shut, afraid of what she might see, and inched forward. Her foot hit a rock and caused a pebble to slide down the side of the gully. And that's when she heard it. The smallest of sounds.

"Buckdancer, is that you?" Abby called softly.

She was answered by a feeble whinny.

Abby heard the clatter of rocks, as Buckdancer hobbled forward into the light.

"Oh!" she gasped. He was clearly much weaker than two days before. His knee was swollen to nearly twice its size.

Abby didn't hesitate. Holding tightly to the bucket and the canvas bag, she slid down the side of the gully on her bottom. The pan of water she'd placed between the rocks was bone dry.

"You must be thirsty," she said, as she set the bag

on the ground and slowly stood up with the bucket. "Abby's got a drink of cool water for you. Would you like that, fella?"

The wounded Mustang snorted his reply, but he didn't move.

Abby kept talking in a soothing voice as she inched forward. "I've got this bucket in my hand. It won't hurt you. I'm going to set it in front of you, so you can have a drink."

Buckdancer watched her warily as she approached. He even stumbled backwards a bit, but he didn't try to bolt.

"There you go." Abby lowered the bucket of water in front of him, and stepped back. "Go ahead, drink up. It's delicious."

Abby turned and walked slowly back to the canvas bag. Behind her she heard a few snorts, followed by loud slurping, as Buckdancer sucked in the much needed water.

"One down." Abby breathed a sigh of relief. "Now for the hard part. Tending that leg."

Abby pulled open the bag. Inside was a mason jar of hot water, some leaves of sneezewort, and a small jar of vegetable oil.

"Waddy told me that when a horse gets a sprain, the first thing you need to do is get the swelling down," she explained to Buckdancer. "I can't tell if your knee is sprained or not. My guess is the swelling has something to do with that gash above your knee. The poisons in your wound have probably drained into your knee. What we need to do is whip up a little bran paste so the swelling doesn't get any worse."

Buckdancer slurped at his water, raised his head, and listened. Then he drank again.

"You look like you really understand me," she said, with a smile.

Abby pulled the rusted tin pan out from between the rocks and placed it in front of her. She poured the bran and warm water in it and stirred them together with a stick. "I'm mixing this up, see?"

Buckdancer cocked his head alertly.

"Looks good enough to eat, doesn't it?" she said. "Add a touch of molasses, and you'd probably think you were in heaven."

Buckdancer hobbled two steps forward, throwing his head back each time his injured foot touched the ground.

"That must hurt like the dickens," she said, as she added the sneezewort leaves to the paste. "This sneezewort will help your wound heal. Waddy said the Indians taught him that."

She picked up the little jar of vegetable oil. "This

is to keep the bran moist. Otherwise it'll dry up and fall off your leg."

Abby dug in her bag for the greens and apples. "All right, boy, I've got a delicious treat for you. What do you say we make a deal? I'll give you these apples, and you'll let me smear this bran on your leg."

Buckdancer snorted and shook his head. She knew he was listening. But she had no idea if he would allow her to get anywhere near him, let alone his wound.

Slowly Abby stood up. She held an apple in front of her with one hand and the pan of bran in the other. As she inched her way towards Buckdancer, Abby sang the same soothing tune her mother had always sung.

"Hush little baby don't say a word,
Mama's gonna buy you a mockingbird."

The Mustang listened and watched as Abby drew nearer and nearer. But still he didn't try to move.

Now the apple was under Buckdancer's nose. He sniffed it curiously. Then, very delicately, he took it from Abby's fingers.

Abby smiled, but kept singing. The horse devoured the apple hungrily, so she handed him another. And another.

When Buckdancer had finished all of the apples,

Abby handed him a bunch of greens. He chomped those too. Bits of foam and apple spattered the sides of his mouth.

Still singing, Abby ever so carefully reached up to touch his neck. Her fingertips brushed the black mane and slid down firmly onto his thick yellow coat. Buckdancer kept chewing.

Abby's heart leapt up. It was hard to keep the excitement out of her voice. Buckdancer was actually letting her touch him!

She offered him some more greens, then slid her hand down his shoulder to his leg. Buckdancer stopped chewing and eyed her suspiciously.

Without dropping a note of her song, Abby scooped her hand into the pan to show him the bran poultice she'd made. He took a nibble of it, and Abby nearly laughed.

She changed the words of her song.
"This is a poultice that's good for you;
It'll heal your leg and it's tasty, too."
The way she was finally able to smear the mixture on Buckdancer's wounded leg was to first offer him a bite, then smear a little on, then offer him another bite.

"A bite for you, and some for me;
You'll feel good soon, just wait and see."

It seemed a miracle, but the wild horse let Abby cover his knee with the bran paste and then bandage it.

Abby worked as quickly as she could. Each passing second filled her with a fierce determination to make sure Buckdancer lived.

"I couldn't save my mama or papa," Abby whispered when she was done. "I couldn't save my baby brother. But, Buckdancer, I'm going to save you!"

CHAPTER TEN

Can't Stop the Roundup

"**O**w!" Abby yelped as she bent over to remove her shoes. Her head throbbed, and her throat burned so badly she could hardly swallow.

"What's the matter, Abby?" Aunt Mary asked, turning up the oil lamp in the front room. "Got a blister?"

It was Friday evening after supper, and Aunt Mary had asked Elizabeth and Abby to join her in front of the fire. The two girls hadn't spoken to each other in nearly a week, and sat as far away from each other as possible at meals.

"It's my head," Abby replied, rubbing her temples. "I have a terrible headache. And my throat hurts, too."

Elizabeth raised a skeptical eyebrow in Abby's direction. Right away, Abby knew what was in her cousin's mind.

Elizabeth thinks I'm pretending to be sick so I won't have to help on the spring roundup, she thought.

"But I'm fine," Abby added hastily, with a phony smile at Elizabeth.

Aunt Mary set the sock she had darned back in the basket beside her chair and looked from Elizabeth to Abby, and back again. "I'm not sure what's going on with you two," she declared as she picked up another sock. "But you're going to need to kiss and make-up before we leave tomorrow morning."

"Leave?" Abby repeated. "So soon?"

She heard a snort from Elizabeth.

"That's all we've been talking about," Aunt Mary said. "Why do you think we've been packing those food baskets and loading the wagons?"

Abby couldn't tell Aunt Mary that Buckdancer had been the only thing on her mind. For two days, she'd raced through her chores at lightning speed, just so she could spend time with Buckdancer.

Every day Abby carried fresh water and food to the gully. The second day she'd been thrilled to see that his swelling was actually going down. But

Buckdancer was still a long way from recovery.

"Everything's happened so fast," Abby said in a hoarse voice. "I didn't realize you were leaving tomorrow."

"You're going, too," Elizabeth said, folding her arms across her chest. "Isn't that right, Mama?"

Aunt Mary nodded. "We'll be off at first light. The branding camp is a ten mile ride away. We'll spend the night there and enjoy the celebration. Then we'll return Sunday evening."

Abby tried to swallow and winced in pain. "So we'll be gone for two days?" she rasped.

Aunt Mary nodded.

Abby frowned. That meant she wouldn't be able to get back to Buckdancer until Monday. He'd be without water and food for three whole days!

Aunt Mary patted Abby's hand. "Don't worry, Curly's staying behind to look after things. Soon as we get back, he'll join the boys at the branding camp."

"I'll stay with Curly," Abby said, leaping to her feet.

"Nonsense," Aunt Mary said, dropping her darning in her lap. "You're coming with us, child."

"But I could feed the chickens and collect the eggs," Abby said. "Curly can't take care of this whole ranch by himself."

"Abby is afraid she's going to have to work at the

branding camp," Elizabeth said to her mother.

"That's not true!" Abby shouted angrily at Elizabeth. The effort made her throat flare with pain, and she pressed her hand to her neck. "I'm always ready to work. That's why you brought me here, isn't it? To work for you?"

Aunt Mary looked shocked. "What are you talking about?"

"I do my chores," Abby continued. "I do the dishes, I help Silas in the cookshack, I clean the house. If that's not enough, than maybe you should find yourself another orphan. I hear there are plenty of them being shipped west. Whole trainloads."

"Abby!" Aunt Mary stood up, and the darning dropped to the floor. "That'll be quite enough!"

The room had begun to spin. Abby clutched the arm of the chair to keep her balance. "And if you need to ship me to the poorhouse, go ahead," she whispered. "Elizabeth won't miss me, I can tell you that."

Aunt Mary shot her daughter a sharp look. Elizabeth stared guiltily at her hands folded tightly in her lap.

"Abigail," Aunt Mary said evenly. "You're overtired. We all are. It's time for bed. You get some rest tonight, and things will look much better in the morning."

"You mean I can stay at the ranch?" Abby asked.

"Of course not," Aunt Mary replied sharply. "Now go to bed. I don't want to hear any more about it."

The room had stopped spinning, but Abby's head and throat still hurt. She stumbled off to bed, certain of only one thing. She absolutely, positively would not leave Buckdancer!

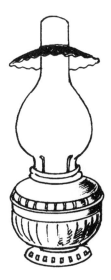

CHAPTER ELEVEN

Run Away and Hide!

"Only a few yards more," Abby whispered to herself as she carefully felt the ground in front of her.

It was pitch black outside. The sun hadn't even thought about coming up yet. Still, Abby could hear sounds of life coming from the barn and bunkhouse as she tiptoed away from the ranch.

Her canvas bag was heavy. She'd stuffed it full of roots from the cellar and apples. She was also toting the flour sack full of bran and a jar of hot water.

"Whew!" Abby set the bag on the ground and took several deep breaths. A wave of dizziness made her stagger backwards. "I should have eaten breakfast."

Abby decided to kneel on the ground for a few seconds, until she could get her bearings. She felt miserable. Her throat was still raw, and the night before, while washing up before bed, she'd noticed a rash on her neck and chest.

"It's from worrying about leaving Buckdancer for so long," she'd told her reflection in the mirror.

Just before bed, she made up her mind not to go to the branding camp. Aunt Mary only needs me to serve food and clean up, she thought. But Buckdancer needs me to live.

Abby had slept in her clothes that night, so she could slip away before dawn.

Now she huddled on the ground, shivering, as the first rays of light peeked over Box Canyon.

"Brrr! Why is it so cold?" Abby said between chattering teeth. She felt her forehead with the back of her wrist. It was damp and clammy. "And why am I so sweaty?"

In the corral behind her the horses were snorting with excitement. "Curly and Big Tim are probably getting them ready to go," she murmured, looking nervously over her shoulder toward the ranch. "I'd better hurry, or someone'll see me crossing the pasture."

Abby rose to her feet and stood for a moment,

trying to steady herself. "Am I woozy," she said. "Must be from lack of sleep."

Clutching the flour sack and canvas bag close to her body, she hurried the rest of the way to the gully. Before she'd even neared the edge, she was greeted with a loud whinny.

"You know it's me, don't you, Buckdancer?" Abby asked as she peered over the ledge. "Are you telling me you're hungry? Is that what you're saying?"

Buckdancer hobbled forward a step. He wasn't exactly rushing to greet her, but at least he wasn't trying to hide. Abby took it as a good sign.

"How's your water?" Abby asked, checking the bucket she'd left with him. It was still half full. Then she dug in her bag for an apple and held it out to the Mustang.

Crunch! Buckdancer devoured the apple in one eager bite.

Abby swatted at her pinafore. "Where's your table manners?" she scolded with a chuckle. "You're getting slobber all over me."

She pulled another apple from the bag. The effort made her feel lightheaded. She took a deep breath and knelt in front of the Mustang. "While you chew on that, I'll take a quick look at your leg."

Abby was careful not to touch the horse unless it

was necessary. She didn't want him rearing up and kicking her. She leaned forward and peered at the leg. "The swelling has definitely gone down. But I think we need to do something about that wound."

The gash above the leg still oozed a milky fluid. Abby was afraid it might be getting infected.

She pulled the canvas bag toward her and took out all of her supplies. At the bottom, in a little tin, she'd packed some dried marigold leaves.

"My mama believed that pot marigold was good for just about everything. Anytime any of us ever cut ourselves, she rubbed marigold leaves on the wound. And it really did heal faster."

Buckdancer had finished chewing and was watching her, his ears pricked forward.

Also in the bottom of the bag, carefully wrapped in cloth, were Abby's treasures. She removed the little gold necklace and held it up for Buckdancer to see.

"This belonged to my mama. It's all I have left of her. I'm not sure why there's only half a heart on this chain," she said, her eyes welling with tears. "But that's how my heart feels. Broken clear in two."

While she was putting the locket away, Buckdancer leaned forward, snorting warm breath onto the top of her head. She felt his soft muzzle nibble on her hair.

"My hair may look like hay," she said with a giggle, gently touching the horse's velvety nose. "But I promise you it's just hair."

She unscrewed the lid on the hot water jar and poured some water into the tin pan, along with the bran and the marigold leaves. While she mixed the poultice, Buckdancer nibbled on the edge of the canvas bag, knocking it over.

The tintype of Abby's father fell onto the ground. As she picked it up, a sudden chill made her shiver. "Brrrr. I don't know how it's possible for it to be so cold out here and me sweating so." She put her hand to her moist forehead. "But I am."

Buckdancer snorted in response.

Abby held the picture up for the horse to see. "This is my papa. He was a newspaper man. Very smart. He liked to read and write stories about the Wild West. But I know he would never have been comfortable living here."

The poultice was ready. Abby carefully placed the picture back in her bag and began to apply the sticky paste to Buckdancer's knee.

"Papa liked houses and towns and people." Abby slowly worked the bran mixture up onto Buckdancer's wound. "Mama was the same. She loved entertaining in her parlor. She even had a ladies' book club. They would read books about, well, most anything, then all get together to talk about them."

Buckdancer flinched, jerking backwards.

"Easy boy," Abby cooed. "I know this hurts, but it's good for you. So you're just going to have to trust me."

Somehow Buckdancer understood her words, because he didn't move again until she was finished applying the poultice.

Abby rinsed her hands in the leftover water from the jar and began putting her things back in the bag. As she was rewrapping the tintype, two blue ribbons fell into her lap.

"Oh, Buckdancer!" Abby pressed the ribbons to her cheek. "I showed you all of my other treasures, but I didn't show you these. They belonged to my brother Ben. He was just a baby, barely a year old, when he—he got sick."

She held up the ribbons, letting them flutter in the breeze. We tied his booties with these. Ben was always pulling at them, untying 'em. He just didn't like shoes. Liked to be free to wiggle his toes."

Buckdancer ducked his head under the ribbons. For a moment they fluttered against his mane.

Abby stroked his neck and he didn't pull away. She picked up several strands of his hair and in a moment of inspiration, carefully braided one of the ribbons into his mane.

"There!" she exclaimed. "You look better already."

As if in reply Buckdancer tossed his mane, letting loose with a loud whinny.

He was answered by a fierce gust of wind that whistled down the canyon.

Abby wrapped her arms around herself, shivering. She glanced nervously at the sky. "Dawn's broken, but dark clouds are moving in. Looks like bad weather is on the way."

She bent over to pick up her canvas bag and completely lost her balance. She fell heavily onto her knees.

"I don't feel well," she groaned. "My head is going round and round."

Thunder rumbled ominously in the distance. Buckdancer hobbled back toward the side of the gully, his head jerking back with each step on his lame leg.

Abby lifted her head to look at him, but her vision was blurred. "It's gonna be a bad storm, isn't it?" She shut her eyes.

Buckdancer whinnied again.

Abby forced herself to her feet as a bolt of lightning zigzagged across the sky and, less than a second later, thunder boomed just above them.

Abby clutched her stomach. Her insides were cramping. Her throat burned. She tried to take deep breaths of air through her nose.

She turned and faced the ranch as the sky erupted in thunder and lightning.

"Gotta get back," she rasped, stumbling blindly across the pasture.

Halfway to the ranch, Abby again felt terribly dizzy. The horizon started to spin. Abby reached out with one hand to steady herself.

Lightning lit up the darkening sky.

Then her knees buckled under her. "I'm not going to make it," she gasped.

And everything went black.

The Fever

Abby's eyes fluttered open.

I'm in a room, she thought. Is that Aunt Mary?

A blurry face bent over her, and a hand smoothed her damp hair back from her forehead. A cool cloth was pressed across her eyes.

Mmm, that feels good, she thought.

Abby started to drift off again. Back into that misty world of the past. She was riding her pony, Toby, trotting in a wide circle around her mother. Little Ben was laughing and laughing. Then he faded from view.

Hot. I feel hot, Abby thought. She moaned. Sweat dripped down her neck.

"Curly found her in the pasture," a deep voice spoke from across the room, "halfway to Box Canyon."

Captain Joe? Abby turned her head.

"She was burning up, and half out of her mind, muttering something about a horse."

Buckdancer? Abby wanted to sit up, but she couldn't get her body to move. Everything hurt.

"When Mary found her missing," Captain Joe explained, "we put a hold on the roundup."

"I was so worried." Aunt Mary's voice shook with emotion. "Afraid she'd run off. A child that young, with no experience, wouldn't last two days in the wild."

The cloth was lifted from Abby's eyes. A strange man bent his face near hers. He wore wire-rimmed glasses and smelled of camphor. "Her body is covered in the rash. And see that pale area around the mouth? It's one of the sure signs. That, and the raspberry tongue."

The man tugged at Abby's jaw, pulling her mouth open. "See how her tongue is swollen and bright red?"

Abby swatted feebly at the face swirling in front of her. Don't know you, she thought. Go away!

"The child's got the fever, all right," the doctor

announced, stepping away from the bed. "Heard there's been a bad outbreak of it all around Laramie."

"The Stoffards were just over at Laramie," Captain Joe rumbled. "And their daughter Mabel was feeling pretty poorly."

"It's the children that suffer the most," the doctor said solemnly. "Whatever you do, keep Elizabeth away from Abby. Scarlet fever is highly contagious."

Scarlet fever? Abby raised her head and croaked, "No. Please, no!"

Someone rushed forward and placed another cool cloth on her head. "There, there, honey. Aunt Mary's here. You're going to be all right."

"I didn't think she could hear us, Doctor," Captain Joe whispered.

"She hears, all right," the doctor whispered back. "But her mind is confused. The fever's made her delirious."

"Buckdancer!" Abby wailed, throwing the wet cloth off her head. "Have to help Buckdancer. He's hurt!"

"Who is this Buckdancer?" the doctor asked.

"I don't know," Captain Joe replied. "Never heard of him."

Abby batted at the sheet covering her body. She had to get to Buckdancer!

"Doctor? What can you do about the fever?" Aunt Mary asked quietly.

"Maybe we had best step outside to talk about it."

The blurred shapes left the room. Abby was alone.

Images of Buckdancer, hurt and bleeding, swirled through her brain. They were followed by thoughts of the bobcat, alive and attacking. Abby thrashed her head back and forth on her pillow.

Suddenly she heard a whinny.

"Buckdancer?" Abby murmured, barely able to raise her head. "Is that you?"

Abby was certain the wounded horse was calling her.

"Have to go to him," she mumbled, throwing back the sheet. She flung herself out of the bed and hit the floor with a thud. But Abby didn't feel a thing. All she could think about was Buckdancer. He needed her.

Abby blinked, trying to make the room swim into focus. She found the door and crawled toward it. Her nightgown was soaked with sweat, and her arms were weak, but still she crawled forward.

When she finally reached the door, she pulled it open, then fell into the hall. She lay helpless, her cheek pressed against the wood floor. "Help," she mumbled. "Have to get help."

Elizabeth was standing at the far end of the hall. "Abigail!" she cried. "What are you doing out of bed?"

Abby was able to muster enough strength to lift her head. "Elizabeth, help me. Please."

Elizabeth pressed a handkerchief to her mouth and backed away. "Oh, Abby, I'd like to," she cried, "but I'm not supposed to go near you."

"It's not me," Abby moaned. "It's Buckdancer. His leg is hurt."

Elizabeth leaned forward. "Is Buckdancer a horse?"

"Yes!" The room began to swirl again.

"He's at the bluff," Abby gasped. Then her eyes rolled back in her head, and she collapsed.

Abby on the Mend

The room was bathed in sunlight. Abby had no idea how long she'd been lying in bed, but suddenly she felt hungry. Very hungry!

Abby pulled herself to a sitting position and looked around. She pressed her hand to her forehead. It was cool. Finally!

She checked the back of her hands. "No more spots," Abby whispered.

Abby was about to throw back the covers and leap out of bed when she noticed a woman asleep in the chair opposite her.

"Aunt Mary," Abby said gently.

Her aunt was wearing the same green dress she'd

been wearing when the doctor had first appeared. Her hair, which was always drawn into a neat bun at her neck, was mussed. Long blonde strands fell across her drawn and tired face.

Suddenly Aunt Mary's eyes opened. She stared at Abby for several seconds. Then her face blossomed into a huge smile.

"You're better, Abby," she declared. "I can see it from here."

Aunt Mary sprang to her feet and ran to the bedroom door. "Joe! Elizabeth! Come quick!"

Abby heard footsteps pound down the hall. Then the door was thrown open. It was Elizabeth.

"Thank heavens!" she gasped, clapping her hands together. The relief on Elizabeth's face was genuine.

Captain Joe appeared behind Elizabeth, resting his hands on her shoulders. He took one look at Abby and shook his head in wonder. "I do believe we've had a miracle."

Then he and Aunt Mary rushed over and smothered Abby in hugs. "I am so happy!" Aunt Mary said as she smoothed Abby's hair off her forehead, straightened her nightgown, and squeezed her again and again. "Oh, dear child, I can't tell you how happy I am."

"Silas!" Elizabeth shouted down the hall. "Quit

dishing up breakfast and come here!"

Then she ran to the window and yelled for the ranch hands. "Hey, Curly! Everybody! Abby's well. Come see!"

Abby smiled. Maybe everyone really does care about me, she thought. The attention felt good, but she itched to question Elizabeth about Buckdancer.

Elizabeth joined her parents at the side of the bed. "We were all so worried about you," she said, clutching Abby's hand. "Curly and Big Tim have been stopping by every morning and every night. And Silas keeps whipping up new batches of Anything'll-Do broth, hoping you'll be well enough to eat it."

The weather-beaten shape of Big Tim suddenly appeared at the open window. "Well, I'll be hogtied," Big Tim declared, his eyes glittering with pleasure. "If it ain't our Miss Abby, come back to join us."

Abby smiled and waved. "Howdy, Big Tim! Have I been gone long?"

Big Tim tipped his hat back on his head. "Too long, if you ask me. By my recollection, it's been nearly a week since we were supposed to leave for round-up."

"A week!" Abby's smile slid off her face. "Oh, no!"

"What's the matter?" Aunt Mary asked.

Abby turned to Elizabeth. "Buckdancer . . . Is he . . . ?"

A sly smile crept across Elizabeth's lips.

"What?" Abby demanded. "What is it?"

Elizabeth wiggled her eyebrows at Big Tim and then said in a very mysterious voice. "We have a little surprise for you, Abby."

Abby opened her mouth to speak, but Elizabeth raised a firm hand. "Not another word. Just do as I say."

While Big Tim turned and whistled for Curly, Elizabeth tied a bandanna around Abby's eyes.

"All right, Papa," Elizabeth announced. "She's ready."

Captain Joe scooped Abby up in his arms and carried her down the hall, through the dining room, and out the back door.

When she heard the *crunch, crunch* of Captain Joe's boots on gravel, Abby knew they were crossing the ranch yard. Soon they were joined by more footsteps and jingling spurs, as their group got bigger.

When they'd covered quite a distance, Elizabeth barked in her best imitation of her father's military voice. "Company—halt!"

Everyone stopped walking at once.

Abby was still in Captain Joe's arms when Elizabeth removed the blindfold. Elizabeth stepped back and cried, "Look!"

There in the corral, with his head held high and his dark mane blowing in the wind, was Abby's magnificent Mustang.

"Buckdancer!" she cried.

The Mustang wheeled to face them, his nostrils flaring.

"Captain Joe, would you set me down, please?" Abby asked.

He grinned and nodded. The second her feet touched the ground, Abby ducked under the railing into the corral.

"Careful," Big Tim warned. "He may be limping, but he's still a wild one."

"Don't worry," Abby replied, steadying herself against the rail. "Buckdancer knows me. Don't ya, fella?"

When the Mustang saw her, his ears pricked forward, and he whinnied loudly.

"Son-of-a-gun," Curly announced from his perch on the corral gate. "He *does* know you."

As if to prove the cowboy's words, Buckdancer took three steps toward Abby.

"You're still limping," she said, eyeing his wounds. "But that gash is almost healed, and your knee looks much better."

"Somebody did one nice job of doctorin' that

horse," Waddy Hancock remarked, leaning against the fence rail. "Course, whoever it was had to go and use a whole mess of bran from our barn to do it . . ."

"Ah, Waddy, don't be such a skinflint," Big Tim said, swatting good-naturedly at the foreman with his hat.

"Yeah, Waddy," Silas cut in. "I believe my supply of apples and greens suffered more damage than your horse feed."

Abby smiled guiltily over her shoulder at the cook. "Sorry, Silas. But I had to do it."

"I understand," Silas said, nodding solemnly. "And just to show you what a generous soul I am, I've brought your fine Buckdancer some breakfast."

Silas dug into the pocket of his apron and handed Abby a bunch of greens and two shiny red apples.

Abby could barely see to take the food because of the tears in her eyes. "Thank you, Silas."

She turned to look at Waddy, Big Tim, and Curly. Then at Elizabeth and her aunt and uncle. "Thank you all for saving me. And Buckdancer."

She held an apple out in front of her, and Buckdancer limped forward. He sniffed the apple, then worked his way up her hand, and nibbled at the lace on the base of her sleeve.

Abby giggled softly. "Yep, it's me. I bet you thought I was never coming back."

CHAPTER FOURTEEN

Two Hearts Are One

The next day, Elizabeth and Abby sat side by side on the back porch peeling potatoes and watching Buckdancer. Abby had recovered enough to sit outside, but she still wasn't strong enough to run around the ranch.

"He sure is handsome," Elizabeth remarked as she dropped her peeled potato into the tin pot that sat between them. "And full of spirit."

"And strong," Abby added, as Buckdancer circled the corral. "Why, look at him. He's hardly limping any more."

Buckdancer turned to look at the girls as if he'd heard them.

"You know we're talking about you, don't you?" Abby said.

Buckdancer answered her with a defiant toss of his head and a loud snort.

"I love the way his mane flies in the breeze," Abby said, watching him circle the corral once more.

"Mane?" Elizabeth repeated. "Oh! I almost forgot." She dug into the pocket of her pinafore and produced a single blue satin ribbon. "Curly said this was tangled in Buckdancer's mane when they brought him up from the gully. Couldn't figure how it got there."

Abby set her potato and knife back in her bowl and wiped her hands clean. Then she gently took the ribbon from Elizabeth. "That belonged to my brother, Ben. It was the tie for one of his booties."

Elizabeth studied Abby's face intently. "I guessed you must have braided it into Buckdancer's mane," she said in a quiet voice.

Abby nodded. "I wanted to give him something special to help him get better."

Elizabeth set her bowl on the chair beside her and went into the house. When she returned, she was carrying Abby's canvas bag. "Curly also found this near Buckdancer. He gave it to me to keep for you."

Abby hadn't really shared any information about

her past with Elizabeth. She decided it was about time she did.

"When my family . . . passed on," she began quietly, "I wanted to keep something to remember them by. The Lloyds took almost everything we had, but I managed to save these."

Abby held up her treasures. First, the tintype of her father. "This was my papa. Your Uncle Will."

As Elizabeth carefully held the fragile glass, tears welled up in her eyes. "He's very handsome. You must miss him terribly."

Abby nodded. "So much, I ache inside."

Then she held up the other ribbon to Ben's booties. And lastly she presented the gold necklace with the broken heart.

Elizabeth took one look at it and let out a startled cry. "Oh! You have to show this to Mama!"

Aunt Mary heard the commotion on the porch and came running out to see what was the matter. Elizabeth's jaw was moving up and down, but no words were coming out.

Aunt Mary took one look at the heart, gasped, and disappeared into the house.

"Elizabeth! What's going on?" Abby asked.

Aunt Mary quickly returned, cradling an identical gold necklace in her hand. She held up the broken heart pendant. "Your mother gave this to me when Joe and I went west."

Aunt Mary was so full of emotion she could barely speak. "She always said that we were two hearts that beat as one, and that as long as we were apart, she would feel that she only had half a heart."

Aunt Mary held out her half of the heart with a shaky hand and pressed it against Abby's half. The two pieces snapped together perfectly.

"Do you see, sister?" Aunt Mary called up to the heavens. "Our hearts are finally reunited."

When Aunt Mary pressed her heart against Abby's, something inside Abby clicked. It was as if her own heart were no longer broken.

When Aunt Mary turned to Abby and opened her arms, Abby fell right into them. "This is a very big day for many reasons," Aunt Mary said. "Captain Joe made a decision last night."

"What, Mama?" Elizabeth asked, eagerly.

"He talked to Waddy and the boys, and he's decided that you can keep Buckdancer for your own horse, Abby."

"My own?" Abby gasped.

Aunt Mary nodded, happily. "Everyone on a ranch has a horse. And Buckdancer will be yours. Curly said he would help break him after Buckdancer's knee has healed."

Abby's brow was suddenly creased with a frown. "Break Buckdancer? I could never allow that."

Elizabeth touched Abby's arm. "*Break* is just an expression. It means Curly will work with him until he's no longer wild. Then he'll saddle him up so you can ride him."

Abby tried to imagine Buckdancer with a saddle on his back and a bit in his mouth, chewing oats from a bucket. She hated the thought.

"Buckdancer is a wild horse," she said firmly, watching him circle the corral once more. "He deserves to run free."

Buckdancer finished her statement with a shrill whinny.

"See," Abby giggled, "he's just itching to break loose."

"It's your decision," Aunt Mary said, touching the

gold heart once more. She quickly dabbed at her eyes with a handkerchief, then cleared her throat.

"You girls get to work now and finish those potatoes. In the meantime I'll talk to Joe. And as soon as he and Waddy think that Mustang's well enough, we'll take Buckdancer home."

Abby nodded. "Back to Box Canyon."

Finally Home

The sun was just peeking over the top of the red cliffs when Abby and Elizabeth arrived at Box Canyon.

Abby had planned to release Buckdancer by herself. Then she realized this was a very special moment and ought to be shared with a special friend.

"Giddyup, Baldy," Abby clucked to the big bay she was riding. By now she was well on her way to becoming a regular ranch girl, and Big Tim's horse had become one of her favorites.

Elizabeth rode beside her on her palomino, Sugarfoot. Buckdancer followed along behind them.

Abby turned in her saddle to look at the Mustang. "Buckdancer knows something's up. Look at the way that he prances behind Sugarfoot."

Elizabeth chuckled, as the horse skittered sideways with excitement. "To watch him dance, you'd never guess he was ever lame."

Abby nodded. "Waddy and Curly took good care of him. Two weeks of food from the barn and he's practically back to new."

Elizabeth smiled at Abby. "Same goes for you. You look better than ever. Tanned, not so scrawny. Why, even your hair looks good."

"I combed and braided it." Abby turned her head sideways to display the braid that stretched to the center of her back. "It's about time, huh?"

The girls had reached the opening to Box Canyon, but neither one wanted to dismount. It was Buckdancer who gave them the signal.

He let loose with a shrill whinny that echoed around the canyon walls.

"Okay, I get the message," Abby said, hopping nimbly off Baldy's back. She walked back to Sugarfoot and untied Buckdancer's rope. "Just give me a second here, and you can be on your way."

Abby coiled the rope up till she reached Buckdancer's nose. Then she dug into her pocket for the apples Silas had slipped her that morning at breakfast. "I'm going to miss you," she murmured as she slipped the halter off his head. "But I'll be watching for you. From right over there." Abby pointed to the base of the cliff. "And every spring when you come tearing out of that canyon, I expect you to at least give a nod in my direction. Is that understood?"

Buckdancer didn't respond. His ears were cocked forward, listening.

Elizabeth, who was still in the saddle on Sugarfoot, holding Baldy's reins, called, "Abby, do you feel it? That rumbling?"

Abby nodded. It felt like an earthquake beneath her feet.

"Better get Baldy and Sugarfoot out of here," Elizabeth cried. "Before it's too late."

Abby leapt onto Baldy's back and gave him a nudge to get going. "Hi yaw!"

The girls galloped away from Buckdancer as the rumbling grew louder and louder. Suddenly a sound like rolling thunder filled the air.

Buckdancer whinnied loudly.

He was answered by another whinny.

"Whoa, fella!" Abby reined Baldy to a halt.

Buckdancer reared up and batted the air with his forelegs just as the herd of Mustangs burst out of the mouth of the canyon.

Finally Home

The General was in the lead, followed by the palomino mare. They led the herd in a wide circle around Buckdancer. The General snorted a loud greeting, and Buckdancer took his place in the band.

Abby wiped the tears from the corners of her eyes as she watched.

Elizabeth rode back to join her. "It's hard to let him go, isn't it?"

"I thought Buckdancer was an orphan like me," Abby said, fighting hard to keep her chin from quivering. "But I was wrong. That's his family. The entire band of wild horses."

"And here is your family." Elizabeth reached out and took hold of Abby's hand. "Right here on the Double Diamond Ranch."

Abby squeezed her cousin's hand. Then the two girls watched as the band of wild horses pounded back toward the canyon.

At the gap in the cliff, Buckdancer separated himself from the others for the briefest moment. He paused, looking back at Abby.

She raised her hand in farewell.

When Buckdancer had completely disappeared from view, Abby turned to Elizabeth and smiled through her tears.

"Come on, Elizabeth. Let's go home."

FACTS
ABOUT THE BREED

You probably know a lot about Mustangs from reading this book. Here are some more interesting facts about this feisty American horse.

∩ Mustangs generally stand between 13.2 and 15 hands high. Instead of using feet and inches, all horses are measured in hands and inches. A hand is equal to four inches.

∩ Mustangs come in all colors. Often, like many horses of Spanish origin, they have an eel, or dorsal stripe, a dark stripe that runs from the withers along the spine to the top of the tail. Common colors among Mustangs include roan, dun, and buckskin.

∩ Although the conformation, or build, varies from horse to horse, Mustangs generally have small, sturdy bodies with short, strong legs and hard hooves. Their hooves are so hard that they can travel over rough ground without injury and without wearing shoes.

∩ The name Mustang comes from the Spanish word meaning group or herd of horses.

∩ Mustangs are descended from the horses that were first brought to Mexico by Spanish settlers in the sixteenth century. By the seventeenth century, the Spaniards had begun to breed their horses near present-day Santa Fe, New Mexico. Some of these horses ran away and became feral, or wild. These feral herds then moved north into the western plains of the United States.

∩ When cattle ranching took hold in the United States in the nineteenth century, large numbers of Mustangs became cow ponies. Cowboys caught and trained Mustangs to perform a variety of jobs. Mustangs learned to cut, or separate, a single cow from the herd. They served as roping horses and as "night horses." Night horses must be especially sure footed and able to see well in the dark.

∩ Many of the Native American tribes also caught and tamed Mustangs. These horses became an important part of life on the Plains. Horses enabled Native American tribes to hunt large number of buffalo and to make the seasonal moves of the village more easily.

∩ Members of the Nez Percé tribe, who were known as excellent horsemen, developed the Appaloosa breed from feral Mustangs.

∩ Occasionally an Arabian or Thoroughbred imported to the New World from Europe ran away from home and joined a Mustang herd.

∩ In 1900, approximately one million wild Mustangs roamed the western United States.

∩ Over the years, many Mustangs have been captured and tamed. Others met less happy fates. Before the passage of a law to protect them, Mustangs in the western United States were rounded up by helicopter, killed, and turned into dog food.

∩ In 1971, the Wild Free Roaming Horse and Burro Act was passed. This law protects Mustangs from being rounded up and killed. The Bureau of Land Management, an agency of the United States Federal Government, is responsible for the well being of these feral horses.

∩ Today there are approximately 35,000 wild horses in the western states. They roam mostly in Nevada and Wyoming. When necessary, the Bureau of Land Management rounds up the horses and puts some of them up for adoption. In this way they keep the wild horse population from becoming too large for the limited amount of grassland available to them.

∩ Since older horses are harder to tame, Mustangs put up for adoption are less than five years old. Even so, of the 130,000 horses adopted under this program, 13,000 of them have been returned to the Bureau of Land Management because they were too difficult to keep.

∩ Today there are a number of organizations that exist to protect wild Mustangs. They include: the International Society for the Protection of Mustangs & Burros of Scottsdale, Arizona; the National Mustang Association of Newcastle, Utah; and the American Feral Horse Association of Boise, Idaho.

Ω In addition, several breed registries, like
the North American Mustang Association &
Registry of Mesquite, Texas, help to preserve
the Mustang's genetic heritage by encouraging
registration and good breeding practices
among domesticated Mustangs.

KATE'S
SECRET PLAN

*The story of a young Quarter Horse and the persistent
girl who will not let obstacles stand in their way*

Written by **Susan Saunders**
Illustrated by **Sandy Rabinowitz**
Cover Illustration by **Christa Keiffer**
Developed by Nancy Hall, Inc.

CONTENTS

CHAPTER ONE

Happy Birthday!

Kate McGill was dreaming about horses: a big, beautiful herd of them, chestnuts and bays and grays. They thundered across the Canadian prairie. Their manes and tails streamed in the wind.

Kate galloped after them. But she was riding lazy old Brownie, so she couldn't keep up. She was falling farther and farther behind . . .

"Come on, Brownie!" Kate urged in her dream. "Faster! Faster!"

Then one of the McGill roosters crowed right under her bedroom window. A dog barked. And Kate

slowly opened her eyes.

A golden sun was floating over the low hills beyond the barn. Kate scrunched down in her bed and pulled the blankets more tightly around herself. It was early June in southern Alberta, Canada. But it was still chilly.

Suddenly Kate remembered what day it was: June 8th, 1926—it was her tenth birthday!

She flung her covers off and hurried to dress. "Happy birthday to me, happy birthday to me!" Kate sang to herself. She zipped up her riding pants and pulled on her western boots. Louder, she added, "Happy birthday to both of us . . ."

"Both of us" meant Kate and Brian. And a couple of knocks on the other side of Kate's bedroom wall told her that Brian had heard the song. It was Brian's tenth birthday, too, because Kate and Brian were twins.

Both of them were tall for their age, and pencil thin. And they both had bright blue eyes, reddish-blond hair, and freckles like their dad.

But Kate and Brian were less alike in other ways.

Kate had always been crazy about horses. Mr. McGill often said that she was born with horse sense.

As a toddler, Kate begged to sit in the saddle in front of her father. She had been riding alone since she was three. That's when her dad plopped her bareback onto George, a poky, fat plow horse. Kate covered lots of miles, steering George round and round the corral.

When she was six, Kate started riding Brownie.

"Brownie is slow, but steady," said Mr. McGill. Which was important when Kate was younger. But now she often wished she had a mount who was livelier.

Brian could ride, too, of course. He helped out with horseback chores on the ranch, like rounding up cattle or riding the fence line to look for breaks in the barbed wire.

Almost daily in the summertime, though, Brian rode straight over to the Frasers' farm. He and Asa Fraser were best friends. And Asa was almost as crazy about baseball as Brian was. They spent every spare moment they could practicing pitching, catching, and batting a baseball.

Brian said that he could take horses or leave them. What he really wanted was to be a baseball player and live in a big city with trolleys and electric lights.

Not Kate. Kate never wanted to live anywhere but on a ranch.

She ran a brush over her hair and smiled at

herself in the mirror. "I'm ready for a birthday!" she said.

She bumped into Brian in the hall.

"What do you think we're getting this year?" he asked as they headed toward the kitchen. "Mom and Dad haven't said one word."

"I couldn't even make Peter give me a hint!" Kate replied.

Peter was the twins' older brother. He would be leaving the ranch soon. He was starting classes at the new university in Edmonton, the capital of Alberta.

"I hope they don't make us wait all day for our presents," said Kate, who wasn't very good at waiting.

"But Dad has to drive to the train. He's picking up the Willises," Brian reminded her. Joe Willis had just been hired as the McGills' new foreman. "Then Mom and Dad will have to get them settled."

Kate groaned: "That'll take up most of the morning. And the afternoon, too. It'll be dark before we have our birthday!"

She pushed open the door to the warm, sunny kitchen.

"Greetings to the birthday girl and boy!" Mr. McGill boomed from his chair at the head of the long wooden table. He was a big man, with curly red hair and twinkly blue eyes.

"Happy birthday, both of you!" said Mrs. McGill. Her dark-brown hair was wound neatly around her head in a thick braid, her heart-shaped face flushed from the heat of the big, black wood stove.

Mrs. McGill gave the twins a hug, leaving Peter tending the griddle.

Peter was tall and thin, like the twins, with dark hair and green eyes like their mother.

"Yeah, happy birthday, squirts," Peter said, flipping a pancake. Then he added it to a huge stack already piled on a platter.

"Yum! Pancakes!" said Brian hungrily.

"With strawberries?" asked Kate. Pancakes with strawberries and whipped cream was just about her favorite meal!

"That's right—we had a few jars of berries left from last summer," said her mother.

Canadian summers are short, so Mrs. McGill jarred and canned as many fresh fruits and vegetables as she could.

"Sit down, children . . . ," said Mrs. McGill.

She bent over the platter of pancakes for a moment. When she turned around, the pancakes were topped with strawberries and whipped cream. And they were decorated with eleven flickering birthday candles, just right for making wishes.

370

"Ten candles, plus one to grow on!" said Mrs. McGill.

She set the platter down in the middle of the kitchen table.

"Happy birthday to you . . . ," sang Mr. and Mrs. McGill, and Peter said, "Blow out the candles before our pancakes get cold!"

"And make a wish!" said Mrs. McGill.

Kate and Brian both took a deep breath. Then they blew at the same time.

Kate didn't know what Brian had wished for. But she had wished for the same thing for years—a new horse.

"Since we'll be busy with the Willises today . . . ," began Mr. McGill.

Kate and Brian looked at each other and groaned.

" . . . we thought we'd give you your presents as soon as we've eaten. It may be the only free moment we have," said Mrs. McGill. "Is that all right with you two?"

"You bet!" said Brian.

"Oh, yes!" said Kate.

"Let's dig in," said Peter, piling pancakes, strawberries, and whipped cream on each of their plates.

Breakfast was delicious, but Kate hardly tasted it.

She was much too busy trying to imagine what her present from her parents might be.

Maybe a new saddle blanket—her old one was almost worn out. Or a new bridle—she had seen a beautiful headstall with silver buckles the last time they were in Medicine Hat.

Or what if the present was something boring, like a new chest of drawers? Or a bed?

Just a week or two ago, her mother had said, "Kate, your bedroom furniture is older than I am."

"I have a feeling it's furniture," Kate said to herself. And her heart sank.

The Best Gift Ever

Mrs. McGill said, "Well I think it's time for those presents."

"I believe that it's Brian's turn to go first this birthday," said Mr. McGill. The twins took turns opening presents first from year to year.

"In that case . . ." Mrs. McGill hurried into the pantry off the kitchen. She returned with a large square box, which she handed to Brian.

"It's awfully light . . .," said Brian, sounding disappointed. "Is it clothes?"

"Maybe. You'd better open it and see," said his father.

Brian tore the brown paper off the box and pulled

it open . . . The box was full of wadded-up
newspapers!

Brian's face fell. "Is there anything in here at all?"
he asked his parents.

"Just keep looking," said Mrs. McGill.

So Brian dug around in the paper and pulled out a
big white envelope.

"That's it . . . ," said his father.

Brian shrugged and opened the envelope.

Inside it was a square of cardboard. A picture of a
baseball player was glued to one corner of the
cardboard. A newspaper advertisement for an
Edmonton hotel was glued to another. An old train
ticket from the Canadian Pacific Railways was stuck in
the center of the cardboard.

"Is it a puzzle?" Brian asked, looking puzzled
himself. "Are these clues?"

"Kind of," said his mother.

"I don't know what a baseball player and a train
have to do with each other," said Brian. "And a hotel?"

Peter rolled his eyes. "Let's put you out of your
misery," he said to Brian. "Turn it over."

On the back of the cardboard, Mrs. McGill's tiny
print explained the gift.

"A baseball game!" Brian shouted as soon as he
had read it. "I'm going to a real baseball game—in

Edmonton! This is great!"

"But how will you get there?" Kate asked, since Edmonton wasn't exactly around the corner from the McGill Ranch. In fact, it was hundreds of miles away. Neither she nor Brian had ever been there.

"Brian and I will take the train to Medicine Hat," Mr. McGill said, pointing to the train-ticket clue. "Then we'll switch to the Calgary train, and then to the Edmonton line. We'll stay in a hotel in Edmonton and see a baseball game—maybe two!"

"Peter will go on the train with them and get settled at the university," Mrs. McGill told Kate.

"What about us?" said Kate to her mother, feeling left out.

Baseball tickets weren't that interesting to Kate. But a trip to Edmonton, a stay in a hotel, and a visit to Peter's university certainly were!

"You and I will run the ranch while they're gone," said Mrs. McGill. "Don't you have something for Brian, Kate?"

"Umm." Kate had been thinking about what fun it would be to go to Edmonton. She had almost forgotten her own present for Brian. She pulled an envelope out of her shirt pocket.

Brian opened it, read the note inside, and grinned.

"A present I can always use," he said, holding it

out so that his parents and Peter could see what Kate had written: "Good for two weeks' worth of chores."

"Now you can play ball with Asa all day long if you want," explained Kate.

"Thanks, twin," said Brian.

Peter gave Brian a baseball cap, white striped with blue. "I ordered it from Toronto," Peter told him. "It's the real thing."

Brian tried the cap on and practiced a couple of slow-motion pitches: "This is the best birthday I've ever had!" he exclaimed.

"Kate, I guess you aren't that interested in your present, are you?" teased Mr. McGill.

"Sure I am," said Kate. But how could her present possibly be as exciting as a trip to Edmonton?

"Let's go out to the barn," said Mr. McGill.

The barn: that meant Kate's birthday present was too big to wrap up . . .

"Furniture," Kate mumbled to herself. "I just knew it."

They all trooped out to the barn—even the dogs, Stella and Brutus, joined them.

Mr. McGill led them around to the back of the barn.

The McGills' Model-T Ford was parked outside the barn. Kate almost couldn't believe it, because her dad was so careful with the car.

Brian was surprised, too. "Why is the car sitting out, Dad?" he asked.

But Mr. McGill was saying, "Push open the barn door, Kate. Go ahead . . . "

Kate lifted the latch and slowly slid the door open. She was trying to come up with something nice to say about new furniture. She didn't want her parents to feel bad . . .

Then she stopped dead!

There, in the big box stall under the hayloft, stood a horse. And not just any horse—he was the most beautiful horse Kate had ever seen. He was a golden chestnut—the color of caramel—with a white mane and tail and three white stockings.

"Oh!" was all that Kate could say. "Ooooh!"

"He's yours, honey," said Mr. McGill.

"Do you like him?" asked Mrs. McGill.

Did she like him? "I love him!" Kate said breathlessly.

Chinook

Kate held her right hand out, and walked toward the horse. He gazed at her with his warm brown eyes and nickered softly.

"I think he likes you, too," said Mrs. McGill, as the horse stretched out his neck to nibble at Kate's fingers.

When Kate got close enough to stroke him, the horse stood as steady as a rock. Then he rubbed his head against her.

"How old is he? Where did he come from?" Kate asked.

"He's four years old. We got him from a Quarter-Horse breeder north of Medicine Hat," said Mr. McGill.

"Brian will be riding Peppy now, with Peter off at the university. We thought you were ready for a better horse, too."

Peppy was Peter's cutting horse. Peppy and Peter had won the cutting-horse contest at the Medicine Hat fair many times.

In the cutting-horse contest, a horse and rider had only two-and-a-half minutes to show what they could do. During that time, they had to choose a cow or steer out of a herd of cattle. Then the horse's job was to keep that cow from returning to the herd, no matter what. The rider's job was to sit still and let the horse do its best work.

When everything went right, Kate thought there was nothing more beautiful. And there was nothing she would rather do herself than ride a cutting horse at the fair.

But there was one problem—she was a girl. The cutting contest in Medicine Hat was only for grown-up men and boys under eighteen years old. Not girls.

With Peter in college, Brian would be riding Peppy at the rodeo. And Kate didn't think it was fair.

For one thing, Brian wasn't that interested. For another, Peter let Kate cut on Peppy a few times at the ranch. And she knew that she was better at riding him than Brian was.

"There's no use arguing about it, honey," Mr. McGill had said to Kate more than once. "Girls don't ride in the cutting contest."

And Kate always thought, "What can girls do to win trophies, then? Bake pies, or make pickles?"

Her mom was fond of telling her, "Kate, you were born in 1916, a good year for women—the year we got the vote in Alberta." So why was it okay for women to decide who would be running the government, but not okay for them to ride in a cutting-horse contest? It didn't make sense. When Kate thought about it for long, she got angry. She wanted to ride, not cook. And she was too young to vote!

But Kate wasn't going to make herself mad today. Not with this amazing birthday present.

"What's his name?" she asked, her arms around the horse's neck.

"They were calling him Stockings, because of his white legs," said Mr. McGill.

Kate thought for a minute. Then she smiled and said, "I'm going to name him Chinook—a real Canadian name."

A chinook was a warm, dry wind that blew into southern Canada in the wintertime. It was like magic: In the space of a few hours, a chinook could make the temperature rise forty degrees and could melt snow.

Chinook would be a special name for a special horse.

"You're going to like it here, Chinook," Kate said to the horse, stroking his neck.

He bobbed his head as if he were agreeing, and whinnied.

"Hey—you'll have to let go of him long enough to open my present," Peter said to Kate.

He handed her a soft, flat package wrapped in old newspapers.

As soon as Kate tore open a corner of the package, she knew what was inside. "A new saddle blanket!" she exclaimed, tracing the red, black, and cream pattern with her fingers. "Oh, thank you, Peter."

"It's double-thick wool, and it was hand-woven," Peter told her.

"It's perfect," Kate said.

Brian gave Kate a new hatband he had braided himself, out of all different colors of horsehair.

"The white is from Peppy's tail, the black is from Brownie, and the red is from old George," Brian said. He lifted Kate's cowboy hat off her head and removed the old leather band.

Kate slipped on the new one in its place: "It even matches my new saddle blanket. Thank you, Brian."

Kate liked her new blanket and hatband—but she couldn't take her eyes off Chinook.

"Would you like to try him out?" her father suggested.

"Oh, yes," said Kate. She led Chinook to the corner of the barn where the McGills kept their saddles and bridles.

Kate's dad helped her shorten the headstall of a bridle to fit Chinook's head. Quarter Horses have short heads, widely spaced eyes, and perky little ears, and Chinook had the perfect Quarter-Horse head.

While Brian held the reins, Kate folded her new saddle blanket in half. Carefully, she laid it lightly over Chinook's withers. She smoothed the blanket until it was straight, and stepped back to admire the red, black, and cream stripes against her horse's caramel-colored back.

Once the saddle was in place on the saddle blanket, Mr. McGill cinched it up carefully and then checked to make sure it was tight.

"You're all set," he said to Kate.

The rest of the McGills followed Kate as she led Chinook out of the barn toward the big round corral where Peter practiced on Peppy. Chinook had a quick, easy way of walking. His ears were pricked forward as he looked around his new home.

"I think he's smart," Peter said. "He's taking everything in."

Kate climbed into the saddle. She almost couldn't believe it. Yesterday, she was plodding around on old Brownie. Today, she was riding this incredible horse!

"Do some figure eights to see how he reins," her dad said. "But start out slow, Kate."

Kate nodded. She squeezed her legs just the tiniest bit against Chinook's sides, and he immediately moved forward. That was good. It showed that Chinook was ready to do what Kate asked, as soon as she asked him to.

His walk was smooth and easy. Chinook didn't drag his feet the way Brownie sometimes did.

Kate and Chinook made a circle to the right for the first part of the figure eight.

"How about a trot?" Mr. McGill called out.

Kate squeezed her legs a bit tighter and leaned forward, to speed Chinook up. They finished the figure eight in a comfortable trot.

Then she nudged the horse again and loosened up on the reins. Chinook broke into a lope. His strides were even and flowing.

"Like sitting in a rocking chair!" Peter called from the fence.

Suddenly Chinook lifted his head higher. His eyes and ears were trained on something in the distance, past the barn. Part of the McGill cattle herd was coming in to drink water at the stock tank.

"He's watching the cows," Peter said.

"Chinook will make a good cow horse," said Mr. McGill approvingly.

"He'd make a good cutting horse," Kate couldn't help adding.

"Now, Katie . . ."Mr. McGill began.

"I know—only boys ride in the cutting contest," murmured Kate.

Still, as she watched Chinook watching the cattle, she couldn't help wishing things were different.

Mr. McGill checked his pocket watch. "Almost time to pick up the Willises," he said to his wife, and added, "Peter, help me hitch up the wagon."

"Is it all right if I ride over to Asa's?" Brian asked. "I want to tell him about Edmonton."

"I guess so—it's your birthday," said his mother. "But don't bother Mrs. Fraser. And bring Asa back for lunch if you want to."

"I will," said Brian. "Thanks again for the birthday gifts!"

Kate was busy making more figure eights on Chinook. And circles. And stopping him. And starting again.

Mr. McGill and Peter left for the railhead to meet the new foreman and his family. They hitched a

wagon to the Model T to carry the Willises'
belongings.

Kate hardly noticed they were gone.

She barely heard her mother say that she was
going to the cabin to do some last-minute
straightening up. "The cabin" is what the McGills
called the first ranch house, the one built by Kate's
grandmother and grandfather when they had come to
Canada from Scotland many years before. Made of
huge logs, it was perched on the edge of a small creek
a mile or so from the main house. The Willises would
be living there now.

Kate gave Chinook a really good workout. Then
she walked him around for a few minutes to cool him
off before leading him into the barn to unsaddle and
groom him.

She was just finishing up, painting hoof oil on
Chinook's feet, when the McGills' car drove up outside.

"Emma?" Kate heard her dad call to her mom.
"We're here!"

The ranch dogs were barking a greeting. The
screen door slammed at the house, which meant her
mother was running down the front steps. Kate heard
more voices, and then Mr. McGill called out, "Katie,
come out here and say hello."

Kate turned Chinook into the box stall, where

there was water and fresh hay for him. Then she
hurried outside.

The Willises

The Model T and the wagon were parked in front of the ranch house. The wagon was piled high with trunks and boxes. Peter and Kate's mom and dad were talking to the man and woman who stood beside the car.

The woman held a plump baby in her arms. A dark-haired little girl was pressed against her. Leaning on the back of the wagon was a wiry blond boy. Kate knew he was just a few months older than she and Brian. She hoped he liked to ride better than Brian did—sometimes it was nice to have company on horseback.

The dogs were sprawled beside the boy, thumping

the ground with their tails. Absently, the boy started to scratch Brutus's back with the toe of his boot.

Mr. McGill caught sight of Kate and said, "This is Kate, one of our twins. It is Kate's—and her brother Brian's—tenth birthday today!"

"Well, happy birthday, Kate, and many happy returns!" the woman said. She was short and round, with curly blond hair and an open, friendly face.

"This is Mrs. Willis, Kate," said Mrs. McGill. "And this is Mr. Willis."

Kate shook hands with them both.

Mr. Willis didn't have much to say. He looked stern.

"Maybe he's just sad," Kate thought. Her parents had told her how the Willises moved from the United States to northern Alberta, where they bought a small ranch of their own. But bad luck and hard winters meant they had lost it.

Mrs. Willis wasn't stern, though. She gave Kate a warm smile, and a hug with the arm that wasn't holding the baby. "Please call me Cora," she told Kate.

"This young fellow is Michael," Cora Willis said, gesturing to the baby in her arms, "and our girl is named Mary." Mary smiled shyly at Kate. She had a sprinkling of freckles across her nose and big blue eyes.

"And that there is Jimmy," Mr. Willis said, pointing at the boy leaning against the wagon.

When Jimmy kept scratching Brutus's back without looking up, Mr. Willis added, "Jimmy, come over here and shake hands." Jimmy slouched over to the steps where Kate was standing and stuck his hand out. He still hadn't raised his eyes.

But when Kate said, "Nice to meet you, Jimmy," and put out her own hand, Jimmy's eyes met hers.

Jimmy Willis's eyes were bright green. And they were definitely not friendly. Then he looked quickly away.

"What is that all about?" Kate wondered, uneasy.

But no one else seemed to notice.

"Let's go into the house for lunch," her mom said to the Willises.

"Oh, we couldn't," said Mrs. Willis. "We don't want to trouble you . . ."

"No trouble at all," said Mrs. McGill. "You don't need to start cooking the minute you get to the cabin. And the children must be hungry."

The big round table was already set. Mr. McGill put Mr. Willis in the chair on his right, and Peter on his left.

Brian and Asa Fraser came racing up the front steps and into the house just in time to squeeze in next to Peter at the table.

Jimmy Willis slid into the empty chair beside his father. Mary sat next to Jimmy, and Kate sat beside Mary.

Kate could see Jimmy glancing around the sunny dining room. He studied the photographs of Kate's grandfather and grandmother in their carved wooden frames. He looked up at the oil lamps made of elk horns that hung above the dining-room table, and at the glass-fronted cupboard filled with the McGills' good china. Then he stared at the silver cups and trophies lined up on the mantel above the fireplace.

Mr. Willis noticed them, too. "Are those prizes from Medicine Hat?" he asked Mr. McGill. Kate's dad must have been talking about the contest on their way back from the railhead.

"That's right," said Mr. McGill. "Peter and Peppy have placed in one of the top spots for the last four years." Mr. McGill nodded at Brian, across the table, and went on, "I hope that Brian will add to the collection this summer. Right, son?"

Jimmy's bright-green gaze focused on Brian.

Brian wriggled in his seat, looking a little uncomfortable.

"Yes, sir," he mumbled.

"Why not? If you've got the right horse, it's easy to

win," Jimmy suddenly muttered under his breath.

"What?" said his father.

"Nothing," Jimmy said.

But Kate had heard him plainly.

Mrs. McGill and Mrs. Willis had been heaping the table with food from the kitchen: roast chicken, smoked venison, potato salad, pickled green beans, deviled eggs, and dozens of hot rolls. Now they sat down, too, and everyone started serving themselves.

"Have you been having a good birthday, Kate?" Cora Willis asked as she helped Mary with a platter of chicken.

"The best ever!" Kate said. "Mom and Dad gave me a wonderful Quarter Horse! He's four years old, he's the most beautiful color, he's . . ."

But she stopped herself.

"I probably sound like I'm bragging," she thought. She could almost feel Jimmy's cold green eyes drilling into her.

Luckily, Mary said shyly, "I wish I had a horse to ride."

"Mary . . . ," said Cora Willis, shaking her head, ". . . you know we can't afford . . ."

But Kate interrupted her. "Mary, you can ride Brownie. Brownie used to be my horse, and she is one of the nicest horses in the world."

"Can I really?" Mary said, clapping her hands together.

"I promise," said Kate.

"Oh, goody!" Mary said.

Brian turned to Jimmy. "Do you play baseball? Maybe you and Asa and I could . . ."

"I don't have time for games," Jimmy muttered. "I have to help my father."

From the way he said it, it was easy to tell that Jimmy thought Brian and Asa—and Kate, too—rarely did anything but play.

Which was unfair—there were chores to be done every day on a ranch. And Brian, Kate, and Asa Fraser did plenty of them!

Brian's face flushed bright red. Kate knew that it would be a long time before her brother tried to be nice to Jimmy Willis again. She wasn't feeling very friendly toward him herself!

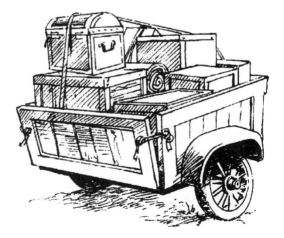

CHAPTER FIVE

Kate Makes Up Her Mind

After lunch, Mr. McGill and the Willises prepared to drive over to the cabin. Before they left, though, Mr. McGill said, "Joe, maybe you'd like to take a look at Kate's new horse first."

Mr. McGill, Mr. Willis, Kate, and Jimmy trooped out to the barn to see Chinook. His head was raised and his ears were pricked as they walked up to the box stall.

Mr. Willis nodded approvingly. "That is one good-looking gelding," he said. "Where did you get him?"

"I bought him from a Quarter-Horse breeder outside of Medicine Hat," said Mr. McGill.

Mr. Willis said, "He has a good build for cutting.

Are you going to train him for that?"

Mr. McGill shook his head: "No, this is Kate's horse, to do with as she pleases." Of course, Kate knew what that meant—to do anything other than cutting.

"What if Mr. Willis is right, though?" Kate thought. "Chinook is built for cutting. Doesn't he deserve a chance to prove himself?"

Chinook was certainly built for the quick stops and turns of cutting. His shoulder and hip angles matched, which gave him good balance. His hocks were strong and low to the ground, and his back was short.

Kate had already seen how he watched cattle. She was almost sure he'd been born with what cutting-horse people called "cow-smarts."

"Kate?" Mr. McGill's voice broke into her thoughts. "Mr. Willis wants to know what your plans are for Chinook."

"Are you going to work on his reining?" Mr. Willis asked.

"Oh. Yes. I think so," Kate said.

But Mr. Willis was already saying to her dad, "It's too bad your boy can't ride this fellow in the cutting, too, in the first-timers' class."

"This horse is wasted on a girl," Jimmy Willis

mumbled in a voice loud enough to be heard.

Kate knew the Willises were just saying what most men thought. But she was suddenly furious! Kate was as good a rider as any boy she knew. And she was sure that included Jimmy Willis!

In a split second, Kate made up her mind. She was going to train Chinook to be a cutting horse. And she was going to win the first-timers' trophy in Medicine Hat this summer. She didn't know how yet— she just knew she would do it, even if she had to cut off all her hair to look like a boy!

Kate already knew a lot about how to train Chinook to cut. She had helped her dad cut cattle in the pasture many times. And she had been watching him and Peter train Peppy for the show ring for the last five years. She had even cut on Peppy herself a few times.

Kate would have to train Chinook in secret, though, if she didn't want everyone constantly telling her how silly she was being.

She glanced up to find Jimmy Willis staring at her. Kate stared right back at him, until he looked away.

"Dad, I'd like to ride Chinook in the pasture this afternoon," Kate said to her father then.

"Well . . . all right," said Mr. McGill. "But take it slow at first. If he has any bad habits, I want you to

discover them walking, not running."

"I'll be careful."

The horn on the Model T beeped.

"I guess the women are ready," said Mr. McGill to Mr. Willis. "I'll show you the rest of the ranch tomorrow."

Kate was standing on the porch with her mother when her dad drove away in the Model T with the Willises. She could see Jimmy's thin face peering out the side.

"I don't like him at all," Kate said in a low voice.

"Who don't you like?" Mrs. McGill said, giving her daughter her full attention. "And why?"

"Jimmy Willis," Kate said. "I tried to be friendly. But all I got back from him was mean remarks about girls, and about Chinook, and . . ."

"Kate, you have to remember what Jimmy's been through recently, losing the ranch," said Mrs. McGill. "Think about what he's had to give up besides the ranch itself—maybe a horse that he really loved to ride. Maybe some dogs. Maybe even his own saddle and bridle. I think the Willises had to sell almost everything they owned."

How would it be to suddenly lose everything? Kate tried to imagine it, but she couldn't. Still, she was sure that she wouldn't be as mean as Jimmy

Willis under the same circumstances!

She would show Jimmy, and she would show Mr. Willis, too. She was going to train Chinook, and she was going to ride him in Medicine Hat. And she was going to win!

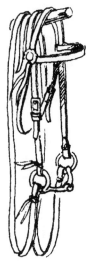

CHAPTER SIX

Mary Rides Brownie

Kate hadn't forgotten her promise to Mary Willis about Brownie. The next morning she found her old mare grazing in the meadow and tied her to the fence beside the barn. Then she walked over to the cabin for Mary.

Mary was helping Mrs. Willis weed the garden. As soon as she saw Kate, Mary jumped to her feet and waved. "Hi, Katie."

"Are you ready to ride Brownie?"

"You bet I am!" Mary replied.

Before Mrs. Willis finished pouring Kate a glass of ice tea, Mary had changed into her riding clothes: frontier pants, an old Western shirt, and a beat-up felt hat of Jimmy's.

"You look a sight!" Mary's mother said, laughing.

Mary was ready to ride. She wanted to run all the way back to the McGill barn—walking wasn't fast enough. And when Mary saw Brownie, she went right up to the mare and patted her neck.

"Mary, this is Brownie. Brownie, this is Mary," Kate said, introducing them.

"She's beautiful!" Mary said.

"Beautiful" wasn't exactly the word Kate would have used. Brownie was fat, swaybacked, and her forelock stuck straight out in front. But Brownie was a nice old mare with plenty of patience. The perfect horse for a beginning rider.

Mary said she already knew how to put a bridle on the horse. Kate helped her slide the bit into Brownie's mouth. Then Kate lifted Mary up so that she could slip the headstall over Brownie's ears.

Kate brought out her old saddle blanket, and the little saddle she had used when she first started riding. It would be a perfect fit for Mary.

Chinook was already saddled and waiting in his stall.

After they had led him over to where Brownie was standing, Kate asked Mary, "Would you like to ride out in the pasture?"

"Yes!" Mary said.

Kate gave Mary a leg up into the saddle. Brownie just twitched her ears and yawned. The rest of her didn't budge.

But once Kate had swung herself onto Chinook, the mare perked up. Kate and Mary set off up the trail to the cabin with Brutus and Stella right behind them.

Mary hadn't been able to ride much when her family had their own ranch. Jimmy had told Kate that most of the Willises' horses were young and barely broken, too wild for a child.

Mary was fearless.

Kate started Chinook out in a walk, but the pace wasn't quick enough for Mary.

"Let's go faster," she said.

Almost before the words were out of her mouth, Mary gave old Brownie a couple of kicks. They passed Kate and Chinook in a speedy trot. Mary bounced so hard in the saddle that Kate worried she might bite her tongue.

Kate nudged Chinook to catch up with them. And the two horses trotted all the way to the cabin and past it. Then the hills rose in front of them.

Kate was going to turn around and head back to the barn, but Mary asked, "Can we ride in there?" She pointed toward the hills.

Kate was about to say "no" when Chinook's ears suddenly pricked forward. Two large calves clattered past them.

"Oh, no!" Kate cried, "They must have broken through the fence, and now they're all running loose."

"What's the matter?" Mary asked, moving Brownie closer.

"I have to put these calves back where they belong," Kate told her. "Why don't you wait for me here? You can sit on that rock and let Brownie eat some grass."

"I can help!" Mary said.

"No, Mary, it's not safe. Stay here like I said."

Kate whistled for the dogs to run forward and nudged Chinook into a fast walk.

As the horse and dogs approached them, the calves stopped short. Their long ears swiveled back and forth while they tried to decide what to do.

Brutus and Stella began to bark. Chinook and Kate moved closer. The calves turned tail and galloped back towards the pen.

Kate swept up a third stray calf on her way in. She pushed all of the animals to the back of the pen. The three calves clumped together, peering out at the riders.

"Now you can help me, Mary. You and Brownie

stand right here in front of them, and don't let them move forward. I'll fix the fence."

Mary tugged on Brownie's reins until the mare stood squarely in front of the cattle. Brutus and Stella sat down beside them. The dogs' tongues hung out, but they were still on the job. All eyes were on the cattle.

Kate wrapped Chinook's reins around a bush. Then she checked the fence.

Two of the cross-pieces lay on the ground, splintered and broken. Kate dragged two logs from the wood pile and lifted them into place. She was about to close the fence when one of the bigger calves dashed past the little girl and Brownie.

Kate jumped on Chinook, and they were off in a flash after the runaway calf. Kate and Chinook cut the calf off in no time, and returned him to the pen.

Mary clapped loudly. "You were great, Kate!"

"Hey! What are you doing?" a voice demanded loudly.

Kate looked over her shoulder and saw Jimmy Willis running towards them.

"Why is Mary here?" Jimmy asked Kate.

"I'm teaching her to ride," Kate answered. "Not that it's any of your business."

"If it concerns my sister, it's my business," Jimmy

shot back. He turned to Mary. "Does Ma know you're here?"

Mary nodded.

"So you girls are playing at being cowboys?" he asked. His lips twitched, and Kate could tell he was amused.

"We're not playing at anything. Some calves broke loose from the pen, and I rounded them up." Kate's eyes flashed.

"And I helped," Mary piped up. "I watched the calves while Kate fixed the fence."

Jimmy walked over to the fence and inspected it. "Not a bad job," he said grudgingly.

"Thanks." Kate grinned.

"For a girl."

Kate turned away. She was tired of being insulted by Jimmy Willis. "Come on, Mary. Let's ride back." Kate flicked Chinook's reins and headed down the trail. When she'd gone several feet, she stopped. She looked over her shoulder and called out, "Jimmy Willis, you're stubborn as a mule when it comes to girls, but I'm going to change your mind. Just wait and see."

Mabel the Milk Cow

Early each morning, Kate was busy with her own chores, and with Brian's, too. While Brian rode over to the Frasers' ranch to throw a baseball around, Kate fed the chickens and gathered the eggs. She fed and milked the McGills' dairy cow, Mabel. Then she fed Chinook, groomed him, and cleaned out his box stall.

When Kate was finished with all that, she saddled up her horse and reined him in the corral near the barn. They did figure eights, circles, rollbacks, and spins until Kate's head was ready to spin.

They were practicing sliding stops one morning a few days after her birthday when Mr. McGill called to her over the fence.

"Joe, Jimmy, Peter, and I are riding out to the back pasture to take a look at the cows and calves there," Mr. McGill said. The back pasture was several miles away from the ranch house. "Want to come?"

Any other time, Kate would have jumped at the offer. But as soon as Mr. McGill said that the others were going, Kate's only thought was, "Now's my chance to start training Chinook!"

It would take the men all day to ride out to the back pasture, look at all of the cows there, and ride back again. Mrs. McGill had probably packed a lunch for them, too. Which meant that Kate would have hours to put her own plans into action.

So Kate answered, "No, thanks, Dad. I think I'll work with Chinook some more."

She hung around the barn while her dad, Peter, Mr. Willis, and Jimmy saddled up their horses. Peter rode Peppy—it was important to keep his cutting horse exercised. Mr. McGill rode his favorite horse, a big bay named Charlie. Mr. Willis rode Star, a young chestnut mare. And Jimmy rode a black horse named Thunder. When he swung into the saddle, Kate saw Jimmy smile for the first time. And she knew Jimmy *did* love to ride, probably just as much as she did.

Once the four of them had headed up the trail toward the back pasture, with Brutus and Stella tagging behind, Kate got busy.

First, she went into the house to tell her mother: "Mom, I'm going to ride out toward the cabin."

"That's fine, honey," said Mrs. McGill. "Say hello to Cora Willis for me."

"I will if I see her," said Kate, hoping that she wouldn't see anyone. "Could I take a lunch with me, like Dad and the others?" she asked her mom.

"I've got an extra roast-beef sandwich," her mother said. "I'll wrap it in waxed paper."

Kate slipped the sandwich into the pocket of her jacket. She was set for the rest of the day. Now for the important part of her plan: getting Mabel the milk cow to the box canyon.

In the hills behind the old cabin, there was a small box canyon. In it, Kate's grandfather had built a corral for his horses. It was hidden away from prying eyes, so it would be perfect for training Chinook.

Kate found Mabel chewing her cud near the stock tank. Mabel was not at all happy about leaving the barn. But with a lot of pushing from Kate and Chinook, she finally ambled away in the direction of the cabin.

Kate made sure that Chinook moved Mabel along the trail at a slow and easy pace. By the time they were halfway to the cabin, she was more certain than ever that Chinook was going to be a wonderful cutting horse.

He kept his ears pricked straight forward, fixed on Mabel. His eyes never left the cow, either. If Mabel took a step or two to either side of the trail, Chinook did the same to bring her back in line. It was almost as though he could read Mabel's mind!

"Cow smarts," Kate said to Chinook, patting his neck. "You've definitely got them!"

As they neared the cabin, Kate crossed her fingers in the hope that Mrs. Willis and the younger children would be indoors. Grandpa McGill had planted a thick row of pine trees along the sides and back of the cabin as a windbreak. If Kate and Chinook—and Mabel—could reach the pines without being seen, they were home free.

Suddenly a small voice called, "Kate? Katie!" It was Mary Willis, standing on the front porch of the cabin with her little brother in her arms.

"What are you doing, Katie?" Mary called to her. "May I ride on your horse with you?"

"I'm just rounding up the milk cow," Kate called back, waving to Mary. "I'd better hurry." She felt a little guilty. She'd make it up to Mary by giving her another riding lesson soon.

Kate gave Chinook a nudge. He pushed Mabel into

a trot. They moved behind the trees and into the hills before anyone else saw them.

Kate guided Chinook and the cow down a dry stream bed and into a small box canyon with a flowing spring at the back. Steep slopes formed three sides of the little canyon. The entrance could be closed off by adding two more crosspieces to a split rail fence. The whole thing wasn't much bigger than the cutting pen in Medicine Hat, and it was totally private.

Now Kate was ready to train a cutting horse!

There was plenty for her to keep in mind. For one thing, she had to remember how to use the reins with both hands to direct Chinook by pulling on one rein and pushing against his neck with the other. She also had to think about what she did with her legs. If she pressed with her right leg, Chinook would move to the left. If she pressed with her left, he would move to the right. Pressing both legs would move him forward.

And Kate always had to remember to sit straight up, in the middle of the saddle. If she leaned forward, or to one side, she could throw Chinook off balance. If she wanted to stop him, though, she should lean her body back, and push herself down in the saddle.

In a real cutting-horse contest, there would be a whole herd of cows to choose from. Choosing a cow that could be worked well was part of the contest. But Mr. McGill felt that a new horse should start with just one cow.

"We've got our cow—now we'll see what we can do with her," Kate said, giving Chinook's neck a pat.

By now, Mabel had moved into the shade of a hill, and she was chewing her cud again. The cow's eyes were half closed. She didn't bother to open them any wider as Kate and Chinook walked toward her. But Chinook was looking hard at the cow, showing what Kate's dad called "cow interest."

When they got closer—about ten or twelve feet away from Mabel—the cow finally opened her eyes. And she shifted her feet a little. Without any directions from Kate, Chinook followed Mabel's movements with his head. Mabel took a couple of steps to the right . . . and Kate nudged Chinook with her left foot to do the same.

Mabel stopped. Kate stopped Chinook by sitting back in the saddle. With both hands on the reins, she made sure that Chinook was facing Mabel squarely. She nudged him toward the cow again, just far enough to make her move a little.

Mabel moved farther to the right. Chinook moved with her. Mabel stopped. Chinook stopped.

Kate nudged her horse a step or two closer. This

time Mabel doubled back to the left. Chinook's head followed her, and Kate directed the rest of his body to do the same.

She had heard her dad tell Peter a hundred times, "You want Peppy to stop, then to turn, and always to control the cow."

Kate let Mabel circle the whole canyon once, with Chinook keeping pace—that was called "tracking" the cow. Then Kate had Chinook move forward enough to stop Mabel. Chinook stopped, too. When Mabel turned in the opposite direction, Chinook moved with her.

"Good boy!" said Kate proudly.

Kate hadn't had to tell him to do it. Chinook was already moving with the cow, on his own.

Paying such close attention was hard work for Chinook. Even though it was cool in the canyon, Kate could see that her horse was beginning to breathe faster.

"If your horse starts breathing hard . . . STOP!" Mr. McGill always said. "Never let him run out of air, or he'll end up getting hurt."

Mabel was looking a little tired, too. A tired cow might not give any milk, which Kate *sure* didn't want.

She waited until Mabel stopped again, and Chinook stopped with her. Then Kate tightened up on the reins and pulled Chinook off the cow, turning him

away from Mabel to show him that the contest was over.

She let Chinook and Mabel rest in the shade for a while as she ate her lunch. Then she started working with them again.

About the middle of the afternoon, Kate had some unexpected visitors. She was concentrating so hard that she didn't notice Jimmy Willis until it was too late.

"Hey, what are you doing back here?" a voice demanded suddenly.

Kate glanced around to see Jimmy on Thunder on the far side of the fence, along with Brutus and Stella. The dogs were wagging their tails happily. They had picked up Kate's trail at the barn and led Jimmy straight to her.

"Traitors!" Kate murmured under her breath about the dogs. Then, louder, she answered Jimmy: "I'm not doing anything—just fooling around."

"You're cutting on Chinook," Jimmy Willis said. "Or pretending to."

"It's not pretending!" Kate said hotly, too angry to worry about Jimmy telling on her.

"Whatever it is, it's bothering the milk cow," Jimmy said. "And your dad sent me to bring her back home." He paused for a second, then added, "Besides, girls can't cut. Everybody knows that."

"I can cut better than you ever dreamed of cutting!" Kate said, furious.

"I don't think so," said Jimmy. "I'll bet I can ride Chinook better than you can."

"You can't, and I'll prove it," said Kate. "The first chance we get, we'll come back here. Each of us will ride Chinook to cut a cow."

"Why would I want to do that?" Jimmy said, sounding as if he were above it all.

"I'll tell you why! Because—if you're better," said Kate, "then you can ride him in Medicine Hat at the fair. If I'm better . . ."

"You won't be," said Jimmy quickly.

Now he sounded interested. As far as Jimmy was concerned, he had already beaten her.

"If I'm better, then I'll ride him at the fair," Kate finished.

"You're a girl! You can't ride him in Medicine Hat, no matter who wins here," Jimmy pointed out.

"If I win . . . you'll help me do it somehow!" Kate said. "Is it a deal?"

But Jimmy had thought of something else. "Who decides who's better?" he asked her.

"We'll go by the rules of the contest, and we'll both decide who wins," said Kate. "Is it a deal?"

"It's a deal," said Jimmy. "Now—I have to get this cow back to the barn."

Brian and Peppy

As soon as Jimmy Willis rode away from the canyon with Mabel, Kate began to worry, just a little. What if—by a stroke of bad luck—Jimmy rode Chinook better than she did the day of their contest? And what if it were Jimmy, not Kate, who ended up winning a prize on Chinook in Medicine Hat?

She didn't even want to think about it!

At breakfast the next morning, she was glad to hear her dad announce, "Brian, you and Peter and I have to get busy on Peppy." Kate hoped to pick up some useful tips on cutting before her contest with Jimmy.

Brian wasn't glad, however. "But Asa's coming

418

over any minute . . . ," he began.

"Asa will just have to wait," said his father. "You and Peppy have to get used to each other if you want to do well in Medicine Hat. And I think we should get started now, before Peter leaves for college." Their trip to Edmonton was only two days away.

"All right, Dad," Brian mumbled. "I'll ride Peppy."

Kate had her chores to do. But she took time out to watch Brian warming up the gray horse in the corral.

Peppy was a little taller than Chinook, and heavier. He had a larger head, and he carried it lower. Peppy was a beautiful steel-gray color, with a light gray-and-cream mane and tail. Kate thought that Chinook was a prettier horse, and that he moved better. On the other hand, Peppy was five years older than Chinook, with five years of cutting-horse competitions behind him.

Peppy and Peter were a real team. But Peppy behaved differently with Brian than he did with Peter—Kate could see that right away. With Peter, Peppy moved freely and smoothly. Peter barely had to nudge Peppy to get him to break into a long, easy lope.

But as Brian reined the horse in figure eights and circles, Peppy's lope got slower and choppier. Soon he was trotting—and Peppy's trot was rough.

Brian and Peppy

"I hate doing this!" Brian said to Kate as he circled the corral. "And Peppy knows it."

"But don't you want to place in the cutting this August?" Kate asked him.

"I don't want to go at all," said Brian. "And I'm sure not going to win anything, not with Peppy acting up and all of those people staring at me."

"I can't think of anything I'd rather do," said Kate.

"And I wish you could!" said her twin. "You're better on Peppy than I am, and that stuff about no girls is stupid."

Kate thought of telling him about her plan for Chinook. But she didn't. What if Jimmy Willis ended up riding her horse?

Mr. McGill and Peter penned some cattle from the home pasture for Peppy to work with—six big calves and three cows. And Mr. McGill turned back for Brian on his bay horse, Charlie. A turn-back man keeps the cow or calf that a cutter is working from running too far away.

Kate never left the corral fence, because she wanted to hear every word Mr. McGill and Peter said. It was the next best thing to having them work with her and Chinook.

"Let Peppy turn with his nose first," Mr. McGill would say to Brian. "And don't pull on him—the rest of his body will follow his nose."

Which was good advice for Kate and Chinook, too.

Or Peter might say, "Don't let him make any false moves. Force the cow to move first by pushing Peppy toward her. Then Peppy will move *with* her."

Or Mr. McGill: "Don't go so fast, Brian. You can slow Peppy down and still handle a cow. In fact, you will handle the cow better."

Kate nodded from her perch on the fence. In the canyon, sometimes Chinook had gotten so excited about what he was doing that he tried to move Mabel—and himself—much too quickly. Now Kate could see how much easier it would be if she made Chinook take things more slowly.

Peter also said, "Be sure that your horse is always facing the cow, Brian, even if you have to pull back on the reins. And always make a clean stop before you turn."

Perhaps the most important advice Mr. McGill gave Brian was: "Study the cattle, and take your time making a cut. You need a cow that moves well, so you can get a good performance out of your horse. Remember—you only have two-and-a-half minutes to show what you can do."

Kate was learning a lot.

But for Brian, having to practice on Peppy meant

taking time out from what he'd much rather be doing: playing baseball. Asa Fraser rode his horse over in time for lunch. He and Brian talked about baseball the whole time, while Kate thought about Chinook and her upcoming contest with Jimmy Willis.

That afternoon, she just rode her horse in the corral. And the next day, she didn't get to ride Chinook at all. After chores, she helped her mother fix a huge farewell dinner for Peter: beef ribs cooked on a campfire outside, a big pot of baked beans, pickled tomatoes, summer squash, and Peter's favorite dessert—a giant German chocolate cake, with lots of canned coconut.

The Willises were invited, and Brian had asked Asa Fraser to come, too, and spend the night.

The grown-ups talked to each other.

Brian and Asa talked about baseball, of course.

Jimmy didn't say a word until just before the Willises left that night. Then he had a chance to speak to Kate alone.

"My dad's going to be exercising your brother's horse the day after tomorrow," Jimmy said in a low voice. "Your father asked him to ride Peppy along the fence-line of the home pasture." He went on, "That's miles of barbed-wire to check for breaks—my dad will be busy for hours. So I'll meet you as soon as I've done my chores, and we'll go to the canyon."

Kate's stomach lurched—their contest would happen so soon? But she whispered back, "I'll have Thunder saddled."

Then she noticed that Brian and Asa were watching them. After the Willises had left, Brian asked Kate, "What did he want? He wasn't being rude to you, was he?"

"Jimmy Willis only opens his mouth when he has something mean to say," Asa agreed.

Kate didn't want to lie to them. But she didn't want to tell them about her plans for Chinook, either-- at least, not yet. So all she could come up with was, "Sometimes Jimmy's not so bad."

"You could have fooled me!" said Brian, frowning.

Kate knew exactly how Brian felt, since Jimmy hadn't really done anything to change her mind about him.

Mr. McGill walked over to them then. "We have a big day tomorrow," he said. "We'd better get to bed."

Kate was sure that Brian and Asa would stay up half the night, jabbering about the baseball game that Brian would be seeing in Edmonton. But she fell asleep as soon as her head hit the pillow.

In what seemed like no time at all, her mother opened her bedroom door and said, "Wake up, Katie.

Breakfast is ready. Don't let it get cold."

Brian and Asa looked bleary-eyed. And Peter looked excited, a little nervous, and sad, all at once.

Mrs. McGill mostly looked sad. And proud, of course. "You're the first in the family to go to college," she said to her oldest son. "And that's wonderful. But that won't keep me from missing you."

"I'll write all the time, Mom," Peter promised. "And I'll be home for the holidays."

"Maybe we'll visit him in Edmonton, too, Emma," Mr. McGill said, his arm around her. "It will be fine." But Mr. McGill looked almost as sad as his wife.

Brian and Asa helped Peter load his trunk and boxes onto the wagon behind the Model T. In one of those boxes was a hooked rug Mrs. McGill had made for him. "So you won't have to step out of bed onto a cold floor," she told Peter.

Mrs. McGill had packed a lunch for them, too.

Soon it was time to go. Kate, Brian, and Peter climbed into the back seat of the Model T, their parents into the front.

Asa waved good-bye one last time. "Write down everything that happens at the baseball game, so you won't forget!" he called to Brian.

Then they were bumping down the dirt road that led to the train. As they passed the cabin, Mrs. Willis and Mary waved from the porch.

"I don't see Jimmy anywhere," Kate's mom said.

"Joe keeps him busy," said her dad.

The dirt road took them past the one-room schoolhouse where the McGills went to school, along with the children from the other ranches in the district: Asa and his little brother, Angus; the three Metcalfe girls; Roberta and David Johnston; and the Robbs.

Peter must have been thinking about their neighbors because he said, "Brian, see to it that you beat Justin Robb in Medicine Hat."

Justin's older brother, Richard, and Peter had been competing against each other in the cutting for years. Peter and Peppy usually did better than Richard and the Robbs' tall black horse, Skyrocket. Now Richard would be going away to college, too. But Justin Robb would be riding in Medicine Hat. Justin was the same age as Brian and Kate.

"You need to keep up the family tradition, son," Mr. McGill added.

"Yes, sir," was all Brian said. But Kate saw him sigh as he gazed out the window of the Model T.

Kate would love to beat the pants off Justin Robb, who bragged too much, anyway. And maybe she would!

The train was waiting for them when they drove up to the railhead, the last stop for this branch of the Canadian Pacific Railway. There was no station, or anything like a building. The tracks just ended in the tall grass of the prairie.

Clouds of gray smoke were billowing from the smokestack. And Mr. Coulter, the engineer, leaned out of the locomotive to call, "How far are you going this time, Mr. McGill?"

"My sons and I are going all the way to Edmonton!" Mr. McGill called back.

Mr. Coulter nodded. "All abo-o-oard!" he said. The train always left at 10:20 A.M., on the dot.

There was just enough time for Kate and her mother to give Peter one last hug. Mr. McGill loaded Peter's trunk and boxes, and a suitcase for him and Brian, into the boxcar.

"Have a good year, son. And work hard. But not too hard," Mrs. McGill said to Peter, with tears in her eyes.

"I will. And I won't," Peter said, grinning at her. "And thanks for the rug, Mom."

Brian had already run up the steps of the passenger car. He was pushing open one of the windows. "You'd better hurry," he yelled to his brother and father. "Because I'm not missing the ball game.

Not even if I have to go to Edmonton all by myself!"

Mr. McGill hugged his wife. Mrs. McGill kissed Peter good-bye. Mr. Coulter tooted the train whistle, fired up the engine . . . and the McGill men swung themselves onto the platform of the passenger car and stepped inside.

Everybody waved.

Then they were gone, heading down the track in the direction of Medicine Hat, then Calgary, and hundreds of miles later, Edmonton.

CHAPTER NINE

Contest in the Canyon

Early the next morning, Kate saw Mr. Willis saddling Peppy. He tipped his hat to her as he started the gray horse up the fence line in a brisk trot.

Kate quickly finished her chores. She was just saddling Jimmy's horse, Thunder, when Jimmy raced up to her.

"I trapped some young steers in the canyon early this morning," he said, out of breath.

"Young steers?" Kate repeated anxiously. She had only worked Chinook on old Mabel. She had no idea how he would act around several friskier animals.

"Three steers and a cow. They'll move better than Mabel, and give us more of a chance to show what we can do," Jimmy Willis said cockily. He seemed awfully sure of himself. "Let's get Thunder and Chinook saddled up," he added. "If we hurry, we'll be back in time for lunch, without anybody missing us."

It was about a mile and a half to the box canyon. The two horses covered the distance quickly in an easy lope.

It was the first time that Kate had actually ridden with Jimmy. She could see what an excellent rider he was, easy and relaxed, his hands gentle on the reins. And it didn't make her feel any better.

"You're good on a horse," Kate said, her heart sinking.

"I've learned a lot from my dad," Jimmy said. "He's one of the best cowboys around."

Maybe he read something in Kate's face, because he added quickly, "We didn't lose our ranch because we were bad ranchers. We lost it because we had bad luck."

When they reached the box canyon, Chinook nickered excitedly at the sight of the cattle Jimmy had penned. The four young animals had been grazing. Now they raised their heads in the air, staring warily at the riders. As Kate and Jimmy rode closer to the fence, they trotted toward the back wall of the canyon.

"We'll each cut twice, all right?" Jimmy said to

Kate. "Go ahead—I'll take the fence down for you." He slipped off of Thunder to remove two of the fence rails.

Kate didn't want to go first! She wanted Jimmy to ride before she did, so that she could watch him and see how well she would have to do to beat him.

But Jimmy probably had the same thoughts. "Ladies first," he insisted with a grin, waving her through the fence.

Kate squared her shoulders and nudged Chinook forward. "I might as well get it over with," she told herself.

She and Chinook moved quietly closer to the cattle. The animals bunched tightly together and turned to face them, their backs to a wall of the canyon.

As far as Kate knew, it was Chinook's first time to walk into a herd of cattle and cut one out. The horse was excited and a little nervous—Kate could feel his tension as he gazed first at one big calf, and then another.

In a real cutting contest, Kate wouldn't have been allowed to help Chinook by pulling on the reins. But now he was still learning. So Kate guided him toward the cow by pulling on the left rein.

Both the cow and one of the steers started

walking away from the herd to the left. The steer's body was between the older cow and Chinook. Kate urged Chinook forward, aiming him at the steer's shoulder. The steer stopped dead.

The cow, on the far side, kept moving to the left. Kate nudged Chinook toward the cow's hip, to push her even farther out of the herd.

Now they had her. The cow was standing about eight feet away from the rest of the herd. Kate quickly moved Chinook into the gap, pushing the cow even farther away from the other cattle, into the middle of the canyon.

"We're really doing it!" Kate murmured. The match had begun. Chinook had been watching the cow closely since Kate had first nudged him toward her. As soon as the cow tried to get back into the herd, the horse lowered his head and stepped in the same direction. The cow stopped, facing Chinook. Chinook stopped, too. The cow suddenly dodged to the right, hoping to get around Chinook. But Chinook dodged to the right as well. The cow stopped again, and so did the horse.

Then the cow dashed to the left! Kate thought Chinook was going to lose her. But he whirled to the left himself. He moved so quickly that Kate had to hang on to the saddle horn to keep from falling off.

But Chinook didn't lose the cow. The cow stopped again, facing him.

"You're already better at this than I am!" Kate said out loud to her horse.

Jimmy Willis laughed. But for the first time Kate didn't feel that he was laughing *at* her. "Good move!" he called out.

Kate turned Chinook away from the cow, so he would know that they were finished with her—that was what cutters calling "quitting the cow."

The cow ran back into the herd, and Kate chose a black steer to work next.

But she and Chinook didn't do as well with their steer. He was wild, and he was fast, too. Chinook was hot and jumpy, and Kate was anxious, and together they made mistakes.

Twice, Chinook turned too far to one side, losing a clear view of the black steer. One of those times, the steer got back into the herd.

In a real cutting contest, that meant points off. Kate just hoped it wasn't going to make the difference between *her* going to Medicine Hat and Jimmy Willis going. Before Jimmy took his turn on Chinook, he and Kate sat for a while to let the horse cool down.

"Chinook will be a champion," Jimmy said. "He's already good, and he's going to be great." He was quiet for a second. Then he went on, "So how are we going to work this out? If I do better today . . ."

If Jimmy Willis did better, competing in Medicine Hat wouldn't be a problem for him. "I'd just tell Dad that I wanted you to ride Chinook in the first-timers' class—and that would be that," Kate said.

But she didn't want Jimmy to ride Chinook. He was *her* horse, and she wanted to ride him at the fair!

"What if I do better?" Kate asked Jimmy.

"If you do better . . ." Jimmy frowned as though he hadn't seriously considered that. After a moment he continued, "You could stick your hair up under a cowboy hat. And sign up in Medicine Hat using a boy's name . . ."

"But how would I get to the fair?" Kate wondered. It would take much too long to ride there—a day and a night, probably. And the train was out: Peppy rode to Medicine Hat on the train, which meant that Chinook couldn't, not in secret.

"Let's worry about that when it happens. If it happens," Jimmy said. "I think it's my turn now."

He picked the friskiest steer in the herd to work with—a red one with a white face. While Kate held her breath, Jimmy and Chinook moved the steer out of the herd.

At first, everything went right. The horse moved

with the steer as if they were linked together. But Jimmy pressed Chinook too hard. Instead of slowing the horse, and the steer, down—Kate remembered her dad's advice to Brian—Jimmy kept nudging Chinook with his legs.

And Jimmy didn't know about making the horse come to a full stop before turning, either. So Chinook was scrambling through his turns, out of balance. Jimmy and Chinook lost the red steer—he raced back into the herd.

Then Jimmy chose the black steer that Kate and Chinook had already worked. Maybe Jimmy thought he would have a better chance with the animal, because he'd seen what the steer was likely to do.

But by then Chinook was too keyed up to pay close attention. The horse made a few false moves, trying to guess what the steer might do. And Jimmy was still pushing him too hard. They lost the black steer, too.

It was over. Jimmy had let two steers get away. Kate had only lost one. So Kate had clearly won!

Jimmy rode Chinook slowly back to the fence where Kate was waiting. She knew she had a relieved smile on her face—she couldn't help herself.

"You won fair and square," Jimmy said to her, climbing down from the saddle. "I'm a good rider. So are you. But you know a lot more about cutting than I do."

He wasn't going to be a sore loser.

"Thanks," Kate said, taking Chinook's reins from him. "Are you still going to help me?" she asked.

"I gave my word," Jimmy said. "And I'll keep it. You'll ride Chinook in Medicine Hat this summer . . . somehow."

CHAPTER
TEN

Brian's False Step

As they rode up to the barn that afternoon, Jimmy muttered, "Uh-oh—my dad's back!"

Mr. Willis was grooming Peppy near the corral. When he saw Jimmy and Kate, he didn't seem pleased. "Good afternoon," he said politely to Kate, before asking his son, "Jim, just where have you been? I looked all over for you—and I could have used some help fixing a break in the fence."

Kate's heart stopped. She could imagine Jimmy answering, "Kate and I were cutting on Chinook in the box canyon."

Jimmy didn't say anything at all for a few seconds. Then he murmured, "I'm sorry, Dad. I promise you that it won't happen again."

"Go unsaddle your horse," Mr. Willis told him. "Walk him around, then wipe him down, and brush him really well. And see to it that he gets some water."

"Yes, sir," Jimmy said. He turned Thunder toward the barn door, with Kate following.

"Thanks for not telling on me," Kate whispered as they pulled their saddles off inside the barn. "And I'm sorry your father's angry."

"He'll get over it," Jimmy said, gathering up the grooming brushes.

"Still . . . thanks anyway," Kate repeated. Now she had learned something else about Jimmy—he could keep a secret.

For the next few days, Mr. Willis kept Jimmy busy—too busy to help Kate with Chinook. She worked her horse on the steers in the box canyon by herself. Then Mr. McGill and Brian came back from Edmonton.

Brian was barely off the train at the railhead when he started in about baseball. "It was incredible!" Brian said to his twin. "We saw two games. In the first one, the Rangers shut out the Hawks: the final score was 9 to 0!"

"'Shut out?'" said Kate.

"It means one team keeps the other team from scoring," said Brian, climbing into the Model T. "In the

438

second game, Bob McElway—he's the Rangers' pitcher—hit a home run! The ball flew so far up in the air I almost couldn't see it, and then it sailed all the way over the left field wall! The Rangers won, 4 to 1!"

"But what about Peter?" Mrs. McGill interrupted before Brian could give a rundown of each of the Rangers players. "What did his college room look like? Was he all right when you left him?"

"And Edmonton?" Kate asked, prodding Brian to get his mind off baseball for a second. "Did you like the hotel?"

"It was fine. I liked the trolley cars," said Brian, before he launched into more facts about the Rangers: "Bruce Culver, the Rangers' catcher, is amazing! He can . . ."

Mrs. McGill started laughing. "Kate, maybe we'll have to get our questions answered by your father."

As they bumped toward the ranch in the car, Mr. McGill told them about Peter's college in Edmonton: "All of the buildings are made of brick and stone. There's a big library, and a playing field. Peter's room is small, but he has a window overlooking a park with trees and flowers. When we left, he'd already met two boys on his floor. He's fine, Emma," Mr. McGill said.

Then Mr. McGill asked them, "How did everything go at the ranch while we were away? Did you find the time to ride Chinook, Kate?"

Mrs. McGill answered for her: "She rode him every day. Sometimes I didn't see Kate from morning till late afternoon."

"Good for you, Katie," said Mr. McGill. "First thing tomorrow we'll get back to work, too, won't we, Brian? We paid Peppy's entry fees when we stopped at Medicine Hat," he told Kate and Mrs. McGill.

Now that her father was back, it was harder than ever for Kate to sneak off to the canyon to work Chinook on cattle. But she did rein her horse in the big corral when Brian wasn't riding Peppy there.

Brian and Peppy weren't getting along any better in cutting practice. Peppy was a smart horse—he could tell when Brian's mind was on other things, like home runs, or pitching a no-hitter, instead of cattle. And if Brian didn't care about what was going on in the corral, then Peppy wasn't going to care, either.

The gray horse would take the bit in his teeth and pay no attention to Brian's hands on the reins. He would turn with his shoulder first, instead of with his nose. Then he started slowing down enough to let calves slip past him.

Once Brian even lost his seat on Peppy.

During their practice, a calf raced to the left. Then it whirled to the right. Brian wasn't sitting straight in the saddle, and Peppy could feel it. Instead of moving smoothly with the calf, Peppy came down hard on his front feet . . . Brian sailed out of the saddle and landed in the dirt!

Brian scrambled to his feet and scowled at the horse, his face red with embarrassment.

"The last thing we need is for you to get hurt—or for Peppy to get hurt—and miss the contest in Medicine Hat altogether," Mr. McGill said sternly. "Try again, son."

But Peppy didn't cause Brian any more problems. Something completely unexpected did.

Asa had come over to the McGill ranch after lunch one day. He and Brian were behind the barn with their ball and bat, pretending to be players on the Edmonton teams: Brian was a Ranger, and Asa a Hawk.

Kate and Jimmy Willis were grooming Chinook near the stock tank. They could see the ballplayers, and hear Brian talking as if he were announcing a baseball game through a loudspeaker: "Bruce Harris of the Hawks is stepping up to the plate . . . Bob McElway, the Rangers' pitcher, is winding up . . . he's throwing . . . Harris swings. He hits! It's a fly ball . . ."

Brian was announcing and running backward at the same time. He held his glove up in the air over his head. His eyes were squinting into the sun, trying to spot the soaring ball.

Brian must have stepped in a hole, because Kate and Jimmy suddenly saw him fall, and heard him cry out in pain.

Asa called to him, "Brian? You okay?"

Brian didn't answer.

Kate and Jimmy Willis stopped brushing Chinook and glanced at each other. "Are you all right?" Kate yelled to her brother.

"I . . . I don't think so . . . ," Brian replied in a strained voice.

Kate dropped her brush and sprinted toward him.

"Mrs. McGill? Mrs. McGill—help!" Asa was shouting. Kate's mother ran down the front steps of the ranch house and over to the barn.

Brian was sitting on the ground. His left leg was tucked under him. His right leg was stretched out in front. He was holding onto it with both hands and staring down at his ankle.

"What happened, honey?" said Mrs. McGill, kneeling beside Brian.

Brian's face was very white. "I . . . guess I . . . tripped," he said to his mother. "I think I sprained my ankle . . ."

Kate didn't know much about medicine. But the

ankle looked more than sprained to her.

It was swelling up, like a sprained ankle. But it was also bent at a funny angle. Kate thought maybe Brian's ankle was broken!

Her mother must have been thinking the same thing.

"Don't move, Brian," Mrs. McGill said. "We'll get your dad." She turned to Kate and said, "The men are on the tractor about half a mile down the south fence—go get your father, right away."

Jimmy Willis was leading Chinook into the barn when Kate ran back to him.

"Brian's hurt—I have to find my father," Kate said.

"I'll saddle Chinook," said Jimmy.

"There isn't time," said Kate. "I'll ride him bareback."

Jimmy led the horse to the corral, so that Kate could climb the fence and slide onto Chinook's broad back.

When she galloped away, Kate was riding Chinook bareback, with only a halter rope for reins.

Chinook flew down the south fence-line. Kate could feel the muscles moving in her horse's strong back. Chinook's skin was warm against her legs. If Kate hadn't been frightened for Brian, she would have been having a wonderful ride.

Mr. McGill frowned when he saw Kate pulling Chinook to a sliding stop beside him.

"Katie, you may feel that you can trust your horse enough to ride him bareback," Mr. McGill said. "But what if he saw something that spooked him? It's possible he could . . ."

Kate interrupted him. "Dad, Brian's hurt. It's his ankle. And Mom wants you, right away!" she said.

"I'll take your horse," Mr. McGill said.

Kate slid down, off Chinook, and her father swung himself up on the horse. The two of them were gone in a cloud of dust, heading back to the ranch house.

"I'll give you a ride back on the tractor," Mr. Willis said to Kate.

The tractor was much slower than Chinook. By the time Kate and Joe Willis got to the ranch house, Mr. McGill was carrying Brian to the Model T. Mrs. McGill was following with a pillow. Asa Fraser and Jimmy stood back, out of the way. Jimmy was holding a sweaty Chinook by his halter rope.

While Mrs. McGill got Brian settled in the back seat of the car, Mr. McGill spotted Kate and Joe Willis.

"Katie, we're driving your brother into Medicine Hat so that Dr. Hall can take a look at his ankle," Mr. McGill said. "I want you to go over to the Willises, and stay with them until we get back. Okay with you, Joe?"

Mr. Willis nodded. "Glad to have her," he said. "If you need to stay in Medicine Hat overnight, Kate can bunk with Mary."

"Thanks, Joe," Mr. McGill said.

When he leaned down to give Kate a quick kiss on the cheek, she asked in a low voice, "Do you think Brian's ankle is broken, Dad?"

"I'm afraid it might be," said Mr. McGill.

He climbed into the car and started the engine. "We'll get back here as soon as we can," Mr. McGill said.

Mrs. McGill waved good-bye as the Model T pulled onto the dirt road. Brian's pale face stared out the back window.

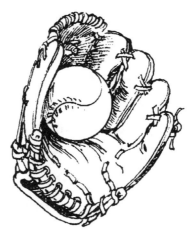

The Plan

As soon as Asa Fraser had saddled his horse and left for home, Jimmy said, "I'm sorry your brother hurt himself. But he sure won't be riding in Medicine Hat. Even if his ankle is just sprained, he only has two weeks until the cutting-horse contest. So what if you borrowed some of his clothes, and . . . ."

"Jimmy Willis!" Kate said angrily. "How can you even think about that right now?"

But at the same time, a small voice in her own head had been saying, "Here's your chance to compete in the cutting in Medicine Hat: you can ride into the arena as Brian McGill. The entry fees are paid—Dad said so. A McGill horse has a stall waiting for him there, at the horse barn. Why shouldn't Chinook get the stall now?"

Jimmy muttered, "Forget it!" He turned his back on Kate and led Chinook toward the barn.

Jimmy and his dad took the tractor down the south fence that afternoon, so Kate didn't see him until evening. Back at the cabin for dinner, Kate told him she was sorry for snapping at him earlier.

"I had been thinking the same thing," she admitted. "Now that Brian is hurt, maybe there was a way I could ride Chinook in Medicine Hat. And I felt terrible for thinking it."

"You didn't make it happen," Jimmy pointed out. "And Brian would want you to compete, if he can't."

"You think so?" said Kate, hoping he was right.

Jimmy nodded. "Now all we have to figure out is how to get you there."

Kate thought again of the train, now that Brian probably wouldn't be competing. But if Brian didn't compete, maybe nobody would be going to the fair. And how could she and Jimmy sneak away to Medicine Hat without anyone noticing?

The McGills brought Brian back from Medicine Hat the next morning. Kate's brother looked a little better—his face wasn't as pale as the day before. But his right leg was encased in a plaster cast to the knee.

The Plan

Mr. McGill carried Brian into the house. Mrs. McGill followed with two brand-new crutches for him to use.

"My ankle's really broken," Brian said to Kate while they settled him in the spare room downstairs.

"But not too badly," said Mrs. McGill, plumping up his pillows. "Dr. Hall said it's more of a crack than a big break."

"He said I can't play baseball for six weeks!" Brian groaned.

"Dr. Hall said your cast will be on for six weeks," his mother told him. "No baseball for two months, at least."

"And definitely no riding, either," Kate was thinking. And her dad echoed her thoughts when he said sadly, "There won't be a McGill in the cutting-horse contest this year."

"Alan, don't make the boy feel bad," Mrs. McGill said to her husband.

Kate thought Brian had looked much more upset about missing two months of baseball practice than about giving up the fair! "Anyway," she said to herself, "there might be a McGill in the cutting, after all."

What her father said next made everything seem easier. "We'll watch the cutting in Medicine Hat, anyway," he told Kate. "Adults cut on a Thursday morning, under eighteen's in the afternoon. You and Joe Willis and I will drive in for the day while your mother stays here and keeps Brian company."

"That's great, Dad!" Kate said, her heart suddenly pounding. She was going to Medicine Hat with her dad, and Joe Willis was going to be there, too, instead of keeping Jimmy busy at the ranch. So Chinook could go to Medicine Hat on the train, if Jimmy was willing to take him. She couldn't wait to tell Jimmy!

The night before the contest, Kate stashed a pair of her brother's riding pants, one of his hats, and a leather belt with "Brian" stamped on it into the back of the Model T.

Mr. McGill, Joe Willis, and Kate would be leaving in the Model T at sunup the next day. No one would be likely to see Jimmy saddle up Chinook and set off up the dirt road to the railhead. Kate had already given him five of her ten silver dollars—birthday presents from her Aunt May and Uncle Randy—to pay the fare to Medicine Hat for himself and her horse.

The train left the railhead at 10:20 A.M., on the dot. An hour and a half later, it would arrive in Medicine Hat.

Kate learned from her father that the fairgrounds were only a ten minute ride from the train station. She and Jimmy had decided to meet at the fairground stable at noon, in the stall her dad had reserved for Peppy, where she would change into Brian's clothes.

Kate was worried about one thing, though: Mr. Willis.

"Won't you get into trouble with your father?" she asked Jimmy.

"If your dad isn't angry, mine won't be, either," Jimmy said. "At least, not much."

"I don't think my dad will be," Kate said. "Oh, he might be upset with me at first. But Dad really wants a McGill cutting-horse at Medicine Hat. And now he'll have one!"

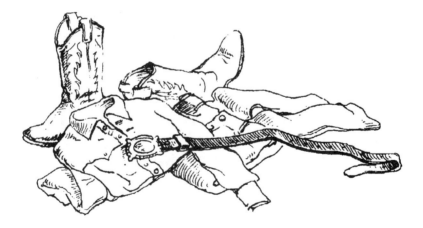

CHAPTER TWELVE

Journey to Medicine Hat

The day of the contest, Thursday, August 10th, dawned clear and cool. Kate and her mother and father ate breakfast by lamplight. Brian was still asleep.

Kate had time to run to the barn to give Chinook one last pat and to whisper "good luck!" in his ear.

Then she and her dad hurried to the car and bumped down the road to the cabin to pick up Mr. Willis.

The cabin was dark, too. But Mr. Willis and Jimmy were both standing on the front porch when the McGills arrived.

Mr. Willis climbed into the Model T, Jimmy raised

his hand to wave, and the two McGills and Joe Willis set off for Medicine Hat.

The yearly five-day fair was the most exciting thing that happened for miles around. The cutting-horse contest was only one of the contests there. There was bull-riding, bronco-riding, and calf-roping. There was also a livestock show, where ranchers could enter their best bulls and cows, and their pigs and chickens to be judged for prizes. There were contests for the tastiest pies, and the prettiest hooked rugs, and the biggest cabbages.

There was something for everyone in Medicine Hat. And it seemed as though practically everyone in southern Alberta was coming to see the show that day. In the town itself, Mr. McGill drove down a street hung with colorful banners that led to the fairgrounds. There, huge brown tents housed the exhibits and the livestock—Kate saw signs that read, "Cattle," "Sheep," and "Poultry." And finally she found the sign she was looking for: "Horse Stable." That's where she would be meeting Jimmy.

Beyond the tents lay the arena, a big, oval corral with high bleachers on both sides of it for the onlookers.

There were people everywhere, walking in and out of the tents, or grooming fat cattle under the trees, or adjusting the saddles on their horses.

"We'd better hurry," Mr. McGill said, pulling the Model T into an empty parking space. "The cutting is about to begin."

He and Kate and Joe Willis climbed into the bleachers in time to see the first grown-up ride into the arena to cut cattle. "This is Michael Dempsey," the rodeo announcer said over a loudspeaker. "He's come to us all the way from Calgary."

Mr. Dempsey was riding a red sorrel with a yellow mane and tail. The horse was bigger than Chinook, with longer legs and a longer head.

Kate had watched the cutting-horse contest in Medicine Hat many times before. But it was the first time she had studied it carefully, to figure out exactly how things worked.

The cattle herd was much larger than anything Chinook was used to. Kate counted twenty-five cows and big calves in the arena. And there were two riders to hold the herd. Once the cutter had chosen a calf and pushed it away from the herd, they held the remaining cattle behind him. Chinook had never seen herd holders. There were also two turnback men, to keep the calf from running away from the cutter, across the arena.

Then there was the crowd: people packed the

bleachers on either side of the arena. Chinook had never had anyone watching him, except Jimmy and the dogs, and now there would be hundreds.

Kate hoped her horse wouldn't be frightened by all of these differences. She began to wonder if maybe she hadn't bitten off more than she and Chinook could chew.

A whistle blew, and Michael Dempsey rode into the herd to choose a cow or calf to cut. He had just two-and-a-half minutes to show what his horse could do.

Kate listened to her father and Joe Willis talk about the cattle.

Mr. Willis said, "I think the spotted cow is blind in one eye. He ought to stay away from her. And that black calf looks wild."

Mr. McGill said, "That red calf is a good one. He's not too nervous, but he moves well—he would really let the cutter show off his horse."

But Mr. Dempsey chose a brown-and-white calf. He pushed it out of the herd, into the middle of the arena. The two herd holders kept the remaining cattle from moving up behind the horse. And the two turnback men saw to it that the calf didn't hightail it across the arena.

The cutting horse got down to business. And he

really did get down. The horse was so focused on the calf that he worked almost in a squat. The calf didn't make a move without the horse being right there with him, almost in his face.

"That sorrel horse is good!" said Mr. Willis.

Cutters lose points if they move their hands at all while the horse is working. Mr. Dempsey's left hand held the reins loosely. His right hand rested on the saddle horn.

After about a minute and a half, he raised the reins a bit to pull his horse away from the brown-and-white calf. Then he rode into the herd for a second time. Michael Dempsey had just started working a white cow when the whistle blew. His two-and-a-half minutes were up.

"Was it good for him to choose another cow to work?" Kate asked.

"I guess he felt that the first one was getting tired," said her father. Then he pointed at the two judges standing just outside the fence near the midpoint of the arena. "I wonder how they marked him," he said.

"I would have marked him high," said Mr. Willis.

"Is eighty points a perfect score?" Kate asked her dad.

"Eighty points for each judge," said Mr. McGill.

"With two judges, one hundred sixty points is perfect."

"But nobody is perfect," said Joe Willis. "High seventies is about as good as anyone gets."

Kate thought that some of the horses she saw in the grown-ups' cutting were pretty nearly perfect. The longer she watched, the more her stomach flip-flopped. Each horse seemed better than the last!

What if she had made a big mistake? What if she and Chinook froze in the arena? Or what if Kate fell off, like Brian? "I'll have gotten Jimmy—and myself—into a peck of trouble for nothing!" she thought.

"What time is it, Dad?" Kate asked.

Mr. McGill pulled out his pocket watch. "Almost twelve," he said.

Which meant that Jimmy and Chinook should be arriving at the horse barn—if everything went well! "I'm hungry," said Kate. "May I go to the sandwich tent?"

Her dad nodded. "Fine. But get back before one o'clock—that's when the cutting for first-timers' starts," he said.

"I'll see you then," said Kate. She added to herself, "Or at least *you'll* see *me.*"

She climbed down from the bleachers. Once she had glanced over her shoulder to make sure her father wasn't watching her, Kate sprinted toward their car.

She grabbed Brian's gear out of the back. Then she raced to the horse barn as fast as she could.

The barn had two alleys running from one end to the other, with horse stalls on both sides of them. She hurried up the first alley, looking first one way and then the other—no Chinook, or Jimmy. She started searching down the second alley. She was beginning to wonder if they had made it at all. What if something had happened to them?!

Then Jimmy Willis stepped out of a stall into the alley and called, "Kate—finally! Where have you been?"

Chinook stuck his head over the stall door. When the horse saw Kate, he nickered. And he had never looked so good to her! Neither had Jimmy Willis, for that matter.

"I couldn't get away from my dad, and yours," Kate said to Jimmy, stroking Chinook's face. "Stand outside the door, so I can change into Brian's clothes."

Inside the stall, Kate kicked off her boots. As she pulled off her riding pants and pulled Brian's on, she asked Jimmy through the door, "Was the train ride okay? Did you have any trouble with Mr. Coulter, the engineer?" She didn't give him any time to answer before asking more questions: "How did Chinook act on the train? Was he scared? Stop it, Chinook," she added, giggling—the horse was nibbling at her hair.

Kate ran Brian's belt through the belt loops of the pants. She put her boots back on. Then she braided her hair into two quick, not-very-neat braids. She stuck the braids up under Brian's black hat.

Kate opened the stall door. "How do I look?" she asked worriedly.

Jimmy stared at her for a second or two. Then he said: "Brian McGill! I guess you made it, after all!"

"I couldn't have done it without you," Kate said.

CHAPTER THIRTEEN

And the Winner Is...

Kate didn't want to ride Chinook into the cutting arena cold. She and Jimmy led the horse over to an open field at the edge of the fairgrounds, where other riders were warming up their horses, too.

"Maybe this will keep us out of my dad's way," Kate said to Jimmy, glancing cautiously around for Mr. McGill's gray Stetson hat.

"And mine." said Jimmy.

At first, Chinook was a little hesitant. But once Kate climbed into the saddle and took hold of the reins, he settled down. For half an hour or so, they did circles and figure eights. "Taking the kinks out of Chinook," Jimmy called it.

Just as Kate was deciding that Chinook had had enough exercise, someone called to her: "Hey—Brian! Is that a new horse?"

Oh, no! It was Justin Robb!

"Hey!" was all Kate called back, hoping she sounded enough like Brian. She noticed that Justin wasn't riding Skyrocket—he was riding a new horse, too, a stocky brown horse. Now they seemed to be heading in her direction.

Kate quickly turned Chinook away. She trotted over to Jimmy, who was standing at the edge of the field.

"Who is that?" Jimmy asked, frowning past her.

"Justin Robb, one of our neighbors," Kate said hurriedly. "Let's get out of here!"

She slid off Chinook. Jimmy grabbed the reins. The three of them dodged into the milling crowd of fair-goers before Justin could reach them.

"Whew! That was close!" said Kate.

"Yeah, but it told us one thing," Jimmy said.

"What?" said Kate, still shaken.

"You look enough like Brian today to get away with this!" said Jimmy.

Then they overheard a man saying, "It's almost one o'clock."

"It's almost time for Chinook and me!" Kate said,

taking a deep breath.

She and Jimmy led Chinook to the back of the arena, and stayed well out of sight behind a loading chute. Over the loudspeaker, the announcer said, "Good afternoon, ladies and gentlemen. The boys' cutting contest is about to begin. We're starting out with the first-timers' class—it's the first time out for either the horses, or the boys, or both. And our first contestant is Harlan Forbes, on a nice-looking paint horse."

For Kate, the two-and-a-half minutes that Harlan Forbes rode seemed like two-and-a-half seconds, two-and-a-half seconds until she might be riding herself. After the final whistle, she stopped breathing altogether, waiting to hear if Brian's name would be called out.

One boy rode, two boys, three, six . . .

When the sixth boy left the arena, the announcer said, "Next we'll be watching Brian McGill, from the McGill ranch—he'll be riding Peppy."

"Come on, Kate," Jimmy said to her. "That's you."

Kate was frozen on her horse. She couldn't move. Not even her mind was working.

But Jimmy grabbed the reins and ran with Chinook to the gate into the arena.

"You'll be fine," he told Kate. "Just let Chinook get

his work done. Good luck!"

A man pushed the gate open so that Kate and Chinook could walk through it. Jimmy gave the horse a pat on the rump . . . and then they were inside the arena. The man closed the gate behind them.

The arena looked huge. Thousands of eyes were focused on Kate and her horse. And one pair of those eyes belonged to her father. Kate wondered what he was thinking right about now . . .

"Make him proud!" Kate said to herself. "This is what you wanted, remember?"

She glanced down at Chinook's little ears—they were already pointed straight at the herd of cattle bunched together at the far end of the pen. Chinook's mind was on his business. She had better get hers on it, too!

Kate nudged Chinook with her legs. They walked past the two turnback men, toward the herd. About twenty feet away from the cattle, Kate stopped her horse for a second to study them. The red calf that her father had talked about was standing behind a cow on the left side of the herd . . .

The whistle blew.

Barely squeezing Chinook with her legs, Kate nudged him forward to push the red calf farther to the left. A few steps more, and the calf was separated from the rest of the herd.

There were plenty of things for Kate to remember: To hold the reins loosely with her left hand. To rest her right hand on the saddle horn. To sit straight in the saddle.

Her legs hung straight down from her hips, with a little bend in the knees. And Kate tried to stay as relaxed as she could. If her muscles tensed up, Chinook would feel it, and he would tighten up, too.

Kate had to leave the cutting to Chinook. She couldn't direct him in any way without losing points. Chinook didn't let her down—he worked with all his heart.

With the two turnback riders, Chinook could stay tighter on the calf than he ever had in practice. The red calf couldn't take a step to the right or the left without Chinook doing the same.

In a way, it was the longest two-and-a-half minutes of Kate's life.

In another way, it was the shortest. When the final whistle blew, and Kate pulled her horse away from the calf, she wished she could have shown Chinook off for the rest of the afternoon!

The crowd seemed to want that, too. Their applause was like thunder!

"A mighty good horse, and a mighty good ride

from a young fellow named Brian McGill!" boomed the announcer.

People were still clapping when Kate and Chinook rode through the gate. Kate began to look around for Jimmy . . . and spotted him sandwiched between two men: Mr. Willis and her father!

She trotted Chinook straight over to them. Before either one could say anything, Kate blurted out, "Please don't be mad at Jimmy. This was all my idea! Chinook is so good at cutting, it just wasn't fair that he couldn't be in the contest. After Brian got hurt, I convinced Jimmy to bring Chinook on the train, and I borrowed some of Brian's clothes, and . . ."

"Slow down, slow down, Katie," Mr. McGill said, starting to laugh. "I'm not mad at Jimmy. As I told Joe, I was sure this whole thing was your idea. And I'm not mad at you, either. In fact, I'm proud enough to burst about the job you've done training Chinook!"

Kate was so pleased that all she could say was, "You are?"

"I am," said Mr. McGill. "But let's watch the rest of the contest. Justin Robb is about to ride."

As the McGills and the Willises looked on from outside the arena, Justin Robb and the brown horse moved into the herd. But Justin made a big mistake. He chose the spotted cow with a blind eye.

If her blind side was toward the brown horse, the cow couldn't see which way the horse was moving. And she wasn't afraid of what she couldn't see. So she didn't stop or turn away, not even when the horse was right on top of her.

Before a minute was up, Justin had lost her. And losing his cow lost Justin a lot of points.

He chose another cow. But he couldn't work it long enough to make up for the points he had lost. The whistle blew all too soon.

Five more boys rode, and then it was over. The two judges met in the arena to compare notes and add up their scores. Then they walked to the announcer's booth to give the results.

"We've got the names of the winners here, folks," the rodeo announcer said over the loudspeaker. "Third place goes to Harlan Forbes from Red Deer Ranch. Harlan, come out here and get your prize."

The crowd clapped as the boy rode his paint horse into the arena to pick up his trophy from the judges.

"Second place was taken by Chester Martin from over near Purple Springs! Chester, congratulations!" said the announcer.

Chester Martin was riding a pretty bay horse with black stockings. The teenager waved his trophy in the air.

Kate was getting more and more nervous. She had thought she and Chinook might win third place. Or maybe second, if they were really lucky. But first place, first time out for both of them? She didn't think so.

"Sorry, Chinook," she murmured to her horse. "Anyway, we gave it our best."

Suddenly the announcer boomed: "And first place for the first-timers' class for boys eighteen and under goes to . . . BRIAN MCGILL! Ride in here, Brian, so we can get a look at you, and at that talented horse of yours—his name is Peppy, isn't it?"

"No!" Jimmy Willis yelled as loud as he could from the gate. "It's Chinook!"

"CHINOOK!" Mr. McGill and Mr. Willis both shouted.

"Chinook!" said the announcer. "That's a fine Canadian name."

Kate and Chinook had won first place? Kate was frozen again! But her dad pulled the gate open for her, and joked, "Get in there, before they change their minds!"

As Kate and Chinook trotted across the arena, the applause thundered around them. One of the judges held up a big silver trophy and said to Kate, "You and your horse did a great job out there, son." He handed the trophy to her.

Kate thought for a second. Then she pulled off Brian's hat and let her braids hang down for everybody to see.

"I'm a girl," she said to the judges. "Kate McGill."

At the same time, the announcer shouted: "She's a girl!"

"This contest is . . . is for boys!" the other judge said, sounding flustered. And he reached out to take the trophy back.

But by then Mr. McGill was standing beside Kate and Chinook. "Kate and her horse won the contest, fair and square!" Mr. McGill boomed.

The crowd must have agreed with him, because people started calling out, "Good for you!" and "She's the winner!" and "She deserves that trophy—she made the best ride!"

The announcer said, "For the first time, a girl has ridden in the Medicine Hat cutting-horse contest! Not only ridden in it, but she has won *first place*! I have a feeling that it's not the last time we'll be seeing . . . what's your name again, young lady?"

Kate called out loud and clear: "Kate—Kate McGill! And this is Chinook!"

"Kate and Chinook!" boomed the announcer. "I'm sure we'll see you next year!"

"You bet you will!" said Kate, patting Chinook's neck.

Chinook bobbed his head and nickered softly in agreement.

FACTS
ABOUT THE BREED

You probably know a lot about Quarter Horses from reading this book. Here are some more interesting facts about this popular breed.

∩ Quarter Horses generally stand between 15 and 16 hands high. Instead of using feet and inches, all horses are measured in hands. A hand is equal to four inches.

∩ Quarter Horses are usually chestnut (reddish brown all over) or bay (brown with a black mane, tail, and lower leg). A registered Quarter Horse can be of any color.

∩ A horse cannot be registered with the American Quarter Horse Association if it has any white on its legs or body above the knees. White on the face is acceptable, but the whole face must not be white.

∩ Quarter Horses are famous for their heavily muscled hind quarters. These muscles allow the Quarter Horse to take off at a gallop from a standing start. Quarter Horses are often photographed from behind to show off these strong muscles.

∩ Quarter Horses were developed from horses imported from England to Virginia and North and South Carolina in the early 1600s. Those horses, who were probably of Arabian, English, and Barb ancestry, were crossed with the Spanish horses that were already in America.

∩ Although the Quarter Horse was developed early in American history, the American Quarter Horse Association was not founded until 1940.

∩ In the late 1700s, Quarter Horses were called "Celebrated American Quarter-mile Running Horses" or "C.A.Q.R.H." They got this name because they are unbeatable at distances of a quarter mile or less.

∩ Before the foundation of the American Quarter Horse Association, Quarter Horses were know by several different names, including "Steeldusts" and "Billys."

∩ Some Quarter Horse fans believe that the Quarter Horse is the most popular horse in the world. In fact, the American Quarter Horse Association is the largest horse registry in the world with over three million entries.

∩ The Quarter Horse's powerful hind quarters also make it a great cutting horse. While cutting, or separating a cow from the herd, a horse needs not only to stop and start quickly, but also to turn on a dime. The Quarter Horse can do that, and at high speed, thanks to its strongly muscled rump and thighs.

∩ Quarter Horses are favorites among cowboys because of their "cow sense" and cutting abilities. They also excel at roping, another important cattle ranch skill, and barrel racing, a popular Western sport.

∩ Although Thoroughbred racing has stolen some of the limelight from the Quarter Horse, Quarter Horse racing is still popular. The All-American Futurity, held every year at Ruidoso Downs, New Mexico, is one of the world's richest horse races. A winner at this race can take home as much as one million dollars.

∩ A good Quarter Horse can run the quarter mile (440 yards) in 21 seconds or less.

∩ A Quarter Horse was the star of the 1994 film *Black Beauty*. Docs Keepin Time, a registered American Quarter Horse, won a Silver Spurs Award for outstanding achievement in entertainment for his performance in the film.

∩ Quarter Horses are also used for general pleasure riding, trail riding, hunting, and jumping. They even perform in the dressage ring. Their athletic ability, coupled with their calm disposition make the Quarter Horse an excellent all-round horse. No wonder they are among the most popular horses in the world!